BLUE
MURDER

A gripping crime thriller filled with twists

CATH STAINCLIFFE

Detective Janine Lewis Book 1

JOFFE
BOOKS

Revised edition 2022
Joffe Books, London
www.joffebooks.com

First published by Allison & Busby Limited
in Great Britain in 2004

This paperback edition was first published
in Great Britain in 2022

Cover art by Nick Castle

ISBN: 978-1-80405-448-2

NOTE TO THE READER

Please note this book is set in the 2000s in England, a time before smartphones, and when social attitudes were very different.

CHAPTER ONE

Day 1: Saturday, 22 February

Promotion! Detective Chief Inspector. Janine Lewis watched The Lemon's lips move and she savoured every terse, acerbic syllable. Detective Superintendent Leonard Hackett, as he was generally known, hated giving her this but he couldn't really put it off any longer. Not unless he wanted suing for unequal treatment: she'd got the experience, done all the training, passed the exams. First woman DCI in Greater Manchester! Certainly the first pregnant DCI the force had ever known. Enough to ruffle a few feathers among the old guard. Send the odd Polly toppling from his perch with shock.

"Thank you, sir," she beamed, when he'd finished. "I'm delighted."

Janine went straight to the canteen afterwards, where she knew the rest of the team would be gathered. As she went in, conversation died down and people turned her way. She made them wait a moment — though anyone with an ounce of wit could see the excitement that gleamed in her eyes.

"I got it!" she grinned.

Detective Sergeants Shap and Butchers cheered and the rest of the room gave her a round of applause.

"Drink, Detective Chief Inspector?" Shap offered. There was plenty of time to get to the bar and back.

Janine shook her head, smiling. "I want to surprise Pete — champagne breakfast."

Shap looked at the clock. "At lunchtime?"

"He's on nights." Pete did shifts at the airport, air traffic control.

After accepting more congratulations Janine left the police station and picked up a bottle of bubbly on the way home. Home was in Didsbury, a family house that they'd bought years back before the prices became completely silly. Comfortable, roomy, it suited them fine.

She parked in the drive, opened the front door as quietly as she could and tiptoed through to the kitchen for glasses. Stifling the childish urge to giggle, she sneaked upstairs with the bubbly in one hand and the glasses in the other.

She kicked open the bedroom door and shock slapped the grin from her face.

Pete. Pete with Tina, Tina the cleaner for God's sake. In their bed. Not alone, not asleep and dreaming of her. Oh, no!

"Ah, you're up already," Janine managed before she fled downstairs, tears spilling. Tipping the champagne down the sink. Hurt and furious, taking one defiant swig. The bastard!

Janine reared from her sleep. A dream? No, not just a dream, a bloody re-enactment. Yes — she had got promotion, yes — Pete had been found in bed with the cleaner, yes — he had left her even though she offered to take him back (after all, their fourth baby was on the way).

And here she was three months on and the feelings still raw, close to the surface.

'Mum!' Six-year-old Tom burst into the room and leapt on her. 'Is it a school day?' He wriggled under the covers with her.

Janine stretched and smiled. 'Nope. It's Saturday. And we are having a lie-in.' She lay back, arms behind her head, relishing the chance. Tom mimicked her pose and gave his own little sigh of contentment. But he could never stay still for long and his squirming prompted her to play.

'What's this doing in my bed?' Janine pretended to be shocked and patted at the duvet. 'What is it?'

Tom began to giggle.

'It's very bouncy.' She pushed him with her hands so he bounced up and down.

'I know — it's a kangaroo!'

'No,' Tom's giggling grew. 'Not a kangaroo, it's me, Tom.' He turned onto his side facing her.

Janine grabbed his shoulder. 'Ah, no. Here's a bony bit. Maybe it's a lobster. Is it a lobster?'

Tom shrieked as she tickled him, his legs kicking.

'What's this — hair? Blimey O'Riley, it's a woolly mammoth!'

'A sabre tooth tiger!' Tom yelled breathlessly.

* * *

Two miles away in Whalley Range, Matthew Tulley leant his pushbike against the side of his shed and surveyed his allotment. It was a crisp February morning, the sun was bright and low in the sky and mist still clung in the shadiest corners. Above, the sky was a fresh blue, here and there a wisp of cloud and a trail of jet vapour. Perfect weather for a tidy-up and sorting the spring beds, lifting some of the root vegetables and preparing the drills for later crops. Lesley could use baby carrots and turnips for their evening meal. He went into the shed to get his tools.

When he heard footsteps and the rustle of clothing he turned to see who it was, took a step to the shed doorway. A look of confusion altered his face as his visitor approached. As he saw the knife.

'What on earth—' Matthew began to speak. His arms went up instinctively. The blade caught his right arm, the pain sudden and shocking.

'No!' Matthew grasped at his arm. The knife came again. Towards his belly and up. Stumbling forward, Matthew felt the agony explode through him, his fingers clutching across his front, felt slick warmth and weight. He fell forward, down over the threshold, his face in the mud, the sensation of grit and cold on his cheek and the smell of the dark soil in his nostril mingling with the metallic scent of blood. Matthew Tulley lost his sight, then his sense of smell, the last thing he was conscious of was the rustling sound of someone running through the plot, scraping past bushes and fencing, feet rocking the ground on which he lay dying.

* * *

Seven-year-old Jade, crouched beside the fencing, prayed that she wouldn't be seen. She wasn't allowed to play on the allotments. If her mam knew she'd be in trouble. Big trouble. No one must ever know. The person was getting closer now, just the other side of the fence. She shut her eyes and pressed herself into the wooden slats, holding her breath. *Don't look, don't look!* When she closed her eyes the picture was like a scary movie, it made her feel sick. The footsteps went past and on. Jade waited, counted to fifty and then a hundred. Cautiously she looked about, listened, and then ran herself. Half expecting a hand on her shoulder or a figure jumping out in front of her. Coming after her next. She reached the alley and ran down to her back yard, slipped in the back door and through to the lounge. Lay down in front of the telly, her heart beating fast in her chest, like a chick's.

* * *

Janine loaded the washing machine and rubbed at her back where the weight was beginning to pull. Six months and counting. A May baby. Nice time of year for it — no need to bundle them up so much. But the nights! At thirty-eight she really hadn't expected another child. Three was quite enough, thank you. Michael was fifteen, after all — technically old enough to father a child himself though she and Pete would skin him alive if he did. They'd done the sex talk, ten minutes of excruciating embarrassment for all concerned, and two weeks later Janine had brought home the pregnancy testing kit. Ironic or what? Watching in dismay as the blue spot appeared, her whole life suddenly knocked sideways by the prospect of seeing her feet disappear from view, her waist double in size, of labour, nappies, feeding, toilet training. Another eighteen years at least of full-on parenting.

Turning for the washing powder, Janine saw Tom pouring his cereal into the bowl and over the table. 'Tom!' He jerked at the noise managing to spill more flakes then righted the box. Ten-year-old Eleanor wandered in, a cardboard box on her head with a hole cut out to see. She reached for the cereal.

'Eleanor,' Janine said, 'take it off while you have your breakfast.'

'Why?' Eleanor said, though it was a bit muffled.

'It'll get soggy.' Janine rescued the milk from Tom and poured some into his bowl and cup.

Tom picked up a straw and started blowing bubbles in the milk; it frothed over the top of the cup in a big ball of bubbles, like a geodesic dome. Eleanor took off her cardboard box and sat down to eat.

Tom stared fondly at his creation. 'An alien world,' he breathed. Janine shot him a warning glance. Any more bubble blowing and the whole thing would collapse, making even more mess.

'What makes wind?' Tom asked thoughtfully.

Was it the moon, or the tides? Janine struggled, her mouth working. She should know this.

'Beans!' Eleanor supplied.

Janine slung two pieces of bread in the toaster and then began to clear up the lunchboxes and PE kits which had been left since the day before. Eleanor was messing about with the radio — tuning into different stations. She'd not found anything she liked. Had stopped searching in fact as she'd got more involved in her impromptu mixing. The telly was on too, blaring from the next room. Janine tried to tune it all out. Tom was stalking round the kitchen in carnivore mode, hands shaped like claws, his teeth bared in a fearsome growl.

'Lunchbox.' Janine instructed her daughter like a surgeon requesting forceps.

Eleanor passed it. 'Lunchbox.'

Opening it, Janine took out a sodden note. Smoke began to pour from the toaster setting off the manic bleeping of the smoke alarm. Tom dived under the table. Grabbing the brush, Janine shoved it up and hit the re-set button on the detector. She chucked the blackened toast in the overflowing bin without a second glance.

'Get dressed,' she said to Tom. He left the room like a jet fighter. Janine unfolded Eleanor's note from school. Read the words — *Head Lice Outbreak*.

'Great!' Janine said sarcastically, scratching at her own head. 'Are you itchy?'

Eleanor nodded. Something else for the weekend list, thought Janine.

Janine had started doing the shopping list when her eldest child Michael surfaced. Still in his pyjamas, with his headphones on, he began to hunt through the cupboards in search of food. Given the chance, Michael browsed — like some sort of animal that had to eat its own body weight every day. A teenage thing. But until she'd gone to the supermarket Janine knew there was nothing much for him to find.

'There's no cereal,' he complained.

'I'm doing a list.'

'What?'

Janine gestured to her own ears — take them off.

Michael ignored her. He peered in the fridge. 'And there's no cheese.'

'Any requests?'

'What?'

Janine began to mime, moving her lips and throwing her arms about as though she was telling him a long and dramatic story. Michael fought to hide a grin.

* * *

Old Eddie Vincent had woken late, barely slept if truth be told, and was drawing back the curtains when he saw the

6

lad coming off the allotments. The lad running, stopping to recce at the alley like a fugitive, breathless and scared. Lad was obviously up to no good. Probably been caught thieving and used the allotments to get away. You could reach the old railway line from here, wasn't only foxes that made use of that to escape notice. Eddie winced as the pain caught him again. Needed his tablets. He turned away from the window and shuffled across the room. Tired. Always tired now.

* * *

Dean Hendrix had legged it, straight off. No messing about. He knew they'd come calling, they always came calling. Usually lads his own age with a copper's sneer on their faces as they asked their questions in some sort of police speak that came out of the ark: *on the night in question . . . at the time of the aforementioned incident.*

He cursed, kicked the settee and paced up and down in front of it, fists balled and his heart skipping too fast for comfort. He grabbed the video and pushed it in the machine. Flung himself down on the leather couch which made a farting sound. The tape started and he watched, frowning and uneasy as he clocked what was going on. He hit the remote: eject.

Swallowing, short of breath, he rubbed his hand round the back of his neck, gathering the hair there into a short ponytail. Should he stay or should he go? The old Clash song sprang to mind, his knee trembling in a spasm as if he was tapping his foot to the remembered beat. Hadn't any option. They'd bang him up for years. He thought of Paula and pushed the thought away.

He leapt up and ran upstairs. Filled a holdall with clothes, slid the cover off the battery compartment of the cassette radio and pulled out the baggie containing the last of his stash.

Downstairs again he put the video and his flick knife into a carrier bag and put that in his holdall. He picked up his house keys, couldn't take the Datsun, he was waiting for a new starter motor. He'd have to bus it.

Dean checked his wallet and got his passport from the drawer in the kitchen. You never knew. Flicked at the pages. Crap photo, looked like he'd just thrown up, skin the colour of porridge and one eye half-shut and his hair, that was before he grew it, a right mess like a bush stuck on top of his head. How could he have walked around looking like that?

He pushed it in the side pocket of the bag and checked round the room. Morning paper; wouldn't do to be leaving that here. Blow his alibi. He'd go to Douggie's. If they found him, he didn't know if Douggie's word as to his whereabouts at the time in question would be enough but it would have to do for now. 'Cos if he had to sort anything else out his frigging brain'd melt.

He rang Paula on his mobile. Call messaging on. He began to speak as he zipped up his bag. 'Paula, look. Erm, I've had to go away for a bit. Erm . . .' He knew he was messing it up. 'I'll talk to yer later.' He picked up the holdall, looked about. 'Paula—' His throat felt dry. He hesitated then spoke again. 'I love you, Paula.' End call.

He pocketed his mobile and made for the front door, pulled it shut, locked the mortise. Adios. He never looked back.

* * *

The kids were squabbling about the computer again. Janine was trying to referee.

'It's my go . . . it's not fair,' Eleanor complained.

'Michael,' Janine began, 'come on, let Ellie have a go.'

'I've only just started,' he protested.

'Phone,' Tom announced.

'See who it is,' Janine sent him to answer it.

'He's lying,' Eleanor said.

'You're lying,' Michael retorted.

'Mum!'

8

Tom wandered back in with the phone. 'You're The Lemon, aren't you?' he said, clear as a bell.

Janine, horrified, stopped in her tracks.

'Mum,' Tom piped at the top of his voice, 'Mum, it's The Lemon!'

Janine snatched the phone from him, she'd told him about this before. Talk about embarrassing.

'No, no!' she hissed at Tom, 'Mr Hackett.'

She stepped into the hall, her face aglow, and tried to sound unruffled. 'Sir?'

Ringing her at home, on a Saturday. Her own enquiry at last? A bubble of hope rose in her chest.

'DCI Lewis, can you come in?'

'Yes, sir. Right away, sir.'

Try and stop me, she thought. Murder. It must be murder.

CHAPTER TWO

Lesley Tulley had found parking space in the Pay and Display beyond the Triangle shopping centre. Sometimes she'd drive round for ages looking for a place. She didn't like the multi-storeys; huge and grim, they made her feel claustrophobic. She had got out to get a parking ticket, already planning which shops she needed to visit and where to start. Her sister's birthday was the following weekend. What could she get? She drew out her mobile and rang her but wasn't surprised when the answer phone kicked in. Saturday morning, after all. Lesley left a message.

A blue van slowed beside her, the driver leaving the car park, his eyes grazing ever so slightly down to her breasts, then back to her face. Eyes gleaming with appreciation. She didn't let herself react, refusing to blush or flirt even when he wound down his window and spoke to her.

Lesley was used to her beauty, the attention it drew. Her large, dark eyes, fine bone structure, glossy brown hair, full mouth, the slim, shapely figure. It was her beauty that had brought her Matthew.

'Queen,' he'd called her, adopting a Liverpool twang. Joking, for he came from the comfortable suburbs and if his mother were still alive she would have been horrified at his

Scouse impersonation. 'My Queen, you are,' he'd said, 'the most beautiful. I want to watch you for the rest of my life.'

She had laughed but he meant it, and before long they were married and he would gaze at her for hours. Even now. She smiled.

In the Triangle Lesley bought the first thing that attracted her; a soft wool scarf, an abstract design of browns and cream. She chatted to the shop assistant about the colour; asked if there were any hats in that chocolate shade. She was peckish but she'd get Matthew's shirt first. It was easy to shop for Matthew. He knew what he liked and what colours suited him. And for school he only ever wore a white shirt and a suit. She crossed to the department store and soon found what she wanted. She put the shirt in her basket and made her way down the escalators to the food section. Got a sandwich and a yoghurt drink.

She ate the snack in Millennium Gardens then went to Boots. There Lesley bought most of the holiday things they needed for their Easter break: sunscreen, mosquito spray, sunglasses. The carrier bag was heavy and she had to shift it from hand to hand as it bit into her fingers.

She hadn't found anything for her sister's birthday yet. Maybe something for the flat? Emma had moved recently into one of the new developments in the city centre. An old warehouse which had been converted into luxury apartments with views over the Rochdale canal and the railway, line. No garden but the buzz of being right in the middle of town, walking distance from the clubs and cafe bars. Lesley hadn't seen the place yet but it sounded very stylish: angled ceilings and curved walls, glass blocks and wooden flooring.

She stared into the window and wasn't sure whether the revivalist lava lamps and brightly coloured quirky clocks and ornaments would appeal to her sister or not. She'd try somewhere else. She crossed Saint Ann's square, went past the church with its arched windows and round pillars. The mellow red sandstone seemed to glow in the harsh light. She reached King Street with its parades of exclusive shops. The window displays vying for attention; some adventurous and arty, others restrained with only a select item or two on show. She settled for a set of six tall wine glasses. Frivolous and fragile but beautifully frosted with spots of colour.

* * *

Janine rang Pete while she was getting dressed. She couldn't remember what part of the shifts cycle he was on. He could be at work, at the airport. She hated it when Tina answered the phone. If he was in he'd probably complain, the short notice, the disruption. But there was no answer. She tried her mum next.

'Janine, hello. How are you?'

'Fine, Mum. Look, it's work. Could you have the children?' She'd never say no though sometimes Janine wished she had a few more options open. Her parents weren't getting any younger and the kids wore them out. Lately Dad had been ill, too, arthritis getting worse and his energy a fraction of what it used to be.

'Of course, it'd be lovely,' her mum said.

Janine chivvied the kids to get ready and hustled them from the house.

'Why d'you have to work?' Eleanor complained.

'That's how it goes, Ellie. If I get called up I have to go in.'

Tom ran to the car. Had he got his inhaler? 'Tom?' He knew what she was asking and patted his pocket.

'Good boy.' She caught sight of his trainers which were in an atrocious state. No time to sort that out today. There was never enough time. It had been even harder since Pete had gone. She hadn't had the heart to advertise for a new home help, and as a result things felt chaotic.

'Can't we go to Dad's?' Eleanor asked.

'Dad's not in,' Janine told her. And you'll probably have to go there tomorrow if this turns out to be what I think it is, she added to herself.

Twenty minutes later she had deposited the children and driven to the new South Manchester headquarters. On the way, waiting at traffic lights, she had checked her appearance in the rear-view mirror. Dark hair with highlights cut just below chin length which framed her face, an attractive face, her eyes large, mid-blue, accented by a barely discernible trace of make-up. She'd a generous mouth, full lips and a good smile. She ran a sheer lipstick over her mouth.

It wouldn't be her first murder; she'd worked plenty of those, but her first time in charge. What if she was wrong? What if she'd been summoned for something completely different? What? What else could it be?

She knocked on The Lemon's door, read the plaque for the umpteenth time, *Detective Chief Superintendent L. Hackett*, and heard him call her in.

'Morning.' He gestured that she take a seat. He looked across at her, intense blue eyes blazing out of folds of skin, mouth puckered, nose wrinkled. Usual expression, like he'd just sucked a lemon or had one shoved somewhere else. He was a sour man, his wit and laughter as acidic as the nickname she had given him.

Janine noticed that Hackett's computer had crashed, a strange pattern of ghostly folders mosaiced the surface. It was common knowledge that Hackett was baffled by IT and refused even to read e-mails.

'Sir.'

Hackett fiddled with a pen. 'Lawson's on long-term sick.'

She nodded. Stress. He'd cracked up after his wife left him. Everyone had seen it coming. Like an accident waiting to happen. Impossible to avoid. That moment when you saw the car ahead, computed the moment of impact and knew beyond any doubt that you would hit it. Lawson had lost it at Easter. Gone home early one day after smashing the mirrors in the gents. Never came back. She'd called, offered to visit but he said it would be better without his old team around. 'Just need to sort it out, Janine, sort my head out, you know.' Heart more like.

'O'Halloran's got the airport thing.' The Lemon continued to list the ongoing murder investigations and the CID officers leading them. He was leading up to giving her a case. It couldn't be anything else! She wished he'd get his skates on. He was tapping the pen against his blotter as he spoke. 'Cragg has got annual leave. He reckons his missus will walk out if he cancels.'

'New Zealand, they've family there,' she said.

He glanced at her, irritated by the interruption. She kept her face set, pleasant and attentive. Wouldn't give him the satisfaction. He tapped the pen faster. 'So I'm going to give you a crack of the whip.'

Her heart squeezed in her chest. About bloody time. Yes! Her own case. Leader of the gang. She fought not to beam at him like an idiot.

'Won't let you down, sir. What is it?'

'Gorton Avenue, allotments off Mauldeth Road West. Man found there by one of the other gardeners. We're treating it as suspicious. You can set up an incident room here. Near enough. Doc's on his way as are SOCOs.' He referred to the scene of crime officers. 'Not sure who'll assist as yet. Janine?'

'Yessir.'

'You report to me on this.'

'Yessir.'

'Daily. Any concerns, queries, cock-ups — you bring it straight to me. Understood?'

'Yessir.'

He sat back indicating she should leave.

She stood and nodded at the computer screen in the corner. 'Alt, control, delete, sir. Only way out.'

His jaw twitched. Only trying to help, Janine thought.

In the corridor she checked there was no one in sight, took two or three steps and then broke into a shimmy, thumbs up. 'Yes! Yes! Yesss!'

* * *

There were buses from the Arndale Centre every quarter of an hour. Dean stood with his holdall. The bus station had a chill feel to it. The buses would lumber in every few minutes and disgorge a bunch of people. The drivers exchanging a word with their mates, nipping out for a fag or a cup of tea. Dean was starving but he didn't want to use up anymore of his cash.

He hoped Douggie was there. He'd tried his mobile but there was no answer. Eejit had probably switched it off. He smiled. Douggie was a good mate. The best but he wasn't all that sharp sometimes. They'd met in Hegley Young Offenders Institution, Deadly Hegley they called it on account of all the suicides. Kids had been dying to get out of there. Literally. Swingers; found dangling in their cells, or bleeders; hacking away at veins with any bit of an edge they could find. Rumour had it that one lad tried to top himself by smacking his head against the wall. Again and again, like trying to crack a coconut. He'd not managed but he had given himself brain damage, which was probably just as good a way out. Then another rumour flies round how it was the screws that did it; bit of punishment got out of hand. Sex and violence with a lad who'd never tell. Couldn't after that, anyroad.

Maybe he'd call Paula from Oldham. Explain that he had to get away. Try and assure her. He had a sudden glimpse of her face, a frown puckering her forehead, swinging her hair in a shake of annoyance that rattled her beads together.

He thought of losing her and felt his eyes smart. She didn't go with anyone else but him. She had wanted that. It was an easy promise to keep — he'd never had such good sex or so much of it. He felt himself swelling at the thought. Paula had taught him the intoxicating art of seduction, of teasing and waiting and playing and making it last and last so they could be up most of the night with dirty soul music on the CD player, stopping now and then for a spliff or some wine or even some food, and then back to it. He groaned, partly because of the sensation in his groin but mainly because of the despair that the prospect of life without Paula raised in him. And he couldn't see his way round the problem.

A gust of diesel-filled air swirled the litter up and cast it around the place. His mouth was dry. Sod it. A can of Coke and a bag of crisps wouldn't break the bank. If he missed the bus there'd soon be another. He pushed himself off the shelter and headed off in search of a kiosk.

* * *

From the bridge on Withington Road, Janine Lewis could see the tent they'd erected to protect the scene of the crime. It would be hidden to passing motorists, as would the whole of the allotments which were on lower ground adjacent to the disused railway line. The cutting was awash with rubbish: mattresses, spilt bin liners and rusting metal. Plenty to clear up if they were going to use this for the MetroLink extension and bring the trams along here to link Chorlton and Didsbury.

She took in the scene before her. The allotments stretched below, in a rough rectangular patchwork, five rows deep and five or six plots across. The railway line formed the boundary to the left, and Gorton Avenue, a row of terraced houses with their yards and a back alley, ran along the right. A similar row, Denholme Avenue, stood at the far end facing her and parallel with Withington Road.

The city was full of housing like this, built to accommodate the workforce that had piled into Manchester to work in the cotton mills, the docks, the warehouses, on the canals and railways. Serried ranks of redbrick terraces, grey slate roofs.

Most of the garden tracts were models of industry, rows of winter cabbages and sprouts, soil dug ready for sowing, canes like wigwams for the coming season's beans and sweet peas, greenhouses, piles of pots and compost heaps. A couple of the allotments had run to neglect, with tall weeds, long grass and ruined sheds.

The whole picture glinted in the silvery winter sun.

The allotments could be reached from either of the stretches of housing. Plenty of escape routes. Someone fleeing the scene could have headed for the houses, or gone along the railway line in either direction or even up the steps to the bridge and away along the road.

She turned back to the tent and the comings and goings of small figures. It was pitched in the corner plot nearest to her, on the back row furthest from the long stretch of houses. Here and there faces peered out of bedroom windows, a child sat on a back alley wall and a small knot of neighbours waited in the alleyway near to the scene. She needed to get the house-to-house started. But first, she had a corpse to view. She opened the car boot and pulled out protective overalls and shoe covers; lucky they were a fit and she was able to close the zip up over her bump.

Janine made her way to the young PC who was guarding the entrance to the scene.

'You got the call?'

'Yes, ma'am, boss,' he stumbled over his words. Couldn't be much older than Michael.

'From the beginning, Constable. Nice and slow.' Janine told him. She knew she'd get a better response if she gave the lad some time to get his act together. He fumbled with his notebook.

'I was on Mauldeth Road West when I heard the dispatch. Eleven o'clock. I got here and a Mr Simon said there was a Mr Matthew Tulley, he knew him, like, on the allotment. He rang from home, Mr Simon I mean.'

Well it would hardly be Mr Tulley, would it? She nodded.

'Mr Simon lives at the end there,' he pointed to the terrace nearest to the road bridge where Janine had surveyed the scene. 'So I come down and have a look and checked for signs of life but there weren't none.' The man swallowed hard. His first body, she assumed.

'Did you touch anything else?'

'Only the body . . . the deceased.' He remembered the correct terminology. 'His neck and his back, when I was checking him.'

'And since then?'

17

'SOCOs arrived and secured the scene.'

'Good.'

An appalling blush suffused the young man's face. Christ, she thought, they'll eat this one alive.

She walked along the path towards the far plot where the plastic tarpaulin had been erected and the SOCO team were busy. Janine ducked underneath the blue and white police tape that cordoned off the area and trod carefully on the metal plates that had been laid down for everyone to walk on, to minimise disturbance of the scene. She could see the body, the head and shoulders on the ground immediately outside the shed door.

Rachel Grassmere, the scene of crime specialist, was taking notes, peering carefully at the floor and adding to the small card markers that had been numbered and placed at points to indicate possible evidence. Other scene of crime officers worked the scene: measuring, recording, filming, collecting, in among the little white markers.

Doc was kneeling beside the corpse, a Dictaphone in one gloved hand. The still cool air held a sickening mix of aromas; the stink of faeces and the nauseating tang of spilt blood. Janine sucked at her tongue to forestall the retching reflex. She wanted it under control before she looked any more closely at what was making the smell.

Rachel Grassmere glanced up and nodded hello, handed Janine a packet of Fisherman's Friends. She took one gratefully, crunching on the lozenge to release the powerful fumes into her nose and mouth, to mask the stench.

'Chief Inspector Lewis,' Rachel Grassmere said.

'This your baby?'

'You could say that,' Janine looked at Grassmere then at her bump. Raised her eyebrows. Grassmere grinned.

Janine studied the body. The man lay face down with his hands beneath him, half in and half out of the shed. His head was turned to the side so she could see the peculiar glassy stare of one eyeball and the right side of his ashen face. His mouth was pulled down in the slack repose that death left. He had black hair. Around him on the earth, his blood had spread, a pool of dark, lustrous liquid. The victim was wearing dark corduroy trousers, an anorak. She couldn't see his footwear clearly, his feet rested inside the shed but they looked like some sort of boot, chunky soles. Had he fallen here? Or crawled out from the shed? She would ask Forensics to try and establish that.

'No visible sign of injury on the back, back of the skull or legs,' Rachel Grassmere told her. 'Doc's just finishing off. We think we've got a shoe-print.' Grassmere pointed and Janine followed her out to where a green plastic butt with a simple tap stood, the ground a little damp around it. 'Looks like a partial sole from a trainer.'

She could barely make out the geometric pattern, would never have known it was there if she hadn't been shown.

'Went to wash his hands, or his shoes?'

'Mr Tulley?' Janine asked.

Grassmere shook her head. 'Different tread.'

Janine waited at the edge of the area observing the SOCOs at their work. She was eager to hear what they had found, what tiny clues pointed this way or that, but knew better than to press for information too soon.

She heard someone call her name and turned to look. Someone approaching. Tall bloke, slim build, nice face . . . she recognised that face . . . Richard Mayne! What on earth was he doing here? He lived down in London, had done since Tom was a baby. He carried a protective suit closely rolled in his hand.

'Richard!'

He smiled. 'Hello, stranger.'

Janine felt slightly embarrassed as she realised what she must look like in the Andy Pandy suit.

'What you doing on my patch, then?'

'Whatever you say, boss. I'm at your service.'

Janine shook her head. 'I didn't even know you were back.' But it was great to see him. He was an excellent copper and a good mate. They'd had a laugh in the old days, competed for their sergeant's badge, enjoyed spinning ideas off each other.

'First day. I never really felt at home down south. Like another planet.'

'Realised what you were missing?'

'Something like that.' There was a hint of mischief in his eye. She wondered what he meant exactly.

Then Rachel Grassmere called to them. 'We'll turn him, now.'

'Come and see what we've got,' Janine told Richard.

He unrolled the suit and began to pull it on.

* * *

Jade was not allowed to play on the allotments. Mam told her very clearly with her mouth pulled back so you could see her gums and the brown bits where her teeth had gone all bad. 'There's bad men go there,' she was told. 'They get little girls like you and hurt them, cut them into little pieces.'

Jade's belly hurt and she wanted to go to Nana's but if she said then Mam might guess something was up and start asking her and she couldn't tell Mam that she'd been to the allotments.

She sat on the back yard wall, watching. There was a funny tent there now like at a Funday and people waiting on the path but there weren't any balloons or burgers. Mam was still asleep and Jade wasn't allowed to wake her up. Not allowed. She was starving. Maybe if she had some food the tummy ache would go away. She jumped from the wall onto the top of the wheelie bin then down. In the kitchen she helped herself to two pieces of sliced white bread. She didn't want jam today. Okay. She didn't even want to think about that.

She went and lay in front of the telly. She picked holes in the bread, pulling pieces away and rolling them between her fingers into small, grey balls. She chewed them one at a time. She flicked the channels. Boring tennis, boring film

20

with no colours, boring car racing, boring golf, Channel 5 was so fuzzy you couldn't tell what was on. She was so bored and her belly still hurt.

* * *

Eddie Vincent stood at his bedroom window looking at the hustle and bustle below. He shivered and moved a little to the edge of the frame, peered out with rheumy eyes through the grubby, grey floral nets to the allotment beyond. He couldn't get warm, no matter what.

Stone-cold from the inside out. There were bobbies swarming all over the place. They'd put some sort of tent up around Matthew Tulley's shed. He ought to go down there — tell them what he had seen. It was his duty. And he had always done his duty. Oh, yes, he thought with rancour, he had always done his duty.

But he was too sick. They'd come calling anyroad wouldn't they? Door-to-door. On the knocker. Hah. He'd loved the door-to-door. Canvassing in the old days. You always had a few grousers, them that nothing were good for and there was no persuading them otherwise. But the rest, they'd turned out for him. And he'd won, hadn't he? Elected to the council for a good nineteen years, and then the Trots muscled in. Lads, wet around the ears, full of piss and wind and big ideas.

Couldn't do a thing while Thatcher was hacking away at everything. Thatcher, Thatcher, Milk Snatcher. He'd seen things change, then. People ground down, kids going hungry, turning wild. Apathy blooming like black mildew. And now: rickets back, TB back. Kids still dragged up in poverty. He hadn't been into Manchester for months but when he used to go he saw all the homeless and the beggars. And the NHS close to collapse they were saying.

Funny place to die, your allotment. He and Maisie had kept theirs on till the end of rationing. Lean years and they'd have been much worse but for the crops they raised there.

Not that you could grow sugar or chocolate or butter or raise a pig. But they picked sackfuls of vegetables and fruit.

When he was overseas, supplies had been regular at first, dull but ample. An army marches on its stomach after all, or crawls on it. It got harder later on. He'd eaten cat in Italy, trapped in the mountains with his chums; dark, stringy meat that made him gag but he forced it down. Not something he'd care to repeat. In fact, he'd no desire to relive any part of his life. His time was nearly up, he didn't think he'd see the year out and with that thought there came a surprising sense of relief.

He shivered again and the pain came, sluicing through his belly. He bent forward gasping, then edged along the wall to the chest of drawers. He picked up the bottle, no lid on it, and shook out a tablet. He swallowed it and turned and took two steps to the bed. He climbed in, shucking off his slippers. He pulled the eiderdown and candlewick bedspread round him, curled on his side. His arms wrapped round his belly trying to warm it. The pillow smelt fetid. He imagined clean sheets, smelling of fresh air, a hot water bottle with its rubber scent, warm milk. The comforts that Maisie would have rustled up for him. Or his mother. Dabbing Calamine on his measles, making mustard baths to break his fever, rubbing camphorated oil on his chest on bitter winter mornings. The curtains were still open, the room full of light but he was in bed now. Too weak to move. He closed his eyes.

* * *

Dean listened to the older ones chatting to the driver as they boarded.

'Cold enough for you, chuck?'

'I hate it. I like the heat, nice and hot I like it.'

'So I hear, but I was talking about the weather.'

'Cheeky bugger.'

'Oy, give her a ticket or we'll be stuck here callin' all day.'

Teasing each other, comfortable, as though the bus belonged to them. The driver whistled all the way. Dean watched the city pass. The bleak suburbs of North Manchester, practically a different country from the south where he lived. No students stayed up this side. No media people, no pavement cafes here or tapas bars. Large areas of old terraced housing had been bulldozed to make way for inner relief roads. Retail parks with their curving paths and burglar-proof metal cabins lay between landscaped areas planted with vicious shrubbery.

They went past the stadium they'd built for the Commonwealth Games 2002 and the Velodrome. Great that. Having the games. Sydney beat them for the Olympics, he could remember everyone waiting for the announcement back then, the feeling that they were up there with a chance. Gutted, they were. There was a big party down in Castlefield, he'd watched it on the telly, and people not knowing whether to laugh or cry. Least, after that, they'd got the Commonwealth, all them athletes in town, brilliant.

With a lurch he remembered why he was running. He couldn't go back inside. He couldn't. Be Strangeways this time. Twenty-two, wasn't he? Oh, Paula. Man, what would he tell her? Sick relative? Mate in trouble? Maybe if he turned it round. Told her Douggie needed him, being hassled or something. Make it sound dangerous so she wouldn't try to come calling. What was he going to do if Douggie was away? The thought drenched his back with sweat. The driver started on a new tune. Oasis — 'You Gotta Roll With It'. *Aw, God*, thought Dean, *if only* . . .

* * *

The SOCOs took positions at the shoulders, hips, knees of the body. Rachel Grassmere readied the camera and gave the count. 'On, three. One, two, three.'

They grunted with the strain as they rolled the corpse. Janine stepped back involuntarily as the mass of guts

23

slithered from the abdominal cavity with a sucking sound and came to rest over the corpse and on the ground. Lurid, multi-coloured coils: a shocking sight. She wished she'd taken two Fisherman's Friends. She thought of the book *Catch 22* where the young air man was complaining about the cold as he held his guts in his fingers. She took a small breath through her mouth. And another.

She gagged then, silently, feeling the sour wash hit her throat. She swallowed hard, kept her mouth tight shut. Everything sticky with blood. So much of it. Trousers and t-shirt stiff with the stuff. The left side of his face darker where the blood had pooled after death. She was amazed there'd been any left in him.

'That is nasty. Very nasty.' Richard said.

'Thank God I skipped breakfast,' said Janine.

She turned away, from the sight and smell, drank in the cold, cleaner air, took a few steps down the plot. He had put a lot of work in here, Mr Tulley. She was no big gardener but she knew enough to recognise the fruits of labour. Rows of cabbages and the tops of root veg at one side. Plots clear and the ground prepared for more. She wondered who he was, this murder victim? What sort of man was he, who'd planted the seeds here and picked the harvest and pottered in his shed? In the hours and days to come she would be finding out everything about him. Nothing would remain private. It would become her property: his life; to study and explore, to sift through and sort and peer into in her efforts to find out who killed him. Who had robbed him of that life, left him to bleed on the cold, winter ground?

CHAPTER THREE

'Chief Inspector.' They called her back. The deceased was now wrapped in a body bag which lay to the right of the path backed by a border of small cyclamens. The juxtaposition made her think of some modern art installation. Doc was packing his bag. Rachel Grassmere stood by the shed doorway. 'Looks like it started in here,' she said.

Janine moved over and Richard followed. She peered inside, careful not to touch the doorframe and spoil any possible prints. The stench of death still tainted the air. The shed was large with potting tables on two walls and tools hanging on the third. Neat and tidy. No smashed pots or spilt compost.

'We've blood spray to the wall either side of the door and the floor here. We'll try for prints on the door frame, the gate, door, tap on the water butt over there.'

She took in the splashes, ochre against the greying wood of the shed. 'Rough wood.' Janine noted.

'Yep. Not promising anything.'

'Probably a knife,' Richard said.

'Well spotted, Sherlock,' Janine said wryly.

Janine retraced her steps to the young PC at the gate. 'Constable.'

'Yes, sir — ma'am.'

'What else do we know about Mr Tulley?'

He rifled through his pages. 'He lives round the corner, Ashgrove. It's a big house on the corner, further up. He's a teacher,' he added, 'the deputy head at Saint Columbus High.'

Deputy head. A professional man, then. Perhaps the allotment had been his way of unwinding, escaping from the demands of busy school life.

'Lives alone?'

The eyes panicked, a fine sweat burst onto the upper lip. 'Don't know.'

More officers arrived to be briefed by Rachel Grassmere for a fingertip search of the allotment and nearby area. Janine watched them gather round for their instructions and she signalled with a wave that she was on her way. She removed the bunny suit and slippers and bagged them. They would be retained in case there were any allegations of cross-contamination by the defence should charges be brought. She would call on Mr Simon, the man who'd found the body, and hear the gist of his story. Richard came over to join her. She asked him to set house-to-house in motion and then come and find her.

* * *

'What's going on?' Mam said.

'Don't know,' Jade said quickly.

'Out there,' Mam hung onto the sink, stood on tip toes to try and see over the wall. 'Something is.' She opened the back door and went out. Jade followed her. Their back gate was broken. The wood had gone all soft and crumbly and one day when Mam was putting the wheelie bin out the top hinge had come loose. Now you had to open it carefully or it swung over and nearly fell right off. Jade never bothered, she just climbed up onto the wheelie bin and over the wall instead.

Jade watched Mam lift the gate open and go out into the back alley. Jade climbed up to sit on the wall. The stone was cold through her clothes.

'What is it?' Mam asked.

'They've found a body,' one of the neighbours said.

'What, down there?'

'Yeah.'

'Do they know who it is?'

'Mr Tulley, deputy at St Columbus.'

They were all excited, like it was a special on *EastEnders* or something. Good and awful all mixed up.

'His insides were hanging out.'

'Good God.'

'Who'd do a thing like that?'

'Like the Ripper.'

'Only saw him last Sunday at church.'

'He teaches our Joanne.'

No one bothered Jade. There was a lump of moss on the wall. It was dry and soft, like a fairy carpet. Jade stroked it. If she looked close there were tiny brown stalks sticking up from the green with little bells on the end of them. She flicked them with her fingers.

They talked for ages then Mam said she felt rough and had to go in. She made a drink and took one of her tablets. Pretty soon she started looking sleepy again. Jade said, 'Can I get some sweets?'

'I don't know how much there is left,' Mam said.

'I'll look.' Jade brought Mam's purse.

'Two twenties and a fifty and two tens.'

Mam gave her twenty pence.

'Can I go to Megan's?'

'Come straight back if they're not there.'

Jade got lollies, they lasted longest. There was no answer at Megan's. When Jade got back she heard her mam being sick in the bathroom. Yeuch. Double yeuch. Jade waited for ages before she went upstairs. Mam was back in bed. Just a lump under the duvet. Sometimes Mam's tablets made her sick and sometimes the vodka did and sometimes just a bug.

* * *

Janine took a bite of chocolate. 'I hate this bit.'

'Waiting to break the news?' Richard asked, opening his packet of crisps.

They were sitting in Janine's car outside the Tulleys' house.

'More the forked tongue. Weighing them up. What's real grief supposed to look like anyway?'

'You do it very well, as I remember.'

She tipped her head to acknowledge this. 'A random attack? Or someone who knew him, knew the allotments? Think we can rule out aggravated burglary. Someone after his Flymo doesn't quite cut it.'

'Might be school not home, trouble in the staff room?' Richard munched. 'So you finally got it — your own investigation?'

'Beat you! The Lemon didn't like it.'

Richard frowned.

'Hackett,' she explained. 'Suits him, don't you think?' She screwed up her mouth, wrinkled her face. 'He's still getting over my promotion to Chief Inspector. But we're short-handed and he's being leaned on to meet his minority targets — and despite my size, I'm a minority.'

'And O'Halloran's still hanging on?' They'd both worked with O'Halloran in the old days.

'Bully Boy. Too right. Lemon won't touch him.'

'I heard,' he hesitated, 'you and Pete.'

She took a breath. 'Tina. Latest home help. Helped herself all right.'

Richard shuffled in his seat. 'Did he know . . . you were pregnant?'

'Oh, yeah. We'd both been in deep shock for a few weeks already. First weekend alone, in Barcelona, for our sixteenth anniversary — big, romantic gesture: all a decoy.'

Richard looked puzzled.

'He was sleeping with her way back then: bastard. Anyway, too much Rioja and bingo: our own special souvenir.' She patted her stomach. 'I'd have settled for a pair of castanets and a straw donkey.'

Richard laughed. She had always been able to make him laugh.

'How are the kids?'

'Tom's six, now.'

'You're joking!'

'Been rough on them. Pete's still on air traffic control, shifts. They barely see him some weeks. They miss him.'

'And you?'

She sighed. 'Good days, bad days. It's not been long. I gave him a second chance, with the baby and all. He moved in with her.' And it still hurt. That he'd been willing to walk away from all they had, the kids, the marriage, their lives. For what?

'What about you?' She broke another square of chocolate off.

'Single again.'

'Really?' She was surprised. Had assumed he'd moved back with his wife. 'You and Wendy?'

Richard nodded and then they both heard the sound of a car slowing. Watched the silver Volvo turn into the driveway and park.

Janine observed the woman, slim, dark-haired, petite, laden with packages as she got out of the car and opened the door to Ashgrove. It wasn't strictly her job to inform next of kin but in a case of murder the spouse was always a prime suspect and she wanted to scrutinise Mrs Tulley's reaction to the news. She recorded the time in her notebook.

She turned to Richard. 'Take notes while we're in there.'

'Yes, boss.'

'Let's go.' She braced herself for the difficult task ahead.

CHAPTER FOUR

Dean stood in the shadow of Oldham bus station and punched in Douggie's number.

'Douggie, yer dub brain, where've you been?'

'An' I love you too, Dean.'

'Yer were switched off.'

'It's the moby. It's rubbish. I got it off this bloke on the market and it only works half the time. So — what's new?'

'I was wondering, can you put us up for a bit?'

'No worries. And is Paula coming too?'

'Nah, just me.'

'You'll need directions, mate. Hang on.' Dean could hear Douggie yelling to someone, something about milk and Frosties. Then he came back on the line. 'Tosser,' he volunteered, 'thinks food grows in the dark while he's sleeping, like mushrooms. Yeah, take the M66 . . .'

'No wheels.'

'What?'

'Starter motor's gone. Give us directions from the bus station.'

Douggie told him which way to go, there was a bus or he could walk it in twenty minutes but it was all uphill.

Like bloody life, thought Dean. 'See you in twenty minutes.'

'You what?'

'I'm in Oldham.'

'Aw, right. Nice one. See yer mate.'

He wanted to be honest with Paula. He was honest with her. Well, some little things he hadn't told her, things from the past. One or two big things maybe but he'd never lied about new stuff. Now all this going down. If he told her it all straight she wouldn't understand. She wouldn't see why he had to run. She'd never had the sort of troubles he had.

Douggie would get it no messing. Douggie knew where he was coming from. He'd walked the same road. Been there, got the t-shirt. Dean turned to face the redbrick municipal building that marked his route up the hill to Douggie's. God, he was thirsty. Freezing cold lager, drops of water beading the can, something with a bite to it, slipping down in long cold pulls. Christ, Douggie better have some dosh 'cos he sure as hell couldn't afford it.

* * *

'Mrs Tulley?'

She nodded. Concern clouding her eyes.

'I'm Detective Chief Inspector Lewis and this is Detective Inspector Mayne; Greater Manchester Police, CID.' They held up their identification cards. 'Can we come in for a minute?'

'Why?'

'If we could talk inside.'

She lead them into the lounge. A large, high-ceilinged room with a white Adam-style fireplace and a contemporary, uncluttered feel. Like Mrs Tulley, thought Janine, the same simplicity in the woman's dress; her long-sleeved, scoop neck top and calf-length skirt, as in the room design.

'Matthew Tulley is your husband?'

'Matthew?' A note of surprise in her voice. 'Yes. What about him?'

'I've some bad news, I'm afraid.'

'Oh, God.' Her face changed, fear flooding in. 'What is it?' Mrs Tulley whispered. 'Has there been an accident?'

Janine noted the woman's assumption. 'I'm really sorry, Mrs Tulley,' she paused, trying to be as gentle as she could with the terrible bombshell she held. 'I'm very sorry to have to tell you that Matthew's dead.'

'No,' Lesley Tulley covered her mouth with one hand and brought the other to join it. Rocked forward slightly. 'No,' she repeated and closed her eyes. She lifted her head a little to speak, 'What happened?'

'Please, Mrs Tulley, sit down.'

She complied and Janine sat down too. Lesley Tulley was gasping, shaking her head. Eyes wide and pained. Janine put one hand on her shoulder, a fleeting touch, some human contact in the middle of the horror. Janine waited, gave her time. Lesley stared at Janine then looked at Richard and apparently failing to make sense of the situation let her gaze slip away.

'What happened?'

'We're not sure at the moment but we're treating his death as suspicious.'

Lesley looked at her confused.

'We believe someone else was involved.'

'Someone hurt him?'

'I'm sorry, I realise how difficult this must be.'

'How . . . ?'

'We believe some sort of weapon was used.'

Lesley shook her head, trying to wake up from the nightmare.

'Is there someone you can call? Someone who can be with you?'

'My sister, Emma.'

'We'll ring Emma in a minute. Have you other family close by?'

'No one. Just Emma and me.'

'We should notify Matthew's family, his parents . . .'

'They're both dead. There isn't anybody.'

'Lesley,' Janine spoke slowly, as gently as she could. 'I'm afraid we will need a family member to identify him but if you don't feel able to—'

'I'll do it.' Tears started in her eyes. 'I want to see him.'

'It's just a formality. We're sure that it's Matthew.' Janine didn't want to leave any false hope lingering. 'I realise this is an awful, terrible shock, but I do need to ask you one or two questions? Can we get you a cup of tea?'

Lesley Tulley nodded as if in a trance. Janine glanced at Richard, he went to make the tea.

'Just tell me if you need to stop at any time,' Janine said.

* * *

'Yo, Dean.'

'All right, Douggie.'

The friends hugged, a swift strong embrace, then parted. 'Come in.'

In the kitchen at the end of the hall a lad sat at the table taking apart a car radio. Dean judged him to be sixteen or so.

'This is my cousin,' said Douggie, 'Gary. It's his dad's house, he's got a few round here. This is Dean what I told you about.'

Gary grunted but continued to work away with the screwdriver.

'So, how goes it?' Douggie pulled out a chair, pulled Rizla papers and a pack of cigarettes from his hip pocket. 'What's the story, Dean?'

Dean remained standing. 'Douggie, a word?' Nodded towards the hall. Douggie looked a bit narked at that but followed Dean all the same.

'This the lounge?'

'Yeah, you'll have to kip in here.'

Dean went in. Sat down, waited till Douggie joined him. Spoke quietly, looking Douggie in the eye all the while. 'Me being here, and my reasons for being here, I don't want no one to know, right?'

Douggie bobbed his head in agreement.

'Not even family,' Dean gestured back towards the kitchen. 'Far as he's concerned I'm here for a friendly visit. Yeah? No whisper of trouble. Not a word. Right?'

'Course,' Douggie replied, an edge of irritation in his tone, denying he'd ever have thought otherwise.

'I'll tell you about it later,' Dean told him. He knew he could trust Douggie once he'd made things plain. Douggie's only problem was he never thought things through, you had to do his thinking for him. Keep it simple and he was fine.

'Toilet upstairs?'

'Can't miss it.'

'Watch me.'

'Har har.'

'And I'm parched, you got any drink in to go with that smoke?'

'Tea?'

'I was thinking more along the lines of something export strength,' Dean raised his eyebrows.

'Nah,' said Douggie.

Dean felt a surge of frustration. He didn't want to be here. He was tired and thirsty, he was bleedin' ravenous and now Douggie was going to tell him there was naff all till his Giro came.

'But it can be arranged,' Douggie, grinning, pulled a large roll of notes from his trousers. 'How about an Indian, an' all?'

Dean smiled, ran his hands through his hair it back from his face. 'What yer waiting for? Mine's Lamb Rogan Josh, extra naan, fried rice, couple of pakoras.'

* * *

Richard filled and switched on the jug kettle and found mugs, tea bags and milk. The fridge was well-stocked with a variety of dairy produce and salad vegetables. The kitchen was tidy, everything tucked out of sight bar the toaster and kettle. Tastefully decorated with pale yellow walls, blond wood counters, grey slate floor tiles. He peered into the door of the washing machine and saw that a very small load had been washed. Something dark, with a white piping stripe, running pants or something similar.

He wondered where they kept the knives. Hunting for a teaspoon he found the cutlery, the deep basket drawer included a block of fancy French kitchen knives, all present and correct. He made the tea and returned to the lounge.

* * *

Jade got her pencil case and her colouring book. She sat at the kitchen table and she did three pages. Didn't go over the lines, not once. Then she did a drawing for Mam. It was loads of flowers and butterflies and a fairy, except one of the fairy's legs went wrong and was too thin and bent the wrong way. She couldn't rub it out because it was felt pen. So she covered it up by giving the fairy a long dress with pointy bits. She had to use dark blue to hide the legs and it was a bit dark so the fairy wasn't so good in the end. She put, *Get better soon, love from Jade*, at the bottom and a row of kisses right across. There were eighteen kisses.

A bit later on there was a knock at the door. Not Megan. Megan always did a special knock, it was their code, it was like a horse galloping. This knock was loud and slow. Four bangs. She thought it might be the man who sells potatoes or the gypsy woman with her lucky charms, but when she peered out through the nets she guessed it was a policeman, he had a clipboard and he was a bit fat with ginger hair. She crouched down and kept very still. Jade wasn't allowed to answer the door if Mam wasn't there, anyway.

When she heard them move away and knock on next door's, Jade crept up to that side of the window on her hands and knees and she heard him say police when next door answered. She felt sick. Maybe she was getting what Mam had. She didn't want to be sick. It was the worst thing in the world. She'd rather have a nosebleed than be sick. Being sick was totally, totally gross. Megan said you had to lie on your back and breathe through your nose if you felt sick. Jade lay on the carpet. It smelt hairy and it tickled the back of her knees.

She lay there for ages. She could see fairy dust swirling in the sun and it moved faster if she waved her hand at it. After a while she stopped the breathing bit and started singing. Just softly. She sang every song she could think of and then she practised doing a crab and she managed to walk like that from the middle of the room to the door without collapsing. Then at last she heard Mam getting up again, which was good because by then Jade was about to die from hunger.

* * *

Richard had handed round tea and sat poised to take notes. Janine had already established the basic facts: names and dates of birth. Married nine years. Fourteen years age difference between them.

'How did . . . you said he was attacked?' Lesley Tulley's eyes conveyed how hard this was to take in.

'We believe it was some sort of knife. There will be a post mortem and that will determine the exact cause of death. He lost a great deal of blood.'

A tiny movement, a nod. 'I can't believe it.' Mrs Tulley looked over to Janine, her face wide with misery.

Janine gave her a moment. And began. 'When did you last see Matthew?'

'This morning. He went off to the allotment.'

'What time was that?'

'About nine, I think.'

'Was that usual, for a Saturday morning?'

She nodded, her lips clenching as she battled tears.

'And you went out?'

'Yes, to town.'

'Can you think of anyone who had a grudge against Matthew? Anything like that?'

Lesley shook her head.

The doorbell rang, the sound shrilling through the house.

'I'll get that,' Richard said.

Janine heard voices outside, clamouring for answers. *Can we have a statement? How is Mrs Tulley? Who's leading the enquiry?*

'No comment, gentlemen.' Richard re-joined them. 'The press.'

Janine got up and moved across to close the curtains. 'Lesley, keep all your curtains closed. Use your answerphone, don't talk to the press.' She switched on a lamp. 'It's important that they only use the information we release to them. Okay?'

Lesley rubbed at her arms, gave a brief nod. Trying to hold it together.

Janine's phone rang. Apologising, she stepped out into the hall. It was her mother. 'Tom sounds very wheezy, Janine.'

Janine's heart sank. 'Has he complained?' Tom was able to manage his asthma pretty well, if he slowed down and complained it was a warning signal.

'No, still bouncing around.'

'I'm sure he'll be fine. I'm not sure how long I'll be but ring me again if he gets any worse, will you?'

'All right. Eleanor wants a word.'

Janine rolled her eyes, strove to summon up a bit of patience for her daughter.

'Mum?'

'Hello, Ellie.'

'They're having bacon and sausages.'

'Well, have some fruit.'

'Grandma's mean,' Eleanor whispered.

'She's not mean, she's just — have toast,' Janine couldn't get drawn into a debate now. 'I'll see you later.'

'The middle of the night,' laden with sarcasm.

'No, not the middle of the night. Bye-bye.'

Janine returned to the lounge her mind running over what else they needed from Mrs Tulley.

'Now, it would be a great help if we could take your fingerprints. It means our forensic people can eliminate them when they are looking at evidence. Inspector Mayne has a kit.'

'It's a bit messy,' he said, 'but it's quick to do.'

Businesslike he showed her how to place each finger on the pad and roll it onto the paper. 'That's fine, thank you.' He sealed the record in its envelope.

She went to wash her hands and when she came back Janine asked if there was a recent photograph of Matthew they could take.

Lesley Tulley froze, a stricken expression on her face.

'Lesley?' Janine spoke clearly as if to a sleepwalker.

Lesley rubbed at her temples and at her hair. 'Sorry photo. Yes. In the study next door.'

They went across the hallway to a smaller room. A desk with computer and accessories occupied the far wall and the others were lined with bookshelves and cupboards. Lesley opened a drawer in the desk and drew out a glossy 7 x 5 print of her husband. She handed it to Janine. 'He had them done for school,' she explained, 'all the staff have their pictures up in the entrance hall.'

The man was definitely the same person that Janine had seen at the allotments. The photo gave him a confident mien, quite different from the face on the victim. He looked healthy, energetic, competent. He wore a charcoal suit, white shirt and striped tie.

'Thank you. We need to take Matthew's diaries, check his recent e-mails.' Janine said.

Lesley nodded. Richard switched on the computer.

'When Emma arrives we will take you to identify Matthew.'

Lesley swayed and put a hand out to steady herself. 'Come and sit down,' Janine invited her.

Before you fall.

* * *

38

Dean and Douggie sprawled among the remnants of the meal from the Star of Bengal and the cans from the Late Shop. Douggie had rolled another spliff. He took a long pull, sucked it in deep and held it there for a couple of seconds. He passed it to Dean. Dean couldn't remember the last time he'd been so blasted. Usually he was with Paula when he smoked, the dope made him more aware of the physical sensations. He'd notice small things, like the feel of the bones in his fingers as he stroked her, the slip of cooler air across his shoulder, the steady tightening of the muscles in his thighs. It made everything stronger, clearer; so he could see the tiny patterns in her skin, smell the traces of soap and hair-oil and the perfume that she always wore. He would hear the rock of her heartbeat mixing with his own pulse drumming in his ears.

He took another drag. Douggie had the giggles. They'd put some old South Park videos on and Douggie flailed helplessly on the floor while the cartoons did their stuff. Dean grinned. Douggie laughed like a cartoon, wheezed like Muttley out of *Wacky Races* — hee-hee-hee — his shoulders pumping up and down. Dean had switched his mobile off. He didn't want Paula to catch him at a bad time. Needed a clear head to talk to her.

He passed the joint back. Douggie stopped giggling long enough to inhale which set him off coughing. 'Get a drink,' he choked. He waved the spliff at Dean, giving it back, and stumbled out. Dean smoked, let his eyes close, leant his head back against the couch. The video finished. He'd better catch the news later, see what was happening back in Manchester. He could hear birds twittering and the see-saw drone of scramble bikes, some dog barking for Britain. Exile, he thought, I'm in bleeding exile. Better than the nick, though. Had the police got interested in him yet?

Douggie came back in, clutching a tub of ice cream, a bottle of strawberry syrup, bowls and spoons. He put them down, took the smoke from Dean's fingers and slid onto the armchair. With a full belly and a couple of tins inside him Dean felt better than he had all day. He helped himself to ice cream.

'The money?' he asked Douggie.

'Errands,' Douggie replied. 'Doing the business.'

Dean knew he wasn't talking groceries. But Douggie wouldn't last another stretch inside. Dean shook his head.

'This is steady,' Douggie said, all wide-eyed, 'low key.'

'For now.'

'Who says it's going to change?' Douggie pulled the tub across the carpet, scooped some out.

'Course it will,' said Dean, 'everything changes, all the time, that's life.' Sounded like some crap song lyric. He shuffled, stretched his hands behind his head, tugging at the hair on his neck.

'It's cool.' Douggie insisted. 'You like a line now and then same as anyone.'

Dean sighed. 'Look, Douggie, less I know the better.'

'Kay.' Douggie shrugged. 'Sure. But if you want to make a bit of ready, I could put a word in . . .'

'There's always room for extra couriers . . .'

'No!' Dean's shout made Douggie jump. 'I don't need it . . . the mess I'm in, I need to stay clean. You understand?'

'Yeah.' Douggie glared.

Douggie'd be asking soon, wanting to know why he was here.

'I don't want to be around when anything's going down.'

'Okay.' Douggie nodded. 'I gotta go to Manchester Monday, not far from yours, this guy . . .'

'Douggie,' Dean said sharply, 'I don't need to know. Nothing.'

'Aright.' Douggie ate some ice cream. Looking at Dean from under his eyelids, mock sulk. 'Suit yourself,' he said and nodded at the sauce bottle, 'pass the Treat.'

But he couldn't leave it alone. Like a kid. 'Dean? What's going on, man? Why you here?'

'Kin' mind reader or what?'

* * *

40

Detective Sergeant Butchers consulted his list. Seven Gorton Avenue, Eddie Vincent, getting on in years. He walked along to the house and knocked on the tatty green door. This place needed work an' all. Guttering loose, rotting window frames, chimney listing to one side, looked like the painting hadn't been touched since it was built. Only little places but a shame to see them being neglected until they were past saving.

Another knock, long and loud. Come on, come on. He waited. He could hear shouts from some local match, football or hockey? Cursing, Butchers made a note on his sheet. He wondered how Shap and the others were doing on Denholme. With both roads framing the allotments the chances were that someone in the houses would have seen something that could help them. But so far all Butchers had got was a lot of ear ache about not having enough bobbies on the beat. He exhaled noisily and moved on.

CHAPTER FIVE

Eddie Vincent, sick and old, was dreaming. Mama was there with her pinny on and a flowery scarf to cover her hair. She was chasing him with the broom and he was screeching with delight. Her eyes dancing, chanting in a daft voice, 'Beware the Boggart who's come to eat. He'll drink your blood and eat your meat.'

Eddie Vincent heard knocking. The bell hadn't worked for years. He considered getting up out of bed and making his way downstairs but knew it was beyond him. He closed his eyes. His mouth was parched. He tried to swallow, to move his tongue and summon up some spit but it was all clemmed up. A drink of water. Over on the drawers but even that was too far. Never mind, he was warm now and the pain had blurred to an ache. Knocking. He'd expected someone, hadn't he? It was there, just round the corner of his memory but he couldn't quite reach it. Happen it'd be clearer in the morning. He'd be brighter in the morning, usually worked that way.

The police, that was it! They'd come back, wouldn't they? The police. If not he'd call them. Ring them up and get them to send someone round to hear what he had to say. But he was too weak now. Slowly, he pulled the corner of the bedspread up to cover his head, leaving a small gap for his nose and mouth. Keep the heat in.

Maisie had laughed at him when he used to do that, she never felt the cold, slept with her arms flung out and often as not half a leg showing. Big and warm, she was. God, he missed her. Even after all these years. Sixteen years. Still such a keen loss. Like a cut that wouldn't heal properly.

Aw, Maisie. He didn't believe in heaven but he'd a notion he'd be nearer to her in death than he was now. Never expected her to go first. He'd always imagined she'd be the one to get a phone call from a stranger or to find him slumped in his chair.

Cycling club. That's where they met. He smiled, let himself drift in echoing memories of those times. Freewheeling down from Hayfield, stopping for sandwiches and Pale Ale at a country pub, cycling behind Maisie, aching to touch her. Getting a kiss for fixing her puncture.

Then the first time they spent the day alone together. A picnic up in Peak Forest near Buxton. Cider in a flask and pork pies and hard-boiled eggs. She kissed him, slow and soft, tasting of apples. She had sighed with pleasure and stretched. She was a lioness, big boned, tawny coloured. She kissed him again, mischief in her eyes. By the end of the long, dreamy afternoon, he thought he'd died and gone to heaven.

* * *

Lesley Tulley's sister arrived within twenty minutes.

By then two uniformed officers had been drafted in to guard Ashgrove from the press pack.

Emma was a taller version of Lesley Tulley; same dark hair, same shaped face but lacking the particular combination of features that made Lesley Tulley a beautiful rather than just a pretty woman. Emma was pallid and trembling as she hugged her sister.

Janine introduced herself and answered Emma's questions as best as she could. She suggested that the Tulleys' GP be contacted in case Lesley required a sedative or sleeping pills. 'It's a huge shock at the moment, she may become more distressed later when it begins to sink in,' she spoke quietly to Emma, aware of Lesley curled into the corner of the sofa.

Janine left them to get ready for the trip to the mortuary and the formal identification and waited outside in her car with Richard.

'She never asked where he was.' Janine pointed out. 'Neither of us mentioned the allotment.'

'She knew that was where he was heading.'

'But he could have been attacked en route, rough area, more people about.'

'What do you make of her?'

Janine considered the question. It was too early to tell, really. She shrugged. Lesley and Emma emerged from the house and approached the car. Richard stepped out to open the doors for them.

Janine drove, Richard beside her. Lesley and Emma silent in the back, faces bleached by shock. At the bottom of Princess Parkway, Janine swung off the roundabout and took the road to the mortuary. The building was adjacent to the police station. From the outside it all looked bright and shiny and proud, glass and steel, reflecting the clear blue of the sky, the glint of the sun. A façade and behind it, inside the mortuary, waiting for them, was something grim and sordid and humbling.

* * *

Before Lesley went in she could feel her heart climbing into her gullet. She held her hand against her throat, the other gripping Emma's. She barely heard the man gently explaining the procedure. DCI Lewis put her hand on her arm saying, 'Take your time, just let us know if it's Matthew.' Though they'd said they were certain. She had to face the reality. To see he was dead for herself. To try and understand. She nodded to let them know she was ready.

A flashback came; her wedding day. Ivory silk dress, little country church outside Chester. Nodding and taking the first slow steps down the aisle. Matthew in a charcoal suit, turning to watch her coming. A quiet wedding, a handful of family and friends. A perfect day.

That night, in the country inn with its four poster bed and real log fire, he'd undressed her, laid her on the bed and watched her. Always watching. When at last he entered her, he slid in deep, just this side of pain, again and again, his gaze locked on hers. 'I love you, Lesley,' he said. 'You are so beautiful.' She cried when she came. He wanted to take her photograph. 'You look so beautiful.'

Suddenly shy, she said 'I don't know.'

'We're married,' he said. They both laughed.

'Mrs Tulley?' She dipped her head now to let them know she was ready and they went in to view the body.

Lesley stared through the glass at the still body of her husband. Unable to speak, she nodded to confirm his identity.

It looked like a model of Matthew, she thought, not the real thing. His skin had a yellow hue accentuated by the lighting, his hair brushed with a parting at one side; he never wore it like that. His mouth turned down giving him a glum expression. He looked older.

She wasn't allowed to touch him, they'd explained to her. The body had yet to be examined. The sheet covered everything but his head. No sign of what had been done to him. The viewing room was cold. A faint antiseptic smell percolated from somewhere as though the hard vinyl floors had just been mopped.

Lesley turned to Emma and the detectives. 'I'd like a few minutes on my own?'

They nodded and withdrew. She hitched her little knapsack over one shoulder and pressed her hands against the glass of the viewing window, tears running from her eyes. 'Matthew,' she whispered, trying the name in her mouth. The sound resonated in the stark room. But what could she possibly say? There were no words. His eyes were closed. It looked as though they had sunk a little. She imagined them drying up, the fluids leaving his body. He would never gaze at her again. His eyes a stunning blue. Hers brown. What will our children look like? A game she had played when it was still a possibility.

The thought brought a sob to her throat. She didn't know how to say goodbye, didn't know that she even wanted to. So she turned and left him.

In the corridor Emma was crying too. Lesley hugged her sister. 'Oh, Emma,' she cried, 'who would do such a thing?' Suddenly a wave of nausea swept through her, she pulled away from Emma, covered her mouth.

Janine Lewis realised what was happening. 'This way.' She led Lesley to the ladies, waited while she went into a cubicle. Impossible not to hear the noise of her vomiting. Janine leant against the wall and tilted her head back trying to squash the rising queasiness. Blame the pregnancy — anything would set her off.

* * *

In The Parkway pub on Princess Parkway, nineteen-year-old Ferdie Gibson, his head cropped so close that his scalp was visible, a badly executed tattoo of an eagle on his neck, rolled up to the bar and ordered two Stellas. The giant-sized TV screen above broadcast Man U's fixture. Ferdie sauntered over to the corner where his mates were. He passed Colin his drink.

'Ow yer doin', Ferdie?' someone said.

'Aright.'

'Tosser,' one of the lads screamed at the screen. 'Did you see that?' He swung round challenging the others to share in his indignation. 'Total crap. They ought to cut his legs off.'

Ferdie sat down, took a swig of his drink, the eagle on his neck rippled. Ferdie waited for the right moment then leant forward. 'You lot, you heard the news?'

'What?'

''Bout Tulley? Someone's done him. He's history.' Ferdie Gibson gave a wide grin. 'Down the allotments, he was.

Knifed they reckon. They took him away in a body bag. He's dead.' Ferdie's eyes gleamed. 'Come on, you lot, I'm buy-ing.' Ferdie flourished a twenty pound note and winked at Colin. 'We,' he announced, 'are going to get plated.' Laughter swirled around the group but Colin glanced away, uneasy. Then Beckham scored and the whole place erupted.

* * *

'I just need to lie down,' Lesley said. Her voice was shaky; even her skin felt tight and tired.

'Okay.' Emma said. 'Anything you want? Tea?'

'No, I'll go up, try to sleep.'

Lesley reached the door and rested there a moment. 'It's like a dream, Emma. I keep thinking I'll wake up,' her mouth quivered and she turned away.

As she walked into the bedroom she tried to compre-hend the fact that Matthew would never be here again. Not here, in this room, not in this bed, not in this house. It was a life she could not imagine. To be without him every hour of every day for the rest of her life. She closed the heavy blue woven curtains, removed her earrings and her clothes. The room was warm but she shivered and she pulled a long, soft, cotton night-dress from her dressing table drawer. She lay down at her side of the bed. How long till she took his pillow away? Grief clutched at her throat and she made a choking sound. Matthew's dead, she told herself. Matthew is dead. Matthew is dead. Sobbing, she repeated it to herself over and over until she was exhausted and had no more tears.

* * *

'Briefing in half an hour. Make sure everyone knows.'

'Yes, boss.' DC Jenny Chen nodded and withdrew.

When Chen had closed the door, Janine slipped off her shoes and stood for a moment, rolling her shoulders back to ease the tension around her neck, then kneading the small of her back. She stretched her arms up towards the ceiling and stood on tiptoe, repeated the movements several times and then made tea.

A decent cup of tea. Eighteen months ago the powers that be had installed monstrous catering machines throughout the division. They dispensed tea, coffee, chocolate, soup, Bovril and, this being the North West, Vimto. She'd tried a taste of the coffee. Once. In a briefing meeting with The Lemon. Janine had taken one mouthful from the polystyrene cup and gagged at the smell, redolent of rotting mushrooms, and at the unidentifiable bitterness which brought back memories of the stuff her mother used to paint on her nails to stop her biting them. The silky texture of the man-made creamer coated her tongue like chalk. She had leant forward as if to take a second sip and discreetly released the mouthful back into her cup, swallowed hard and brought her full attention back to the meeting.

The following day Janine had made time for a lunch break and had returned to her office with a small kettle and cafetiere, a selection of teas and coffees and a dinky mini-fridge which she plugged in and proceeded to stock with mineral water, milk and fruit juices. Sorted.

She put her feet up and began a list of items to cover at the briefing meeting. Initial reports would be given and tasks assigned to the various teams involved in the first frantic stages that followed the discovery of a body. She worked steadily, her concentration betrayed by the way she pulled and twisted her hair with her left hand.

She was interrupted by her phone. It was Michael.

'Mum, can you give me a lift home?'

'Where are you?'

'The Trafford Centre.'

'The Trafford Centre? I'm at work, Michael. Why can't you get the bus? Or try Dad.' Teenagers were like toddlers, Janine thought, the centre of their own universe, constitutionally unable to put themselves in anyone else's shoes.

The phone went dead. 'Hello?' Janine tried to call him back but there was no answer. She shook her head. What was he playing at? 'They seem to think their father's incapable,' she muttered to herself.

There was a sharp rap at the door and The Lemon came in. Janine slid her feet down. Wished she had her shoes on.

'Sir?'

'These actions, Chief Inspector Lewis,' he waved the sheaf of paperwork she had sent through. 'Some sort of joke?'

Janine frowned.

'The forensics alone will wipe out the budget and as for overtime,' his lips compressed with impatience and he threw the papers onto her desk. 'We're not a bloody charity, you can't trot around slapping it all on a credit card either. Get that back on my desk by the end of the day and cut thirty percent.' And he swept out.

Tight bastard, she thought to herself. They all knew that you had to account for every penny spent in these days of Best Value but she really hadn't gone over the top.

* * *

Bobby Mac, a homeless man, was roaring drunk. Wheeling round and round on Market Street, his over coat flying out like a Cossack's skirt. He tried to kick a leg out and stumbled backwards, knocking into a stroller pushed by a young man. 'Piss off,' the lad shouted. 'Watch the baby. Bloody nutter.'

Bobby scrambled to his feet, swung round. Who was calling him? He'd have 'em. People looking at him. 'Piss off,' he echoed, 'go on the lot of you.' He ran at a knot of teenage girls. They scattered, squealing and swearing.

'Come on, now.' One of the *Big Issue* sellers moved towards Bobby. 'S alright. Calm down, calm down. It's Bobby, isn't it?'

'Bugger off,' said Bobby though his manner was less aggressive. 'What you looking at?' He shrieked at the Saturday afternoon crowd gathering round.

The busker playing the saxophone stopped and bent to collect his change.

'I'm as good as you. I was in the army. BFPO . . .' He couldn't remember the number. 'I had a wife and an 'ouse. I had a wife.' He stopped, suddenly bewildered. He rubbed at his mouth with the back of his sleeve, teetering on his feet. The men at the stall selling inflatable hammers, umbrellas and socks, four pairs for a pound, were watching.

'Sit down, mate,' the *Big Issue* bloke nodded to the benches in the middle, 'have a rest. Come on.' He put his hand out.

'They want to clear them off the streets,' a woman's voice rang out. 'Beggars.'

'Keep away.' Bobby's eyes narrowed. Spit flew as he spoke to the paper seller. 'I know your sort. You're just like the rest.'

The vendor moved away, hands raised in a gesture of surrender.

'Well, I'll show you. I'll show you. I know how to look after myself. I was a soldier. BFPO. Yes sir!' he shouted. Fumbled in his coat. Coughed and hawked a gob of phlegm to the floor. He withdrew the knife with a clumsy flourish. 'Used to be bayonets. See?' He pushed it at the boy. 'See?'

'Aw, hell,' said the vendor taking another step back. The store guard at New Look punched in the code to call the police from the Arndale Centre.

* * *

Dean told Douggie everything. By the time he'd finished Douggie was in no mood to giggle.

'What am I gonna do? I'm not going down again, Douggie. No way. It'd kill me, man. And Paula . . .' He stumbled to a halt, eyes hot, mouth dry.

Douggie shrugged. 'Stay here, man. That's fine. Long as it takes.'

* * *

While she waited to start the briefing, Janine took round Eleanor's sponsorship form.

Butchers methodically entered an amount and returned the form. Janine looked. '50p — Total!' she said in disgust. 'Push the boat out, Butchers, why don't you.'

She turned to Richard. 'Come on, our Eleanor's sponsored skip. Good cause.'

He smiled and took it from her. She watched and did a double take as he offered a pound a lap. 'She'll do the whole lot, you know,' she warned him. 'Serious skipper.'

Richard shrugged.

Rachel Grassmere arrived and Janine put the form away and moved to the front of the room in front of the boards that already held details about the case. Time to begin the briefing. Her throat went dry and she felt her chest tighten. Nerves. She took a deep breath and lifted her chin, determined to show the team that she could handle it.

'Good afternoon, everybody. DS Butchers,' she nodded to the plump, ginger-haired man who wore one of his collection of appalling character ties, 'and DS Shap.' Ferret-faced Shap cocked his head, a half-smile on his lips. She knew Shap to be an effective detective, quick off the mark but a little too lax about playing by the rules. The opposite of Butchers, in fact, who had struggled to make sergeant and was a stickler for detail.

'DC Jenny Chen.'

Chen was new, a bit of an unknown quantity. Tall, willowy, gorgeous-looking. Janine wondered whether her beauty would be an asset or a handicap in the job.

'DI Richard Mayne,' Richard lifted a hand in greeting as she introduced him, 'back from far flung parts, he'll be my second in command.'

'And Miss — erm . . .' Damn! She'd gone blank. She stared at the woman, forensic specialist, mid-length blonde hair, lovely face. Rachel . . . Rachel . . . she felt her face get warm. Just as panic began to kick in Rachel helped her out.

'Grassmere.'

Janine smiled, nodded her thanks. 'Grassmere, from Forensics. Good to see you all. So what have we got?' She pointed to the picture of the teacher behind her. 'Victim, Matthew Tulley, age forty-two, deputy head master at St Columbus Roman Catholic High School in Whalley Range. Wife, Lesley Tulley, age twenty-eight, both lived at Ashgrove, Barnes Lane. Last alleged sighting of Matthew Tulley, at home about nine this morning when he left Mrs Tulley to go to his allotment.'

She referred again to the display where there was a sketch of the allotment and nearby streets. 'Deceased discovered and reported at eleven a.m. by a Mr Simon who has the adjoining plot.'

Janine's stomach took a dive as she realised that there were no scene of crime photos up. Oh, hell! 'Where's scene of crime shots?' she said irritably.

DC Chen answered. 'On the way, printer's playing up . . .'

'The white heat of technology, eh?'

That won her a laugh.

'Okay. Mr Tulley was prostrate, face down, feet in the shed, torso and head out. Waiting for confirmation on the weapon, some sort of knife.'

'We heard it was a ritual killing, boss — he was disembowelled,' said Shap.

She raised her eyes to heaven. The men and women here, like any other people, were quick to spread rumours and latch on to any opportunity for sensationalism. 'Bollocks.' A ripple of laughter. 'No, they were intact, actually.' Janine continued. 'The wound was large enough to release the intestines, that's all. I'm off tripe for the duration.'

'Besides,' Grassmere chipped in, 'looks like he moved after the attack. There was no ritual positioning of the body post mortem, no tokens removed, no paraphernalia. Nothing like that.'

'Carry on, Miss Grassmere.'

Janine sat down, allowing the forensic scientist to take the floor. Grassmere outlined their initial findings and some of those assembled made notes in their books, and murmured comments that only their immediate neighbours could hear. 'The post mortem is underway now, fingerprints have gone off so we should have both those by the morning. PNSC have arrived,' Grassmere referred to the Police National Search Centre, 'and they are carrying out a detailed search of the allotments and environs. All sealed off till they're through.'

Janine thanked her.

'House-to-house, you know who you are?' Eight heads nodded in response. 'Carry on till dusk. Cover any sightings of people going to the allotments or coming away, any time before eleven o' clock. Also recent disturbances, unusual events in the area and any information on the victim.'

As she spoke a part of her was observing her performance, assessing her choice of words, her manner, her gestures and identifying areas for improvement. She had to be good, twice as good.

'Reports here for tomorrow morning, eight a.m. sharp.'

A couple of half-hearted groans greeted the announcement of an early Sunday.

'I could make it earlier?'

'No, boss, eight is fine.'

'Friends and associates,' she moved on. 'Inspector Mayne?'

'Appointment arranged for the morning with the headmaster, Mr Deaking.'

'Good.' She referred to her notes. 'We'll be getting a list tomorrow morning from Mrs Tulley of other friends and associates and we'll be establishing her movements this morning as well as talking to her sister. Emma is staying at Ashgrove with Mrs Tulley. Any questions?'

'Deceased have any form, boss?' Shap put in.

'Nothing on HOLMES so far.' She referred to the national computerised database that the police forces share. 'At this point no known suspects. As far as the press goes, we've issued a statement. Word travelled fast and they're camped outside the Tulleys' at present. Two officers are there to keep an eye on things. If nothing emerges in the next 24 hours we will ask Mrs Tulley to make an appeal for information. Anything else? Right, then . . .'

Her closing of the meeting was interrupted by the arrival of an officer with a box of ten by eight digital computer prints from the crime scene. 'Sorry about this,' he wheezed. 'Bloody printer's on the blink.'

Grassmere and Richard helped to pin up the photographs. They depicted the allotments from various vantage points, as well as the nearby housing, Tulley's plot, the shed inside and out, Matthew Tulley prone and on his back and close-ups of his wounds.

'Death in all its glory,' Janine said quietly.

She noted the way the squad settled, a shift in the atmosphere as each person saw what had been done to the man and as each adopted an image of the murder that would drive their work and, for some, haunt their dreams.

CHAPTER SIX

There was no bread left in the canteen when Janine called on her way out, but she managed to get a bottle of milk. She'd just got into her car, when Richard appeared. She wound down the window.

'Fancy a drink?'

'Can't — kids.'

He nodded. 'Maybe we could get a bite to eat some time?'

'Be nice.'

'Tomorrow — depending on . . .'

'Yes. I'd like that.'

'I'll . . . erm . . .' He waved his hand vaguely. She hadn't got a clue what he was trying to say but she nodded anyway. He'd always had that quirky quality, as if his mind moved too quickly for his mouth to keep up. Richard would become inarticulate or his sentences trail off but it was often because he was distracted by some complex idea or insight.

He stepped away from the car and she gave him a fare-well wave.

At her parents' she felt a wave of exhaustion. The start of the second shift — so much to do before she could get any rest.

She was stunned when Pete opened the door to her. Knew immediately something must be wrong.

'What are you doing here?'

'Someone has to pick up the pieces,' Pete said.

Michael came into the hall. Oh, God. He was hurt, his face cut and bruised. 'Michael! What's happened?'

Tom ran out from the lounge. 'Mum, Mum. He was mugged.'

He'd rung her, the Trafford Centre. He'd rung her and she'd practically ignored him. Her stomach lurched with guilt. She put an arm round Michael's shoulder. 'Are you all right? Why didn't you say?'

He shrugged her off. 'You were busy.'

That stung her.

Tom started fooling about, miming a hold-up.

'What happened?' she said again.

'They tried to get his phone,' Pete told her, his face set and anxious, 'then they duffed him up.'

'You should have just given them it,' Janine told Michael.

'I was going to,' he shouted, 'then they just ran off.'

She rounded on Pete. 'You should have rung me.' He glared back at her. She looked away. She didn't want to start arguing in front of the kids. Michael had been through enough for one day.

They were halfway home, en route to the take-away pizza place, when Janine asked Michael what the police had said. In the rear-view mirror she saw him look away. There was an uncomfortable silence. He hadn't reported it. She was shocked, he should report it, of course he should. She bit her tongue. Now wasn't the time.

She got a chance later, after they'd eaten and she was in the middle of clearing up.

'Michael . . .'

He guessed what was coming. 'I don't want to.' He yelled at her and stormed out.

'Bad time?' Sarah, her neighbour and friend, was at the back door.

'Depends.' Janine said. 'If you came bearing gifts.'

'Red or white?'

Janine gestured to her bump. She was on the wagon for the duration.

'Milk or plain?' Sarah amended. They shared a love of chocolate.

Half an hour later they were ensconced in front of the telly. Eleanor sat between Janine's knees, a towel round her neck. Janine drew the comb through another swathe of slippery hair. Spotted the telltale grey blob on the comb. 'Eleven. Other children bring home gerbils, hamsters.'

'When I grow up I'll invent a death ray for nits: one zap and they're dead. And we'll be dead rich and you'll never have to work at the weekend.'

A little dig. Janine exchanged a glance with Sarah. Ellie hated being sent to Grandma's. And Janine worried that the kids needed her around more now that Pete had gone.

Sarah scratched her head.

'Sarah's got them too,' Eleanor said gleefully.

'The whole school's got 'em, not just you kids. Occupational hazard. Staff room stinks of Tea Tree.'

'Done.' Janine told Eleanor. 'Off you go.'

'Remember the present for Holly's birthday.'

'Yes.'

Once she was out of the room Janine rang Pete. 'It's me. I'll have to drop them early.'

He sighed. 'Can't your mum have them?'

'No, you know she had them today. They want to see you, Pete.' She lowered her voice and muttered, 'God knows why.' Flicked a glance at Sarah. 'Be about half-seven, see you then.'

Janine told Sarah all about Michael's ordeal. 'I felt so flamin' helpless. And he won't report it. I started thinking, if I'd only realised, if I'd been home . . .'

'If you weren't such an awful mother.'

Janine acknowledged that. 'I'm a Detective Chief Inspector, I'm leading a bloody murder enquiry and I can't protect my own kids. Can't even keep up with the shopping.'

'What? Not still baking your own bread?'

Janine stuck her tongue out. 'How do we all keep going though?'

'What's the alternative?'

She took another chocolate and passed the box to Sarah.

'How was work,' Sarah asked her.

'Murder,' she said dryly. 'You see the news?'

Sarah shook her head.

'They didn't give details but you know the saying hung, drawn and quartered? Well, this poor bloke had been drawn. Enough to give anyone morning sickness.'

'Janine!' Sarah exclaimed. 'That's revolting. God. I don't know how you do it. I'd be in bits. And then after seeing that you've got to go after whoever's done it. I couldn't do it, no way.'

'Well, I couldn't cope with a roomful of screaming eight-year-olds all day long.' She poured more wine for Sarah, helped herself to some cranberry juice. 'However — there is good news, too.'

Sarah was all ears.

'Well, I think it's good. Richard.'

'Richard?'

'Richard Mayne. DI. We were probationers together. He transferred south when Tom was little, now he's back. Assisting me. And he is seriously sexy.'

'Whoo-oo-oo.'

'Lovely eyes, nice hands, nice lips, gorgeous lips, really, really . . .' she became tongue-tied. 'Good bloke too.'

'You fancied him before?'

'Oh, yeah! One night we were off on a training course, got as far as the bedroom but changed my mind. Pete and I were engaged. Left Richard all hot and bothered.'

'You're blushing.'

'Blame the hormones. There was something special. That spark? But I realised too late. I'd already said yes to Pete.' She paused. How long before the separation would lose its power to hurt her? Before she could talk about Pete and feel neutral, normal? 'And where's it got me?'

'Maybe this is second time lucky?'

'I don't think so,' Janine said dismissively. 'He's asked me out for a bite to eat, whatever that means. I think he was going to book somewhere but he trailed off. This habit he has, not finishing his sentences. Must have missed that bit of literacy hour.'

'Think he's interested?'

'In me? In this state?!' Janine pulled a face. 'Get a grip, Sarah. Bit of flirting, I reckon. Good for the soul. Besides, first shot as senior officer in charge of a rather gory murder, six months pregnant, romance isn't exactly on the agenda.'

She saw the news was starting and turned the sound up. 'Here we go.'

Michael looked in then, glanced at the TV, sneered and walked off. Time was he'd have been chuffed, Janine thought. Proud of her even. Not now. Rebellion, she supposed. Wanting to be different from his parents.

It was the lead story.

"The body of deputy headteacher, Matthew Tulley, aged forty-two, was found on allotments in the Whalley Range district of Manchester today. Police have launched a murder enquiry . . ."

Sarah got up and took a step towards the telly.

They were showing a shot outside the Tulley's house and Janine and Richard leaving. 'That's not my best side.' Janine pointed out.

". . . In Lancashire another two in a series of off-licence robberies . . ."

'Oh, my god!' Sarah turned back to Janine.

Janine turned the sound off. 'You know him?'

'Know of him. Through the union. He was disciplined for hitting a pupil. And last year, the lad he'd assaulted came back to school and stabbed him in the playground.'

Janine's mind was racing. Someone had stabbed Tulley before?

'Can you remember the boy's name?'

Sarah nodded. 'Yeah, Ferdie Gibson, became a sort of shorthand for dangerous pupils, anyone like that we'd call it having a Ferdie in the form.'

Janine grabbed her phone. They needed everything they could get on this Gibson.

Sarah watched her. 'What?'

'First solid lead,' Janine told her. 'Sounds like this could be the bloke we're looking for.'

* * *

Dean lay on the sofa bed in Douggie's lounge with just the glow from the VCR to take the edge off the darkness; he waited till he reckoned the others were asleep. There'd been no sounds from upstairs for a while. The place had cellars: one room with a washer/dryer in, two others derelict under the back of the house. One of them would do. He could have asked Douggie for a safe place but, since he'd learnt what Douggie was wrapped up in, he knew he should be cautious. Safer all round to keep it to himself. He had stretched over and switched on the table lamp, retrieved the carrier bag from his holdall.

The lounge door creaked when he opened it but he figured if either Douggie or Gary heard him they'd assume he needed to take a leak or get a drink. The light in the cellar worked, he went carefully down the wooden steps. Washing machine straight ahead. Turned back on himself to the empty cellars. Doorways into gloom. The first took a bit of light from the bare bulb hanging on the wire at the bottom of the stairs. Enough to spill across the dusty floor over bricks and old milk bottles and to the edge of a pile of junk up against the far wall. The place reeked of coal, the tarry smell rich in the cold, damp air, a whiff of mould too, catching at his throat.

Dean stood and examined the possibilities. He moved closer to the pile of junk. The chassis of an old pram, thick with rust, cardboard boxes, rags. There was a folding chair, striped canvas clotted with black mildew. Dean opened it a little and put the bag in the middle, folded it shut. He lifted up a piece of rotting blanket from the floor and draped it over the chair. Pushed the whole thing round to the right hand side of the rubbish, the darkest part. It wasn't perfect, Douggie or Gary could come down here and start rooting about but it was better than leaving it lying around upstairs. Ripe for anyone to pick up. That my shopping? Bloody 'ell, look at this. What you doing with this, Dean? Looking at him in a new way, thinking all sorts because of what he had in the bag.

* * *

He was lying on the table in the garden. Lesley called to him but he didn't answer. She walked over to him but suddenly there was a crowd around the table and they wouldn't let her pass. 'He's my husband,' she shouted to them, 'please, I have to help him.' People pushed and jostled her, called names. She fought her way through them with a terrible urgency.

Then she was beside him, the others fell silent.

'Matthew,' she took a pace back, her breathing heavy, the sweat cooling rapidly on her arms and legs. Matthew moved. He raised himself up and turned to face her. He smiled.

Why had she been so frightened? He was fine. 'Oh, Matthew.' He held out his arms and she walked into them, he embraced her and she let her tears fall on his chest.

'I thought you were dead,' she said.

'I am.'

She pulled back and he was all bones, a grinning skull.

Lesley woke with a jolt. Her stomach twisted tight, her heart batting against her chest. Sweating. Oh, Matthew. She missed him so. Dread came washing through her. Would it always be like this? How could she bear it?

CHAPTER SEVEN

Day 2: Sunday, 23 February

The kids were never at their best at six thirty on a Sunday morning. Nor was Janine. Yawning and struggling to clear her mind, she scraped together breakfast for them.

Tom sneaked into the room and launched himself onto her back.

'Jesus! Mind the baby,' she yelled. 'Get dressed and get your inhaler.' He shot off. 'And get Eleanor,' she called after him.

Michael was prowling around, hunting through the cupboards. When had she had the chance to get any shopping in? 'Michael,' she told him, 'if aliens had landed in the middle of the night and stocked the larder I think we'd have heard them.'

Pete was on the doorstep when they reached his place. A trendy waterside development in Salford Quays, which he'd rented when he'd slung his lot in with Tina. There was no way he was going to move into the place Tina already had. Liked his comfort did Pete. Janine thought he looked slightly ridiculous in his new setting; fifteen years too old and not nearly trendy enough.

The kids filed out of the car. Tom dived at his dad who caught him and swung him about before sending him inside.

'Least they'll feed us.' Michael's parting comment.

Janine wound her window down a bit. 'I'm not sure when I'll finish. I'll ring. Tom's a bit chesty, I think he'll be all right but keep an eye on him. Oh, and Eleanor's gone completely veggie now.'

Pete looked sick. 'Well, what on earth do we give her?'

Janine started the engine, flashed him a brittle smile and waved as she drove off. Petty maybe but deeply satisfying.

* * *

Emma was still asleep but Lesley had been up since three. She had wrapped herself in a duvet, turned the fire on in the lounge and tried to get warm. The phone went very early but they had left the answerphone on as the police had suggested. She listened to the stilted recording and then the caller spoke. She recognised his voice before she even made sense of the words. Adrenalin coursed through her, raising gooseflesh on her arms and making her heart stutter.

'Lesley? Pick up the phone.'

She shook her head, petrified. Clasped her hands to her ears to shut out the voice. 'Lesley, I know you're there. Pick up the phone. Talk to me, Lesley.'

Her teeth began to chatter and her breath came in little gasps. He was after her. Oh, God! He was after her.

* * *

The team were there on time, though DS Shap looked as though he'd not stopped to wash or shave on the way in. Janine plonked a large box of croissants down on the table alongside the coffee that Richard had ordered for the meeting.

'Dig in,' she told them, helping herself to a chocolate one. Butchers moved with surprising speed for a man of his bulk, as if he was frightened there wouldn't be enough to go around. The others dived in after him.

'Ferdie Gibson,' Janine nodded to the board where Ferdie's details had been added. An unflattering photo of the shaven-headed youth complete with inky blur on his neck. 'We should have known about the stabbing yesterday.'

'Not on file, boss,' DC Chen explained, 'it was never reported.'

'We'll be paying Ferdie a wake-up call after this meeting. Now,' Janine licked her fingers, 'we still have nine a.m. as the last sighting. Witness places Matthew Tulley between his house and the allotments then.' She turned to Shap and Butchers. 'I want all house-to-house accounted for by the end of today.'

They nodded.

'One thing's puzzling me,' she continued. Richard looked expectant. 'Why didn't Lesley Tulley tell us about Ferdie Gibson?'

'Shock?' he suggested.

Janine pulled a face. She looked at the boards again where Lesley Tulley's picture was up beside that of her husband. The picture had appeared in the morning papers, Lesley leaving the house for the mortuary, her face bleak and blank.

'Husband's been killed. We ask her if anyone had a grudge — I mean you'd mention it in passing wouldn't you?' She took a swig of her drink. 'Post mortem?'

Richard held the report. The salient points had already been written up on the boards.

He summarised them for the team. 'Death due to a massive haemorrhage from the wound to the abdomen. Defensive cut on the right arm. Time of death between nine, last sighting, and eleven, when he was found. Also the victim's fingers were clean, no compost or plant material under the nails.'

Janine looked at the team. 'Suggesting?' she prompted them.

'Not much of a fight,' Shap said.

'He'd not done much gardening,' put in Chen.

Janine nodded. 'He died sooner rather than later.'

Richard turned the pages of the document. 'Dr Balloran concludes that the weapon was a sharp knife with a slightly curved blade. All-purpose type used by fishermen, gardeners . . . murderers.'

'All right,' Janine warned him.

'Five inch blade. The attacker was right-handed. Victim in good health, report refers to a recent scar on upper chest.'

'Ferdie Gibson carving his initials,' said Janine. 'Miss Grassmere?'

Rachel Grassmere flicked on the overhead projector. Richard turned off the lights. 'Dabs still being processed,' the forensic specialist announced, 'but we've got a decent one on the tap. The trainer print, here by the water butt.' The screen displayed an enhanced version of the muddy print Janine had struggled to make out. 'Right foot, somewhere between a ten and a twelve from the look of it. Small tear on the outside heel and two puncture marks on the ball of the foot, sort of thing that a drawing pin leaves. It's a dream. The lab's getting us make and model.' She snapped the projector off and the lights in the room came on again.

'Butchers, best eliminate Mr Simon, first on the scene, before we go round checking people's shoes.' Janine told him. Butchers nodded glumly.

Janine stood up brushing crumbs from her clothes. 'Ferdie might be the break we're looking for but we don't know that yet. As ever we have to look closely at next of kin.'

'Mrs Tulley a suspect, boss?' Shap asked.

'Let's just say we haven't been able to rule her out yet. We'll be seeing her today and trying to establish an alibi. Matthew Tulley's diaries.' Janine held up the books. She had spent an hour the previous evening scanning through them. 'Practically all the entries relate to Tulley's job. Meetings about Year 7 intake and Year 9 GCSE options, Governors and staff meetings. A few unexplained entries, star and time, but no indication what the appointment was. No leads there at present. So, the rest of you, you know what you're working on. Back here at five,' she instructed them, 'and let's fill this wall.'

CHAPTER EIGHT

'We'd like a word with your son, Mrs Gibson, is he in?' They put away their badges.

'What's it about?' Her brow furrowed and she glared at Janine and Richard from the doorway. One arm was wrapped about her waist, the other, elbow propped on it, held the fag close to her mouth.

'It's in connection with one of our enquiries,' Richard explained.

'What enquiry?' she said derisively.

'The murder of Matthew Tulley,' Janine spoke sharply. 'Is Ferdinand in?'

'He's got nowt to do with that. That's bloody harassment, that is. That man assaulted Ferdie,' she shook her cigarette at them, 'and he was given an official warning by the school. Bleeding disgrace, deputy head and he's lamming into kids.'

'And then Ferdie knifed him,' Janine pointed out.

'You can't prove that. That never went to court,' her mouth worked furiously, spittle gathering in the corners of her lips. 'Ferdie's never been near him. Just leave him alone.'

'We need to talk to him,' said Richard. 'Now either we can have a few words with him now, clear things up and hopefully eliminate him from our enquiries or we can come back with a warrant to hold him for questioning at the station.'

'Go get yer warrant, then,' she began to shut the door.

Richard stopped it with his hand. 'Don't you think you'd better see how Ferdie wants to play this? He might not be best pleased if you have him dragged down to the station, kept for 24 hours.'

She shot him a look of contempt and closed the door.

Janine glanced at Richard, raised her eyes to heaven and back. 'I still don't know all the ins and outs,' Janine resumed their previous conversation, 'but Michael was pretty shaken up. Got a right shiner.'

They heard Mrs Gibson coming back and bowed to each other: the tactic of sending her to check with Ferdie had worked. The door opened and Ferdie Gibson appeared behind his mother. The close haircut gave him a weaselly appearance, his scalp was a greasy white colour beneath the fuzz of hair. Janine noticed the botched tattoo on his neck. He was barefoot with a Nike top, a fancy Rolex-type watch and Adidas pants on, white stripes and rows of buttons all up the legs. Janine wondered about the buttons; did people undo them when they got hot, leave the fabric flapping like chaps?

'Hello, Ferdie,' said Richard, 'I'm Detective Inspector Mayne and this is Detective Chief Inspector Lewis.'

'What d'ya want?'

'We'd like a word. Inside if you don't mind, more private.'

He shrugged and wheeled to face the nearest room; they filed in after him followed by Mrs Gibson. The small room boasted three sofas and a TV and video. The system looked state of the art, the sofas were an ill-matched trio, all had seen better days.

Ferdie flung himself onto the faded pink, over stuffed couch, his mother took the olive green sofa bed and Richard and Janine shared the low slung settee which had sludgy orange and brown cloth and wooden arms.

Janine could feel the supporting elastic ropes through the thin cushions. In a previous era it would have been up-to-the-minute modern design along with fondue sets, convex mirrors and pedestal ashtrays. Like thirty years ago.

Where were Ferdie's trainers? She glanced at Richard and down at the lad's feet. Richard acknowledged the query. Janine gave Richard the nod — he should ask the questions.

'We're investigating the murder of Matthew Tulley,' he said.

'I want a brief then.'

'Just an informal chat, Ferdie. If you could tell us where you were between nine and eleven yesterday morning.'

Janine detected a change in the boy's demeanour, subtle and fleeting but there all the same. Did he know something?

'I was here, in bed,' he swivelled his head to face his mother, 'that's right, innit, Mam?'

'He never gets up in the morning,' she said emphatically.

'You were here all that time?'

'Had my shopping to do but he was in bed.'

'Till when?' Richard asked Ferdie.

'Dunno. 'Bout one. Called for my mate, went to the pub.'

'Your watch not work?' Richard nodded at the bulky model on the boy's skinny wrist.

'Didn't know it mattered, did I?'

'When did you last see Mr Tulley, Ferdie?'

'Months back. Punched me in the head, you know. 'S affected my concentration, know what I mean. I get these panic attacks.'

Give him an Oscar, Janine thought as she watched him elaborate on his symptoms.

'Still carry a knife, Ferdie?'

''S illegal, innit?'

'But you used one on Mr Tulley.'

'They never charged us.'

Janine wondered why there'd been no crime report. Why hadn't Matthew Tulley pressed charges?

'This mate you called for, what's his name?'

'Colin.'

'And where does Colin live?'

He gave them the address. Janine stood. 'I'll leave you to finish off, Inspector.' Ferdie glanced at her, suspecting something but unsure of what. 'I'll let myself out.'

* * *

Mam was crying. Jade hated it when she cried, it was worse than her shouting and being all stressed out. Jade was on the top step. Mam was in the lounge, on the settee making a horrible moany noise and Jade knew her face'd be all red and lumpy from crying. Jade didn't want to see her but she wanted some breakfast. What she'd really like was Coco-Pops but Mam said they cost a bleeding fortune and she had to have corn flakes or Weetabix.

Her Nana got her Coco-Pops when she stayed there but she only let Jade eat them in the morning not whenever she got hungry. The best bit was how the milk turned to chocolate milk, all swirly and sweet. Jade reckoned she could eat a whole packet and not get sick of them.

Jade hated Sunday. Everything was horrible. She couldn't even watch the cartoons till Mam stopped crying. It wasn't fair. When Mam was going with Alan they went to Wacky Warehouse on a Sunday and Alan'd buy her sweets and she could play while Mam and Alan had a drink and then they'd get a bar meal. Chicken nugget and chips, she always had, and a Coke with ice cubes and two straws. But Alan was going with someone else now.

'Jade,' her mam called 'Jade, come here.'

She ran downstairs and into the lounge. Mam was still in her nightie and there was a pile of squashed up bits of toilet paper on the settee from her blowing her nose. Her face was all shiny and big and red. She looked ugly.

Jade saw the police car drive past the window and slow down. Her belly started to hurt.

'Jade, come here,' Mam sounded like a little girl as she patted the seat beside her. Jade went over and slid onto the settee. Her mother put an arm round her and pulled her close. Mam's breath stank horrible. Jade tried not to breathe.

'You know I love you, don't you?'

'Yes, Mam.'

'Even when I'm not happy, I still care about you. I do my best. You're all I've got Jade. If anything ever happened to you . . .' her voice squeaked.

Jade thought of the tent on the allotments. The bad men who waited there. Nonono, not that. She felt sick.

'I'd like to do more for you, Jade. Get you nice things and that.'

A big bowl of Coco-Pops.

'But we've just not got the money,' a catch in her throat like she'd swallowed a toffee.

Jade squeezed her eyes tight shut. Waited. Mam shivered. 'If I had it, Jade, I'd get you such lovely things.'

'Mam, can we go to Nana's?' Sausages and fluffy mashed potato and onion gravy.

'I don't think so,' Mam whispered.

Jade wanted to hit her. 'Please? Can I go then? Please? I can go on my own.'

'Yer not going on yer own. It's not safe.'

'You could put me on the bus.'

'I don't think we've even got the bus fare, Jade.'

'We could walk. Please, Mam, please?' In the wait Jade smelt hope.

'She might not be in.'

Of course Nana would be in. She was always in except when she went to the doctors. Her knee was bad and her chest all wheezy. 'Like puffin' Billy, I am,' she always joked.

'I'll go ring,' Jade clamoured. Mam hesitated then went for her purse in the kitchen. She fished out 10p and gave it to Jade who ran out of the house to the phone box before her mam could change her mind.

* * *

In the car Janine radioed through and sent Butchers to check out Ferdie's version of events with Colin.

'Pronto,' she said, 'I want him checked out before anyone gets on their sweaty little mobile to warn him.'

'Spitting distance, boss. Five minutes.'

'Ring me when you're done.'

* * *

Butchers found the static van and surveyed it from the outside. There was no noise and only the one car nearby so it didn't look like Colin had company. Butchers stepped up to the door and knocked. He heard clattering from inside and then the door was jerked open. The young bloke stared at him for a moment, then his eyes darted away.

'Colin? DS Butchers. Got a moment?'

Colin stood back and let him in. Butchers eased himself through the narrow doorway and into the kitchenette. He saw steam from the kettle, general clutter.

'Kettle on?' Butchers asked him.

'Only got coffee.'

'Two sugars, ta.' While Colin fussed with cups and jars, Butchers made a small tour of the place. Fish tank that had seen better days, he thought he could make out a couple of corpses in the slimy water, cartons of fags — duty free or black market — and a copy of the evening paper on the table. *Allotment Slaying*.

'You on your own here?'

Colin nodded, brought the drinks over to the table. Butchers sat carefully on a stool and skimmed the paper. Colin watched his every move, the pulse in his neck visible.

'Yesterday morning?'

'What?'

'Where were you, Colin?'

'Here.' He kept swallowing as though the lie was caught in his throat.

Butchers put the paper down. 'Really?'

Colin stared at him.

'Ferdie Gibson. Your mate, or so he says . . .'

'What?'

'What do you know about Ferdie Gibson and that school teacher that's been killed?' Butchers regarded him, neutral expression, open face. Waited.

Sweat broke out on Colin's upper lip. 'Well Ferdie had a go at him but that was ages back.'

'Good friend is he, Ferdie?'

'Sort of.'

'Only at the moment he seems to be relying on you to back up his story. See him, yesterday, did you?'

'No. Yes.' Colin said, panic mixing him up. 'I mean—'

'Or d'you need Ferdie to remind you what's what?' Butchers leaned a little closer, spoke softly. 'You're not cut out for this, are you? Stress. It's a killer, you know.'

Colin was shaking.

'We can deal with Ferdie. You help us out.'

'Don't know what you're on about,' Colin said quickly and grabbed his drink.

* * *

Janine added to her supermarket shopping list while she waited. Ten minutes later Detective Sergeant Butchers reported that Colin had been in bed till one when Ferdie called. They'd sent out for pizza then gone to the pub, The Parkway, and watched the match.

'Thanks.'

'Something else, boss.'

'Go on.'

'He was scared witless, nearly did a runner when he opened the door and saw me, like he was expecting a visit. Maybe no connection to the case but he was guilty of something, shaking like a leaf.'

'Worth putting a bit of pressure on?'

'I should say so.'

72

'Get someone to check out his form, I'll put Chen on obbos for Ferdie Gibson — see where he goes once we've left here.'

She broke the connection and sat back in the seat. What had rattled Colin's cage then? Having to give a false alibi for Ferdie? Though she wondered if Ferdie would have been quite so cocky if he was the guilty party. Then he'd have toned his act down a bit, surely? Whatever it was she'd do her best to ferret it out. And Colin, the weaker link, might be the best place to start.

* * *

Butchers, after calling on Colin, returned to his stint on house-to-house, covering the terraced properties along the two streets that skirted the allotments. More ticks were appearing on his list, each indicating that all residents at an address had been seen. There were now only three households where as yet they had failed to talk to anyone. Pensioner Eddie Vincent and the Smiths on Gorton Avenue, and Dean Hendrix on Denholme Avenue.

He would start with the Smiths, number three, near the main road end of Gorton. Woman and her young daughter lived there. Sunday morning he hoped would be a good time but again there was no reply when he knocked. The bell didn't appear to work. He gazed at the dirty white door. The frame was in need of paint, bare wood showing through. Butchers was a keen DIYer, though he preferred the term craftsman. This weekend he should have been building his barbecue, at the side of the patio. He'd got a great design, simple lines with some nice edging, brick supports, place to keep the plates and the utensils, cover for bad weather.

'You've missed 'em, love,' Mrs Across-the-Road called to him. 'They've gone out.'

'Any idea when they'll be back?'

'No, sorry love.'

'Thanks.'

DS Shap strolled up then.

'Where've you been?' Butchers glowered at him.

'Church,' Shap said sarcastically, 'Sunday, isn't it?' He glanced at Butchers' list. 'Thought you'd have cracked it, by now.'

'You've had a bloody haircut,' Butchers was disgusted.

Shap waggled his hand like a puppet. 'Nag, nag, nag.'

Butchers shoved the clipboard at him. 'I'm off to the shop.'

'Get us a bar then.'

Butchers flipped him a V-sign without looking back.

* * *

Ferdie Gibson was on his mobile to Colin as soon as the door had closed behind DI Mayne. The rozzers had already paid Colin a visit. Must have planned it. How'd they known Colin was going to be his alibi though? Then he got it. That's why the woman had slipped out, to check it out.

'I think they know something,' Colin was freaking out.

'They can't,' said Ferdie. 'Not unless you put ideas in their heads.'

'I didn't, I swear. All they asked me was where I was yesterday morning and whether I went out or if anyone called. I told them I was in bed and then you come round at dinner time.'

'They ask you what time?'

'Yeah, I said about one.'

'Stick to that.'

'You think they'll come back?' Alarm filled Colin's voice.

'How do I know. But if they do, say exactly the same stuff. Off by heart.'

'What if they don't ask the same things.'

Sweet effin' Jesus, thought Ferdie. 'Make it fit, don't change anything.'

'I nearly filled me kecks,' said Colin, 'open the door, copper there. Thought he was going to arrest me.'

Ferdie could imagine it. Colin with his frozen rabbit look. Guilt all over his face. Miracle he hadn't gone down on his knees and made a full confession. Tosser. He should never have let Colin in on it.

'Colin,' Ferdie said, 'just stick to the story and it'll be cool.'

'Right.'

'They don't know nothin', right?'

'Yeah, right.'

'See ya later,' Ferdie broke the connection and flicked on the sound for the TV, leaning forward with interest as the official photograph of Matthew Tulley segued into a shot of the secured scene of crime. He watched the report with interest, a smile on his face, his head bobbing like a hairless nodding dog.

* * *

Richard was eating violently coloured corn snacks. How could he look so healthy, not to mention slim, when he ate such junk? An appalling smell filled the car. Janine looked askance and turned the fan on.

'Ferdie Gibson, what d'you reckon?' Richard asked.

'I don't know. He was edgy. Alibi's a bit flaky, to say the least.'

'If it was planned he'd have come up with something better.'

'Then again, not the brightest button in the box, is he?' she said. 'So maybe it was opportunistic. Runs into Tulley, sees his chance, flips. Ropes his mate Colin in to try and give him some cover.'

Janine pulled the car into the gates at the entrance to St Columbus RC High. The school where Matthew Tulley had taught. The school was deserted, pupils and staff at home for the weekend. They were met at the front steps by Mr Deaking, the headmaster, who was expecting them.

'A terrible business,' he said. He was a short, balding man with a furrowed face. He looked disturbed, pale and pinched as though the blood had been drained from him.

Janine shook his hand.

'Arthritis,' he made an apology for the crabbed handshake. 'Comes to us all if we're around long enough.'

'My father's got it,' Janine told him, 'the bracelet do any good?' She nodded at the copper bangle he wore. Maybe she could persuade her dad to try one.

He shrugged, turned the bangle this way and that. 'Hard to say. Do come in. How is Mrs Tulley? Silly question, I suppose. Poor woman.' He took them across the foyer past displays of artwork, charcoal portraits, a series of brashly coloured still life painting and a number of suspended sculptures made from rubbish as far as Janine could tell.

A few more pleasantries were exchanged and then Janine got down to the matter in hand. 'What can you tell us about Matthew?'

'Bright, articulate, efficient. He was an excellent organiser, dependable. Had to be, we've over a thousand pupils here, a long tradition to maintain. The position of deputy carries a great deal of responsibility.'

'Any problems?'

'Ferdie Gibson . . . terrible business. I never dreamt . . . you've interviewed Gibson?'

Janine nodded. 'Mr Tulley was disciplined?'

'Oh, yes, we nearly lost him. Governors saw sense, thank goodness. Then the boy returned — he was no longer a pupil at the time — and attacked Matthew.'

'But that never came to court?'

'Matthew was exhausted. He'd spent the best part of a year being hauled through the disciplinary process. Then this assault . . . he refused point blank to report it, wouldn't press charges, wouldn't even go to the hospital. Simply wanted to get back to normal and put it behind him.'

'Were there any other incidents like the one with Ferdie Gibson, times when Mr Tulley lost his temper?'

'We all lose our tempers. A room full of moody adolescents can be very trying on a wet day. But no.'

'Was he well-liked?'

'I couldn't say he was one of the most popular teachers. As deputy there's a lot of discipline to dish out but he was a fair man and I don't think anyone bore him ill-will. Apart from Ferdie Gibson. Will you be arresting Gibson?'

'It's early days, as yet.' Janine trotted out the standard response. 'What about friends, acquaintances, anyone he was particularly close to on the staff?'

'Not really,' he sighed. 'Awful blow.'

'Mr Deaking,' Richard said, 'perhaps I could address the school on behalf of the enquiry? Let them know we're doing all we can, who they can contact if there's anything they think we should know, that sort of thing?'

'Yes, of course.'

* * *

Sunday lunchtime and Dean and Douggie had finished off a plateful of bacon sandwiches swilled down with mugs of coffee. Eminem on the sound system, Douggie mouthing the words. Housemate Gary was browsing his way through his second massive bowl full of cereal; mixing together Sugar Puffs, Frosties and Weetos. He ate like someone was going to snatch it away, shovelling it up in an unbroken rhythm, the spoon flying between the bowl and his mouth. He didn't appear to chew at all, just crammed it in and swallowed.

'Could get out?' Dean suggested as Douggie laid the makings on the table and began licking Rizlas.

'Cool by me,' nodded Douggie. 'There's a park up the road. Have a kick about. Gary?'

Gary stopped for a fraction, spoon halfway to his lips, eyes wary. He grunted.

'Fancy the park,' said Douggie, 'play some footie?'

Gary shook his head and resumed feeding. Dean wondered if he was all right. He never said much and seemed to keep well to himself. Had a wild feel about him, like he wasn't tame yet, not used to human company.

They shared the spliff and Dean used the bathroom first. He shaved and wondered what he would look like with a 'tache or beard. He wouldn't mind a little beard, just along the jaw, cropped short. Couple of times he'd stopped shaving but he got sick of waiting for it to look like anything halfway decent.

Paula didn't fancy it. She liked him clean-shaven. Would send him for a shave if he was too rough. Think I'll let you in any of my soft places feeling like sandpaper? She liked his hair. She'd pull her fingers through it, over and over. He loved that.

Maybe his mum had done that when he was small. Sort of thing a mother would do. He couldn't remember. Couldn't remember hardly anything of her. Just a few moments, memories faded and smudged, crumbling at the edges like something left out in the rain or pulled from a fire. He hadn't actually tried to recall any more. He reckoned there was more there and places he could go, people he could look up who would help stir his memories but no rush. Not ready for that yet.

While Dean rolled a couple of smokes for the picnic, Douggie cut a couple of lines of coke, chopping the powder this way and that with the razor blade, scraping it into shape. He snorted one and passed the mirror over to Dean. Dean leant forward and put the rolled-up note to his nose, pressed his right nostril shut with his finger and inhaled steadily along the line, sniffing it clear. It felt cold, like sucking frost up his nose. Then the familiar bitter taste at the back of his throat and a rush of mucous. He sniffed and swallowed, cleared his throat. They did another line each. Dean felt the rush begin. Happy. Sun was shining. Douggie smiled at him. Good mate Douggie.

Dean winked.

Douggie picked up the football. 'Shall we go?' In his Donald Duck voice.

Dean nodded. They stopped at the corner shop to get some beer and fags.

* * *

Shap got no reply at Dean Hendrix's home, he asked the next-door neighbour, who was lurking on her front step, if she'd seen him about.

'No, but we're not the sort for peering through the nets all the time like some. He doesn't keep regular hours, you could never say when he'd be there. That's his car.' She gestured to the red Datsun.

Shap raised his eyebrows. 'Anywhere he might be staying?'

'He's got a girlfriend, black girl, she's round a bit but I think they mainly go to her place. She'll know Mr Tulley, she was at the school.'

'Know where she lives?'

'No. But she works in town, one of those bars, our Kelly saw her serving. 'Ang on.' She leaned back into the house, cocked her head and yelled. 'Kelly . . . Kelly! What's the name of that bar where you saw Dean's girlfriend? The bar . . . Dean next door. Right.' She straightened up. 'Steel, they call it.'

'Thanks,' Shap wrote it down. 'Look, if you see Dean, will you ask him to give us a bell, DS Shap, this is the number, we just need to see if he saw anything yesterday.'

She nodded, took the card from him. 'Have you got any leads then?' Interest lit her eyes.

'Too early to say.'

'Terrible thing,' she lowered her voice, 'they say his insides were all spread out like some voodoo thing.'

Shap smiled, enigmatic, he reckoned, that was the word. He said nothing, enjoying the lurid speculation. He tipped his head, cocked his index finger, a little farewell gesture that he practised in the mirror.

Butchers returned, his face full of something.

'Where's mine?'

Butchers ignored him. Shap shot him a look. Lardy boy had about as much charisma as a garden snail. Why couldn't he have been paired with Chen? Nice bit of eye candy. That'd brighten the daily grind.

'Dean Hendrix,' Shap told him. 'Not home. Got his girl-friend's details, though. Pay her a call later then we've cleared all the houses on Denholme Avenue.'

* * *

While Douggie was paying, Dean saw the newspaper; *Allotment Murder Hunt.* Felt his belly flip round. Turned and went outside. Shaken, and wishing he'd never seen it. Spoiling his day like that.

The park wasn't far. They passed the bowling green which was deserted, the grass lumpy and discoloured. Coming towards them was a little kid, a right shrimp on a massive battery operated tank.

'Look at him,' Dean said.

'Neat.'

'He could crawl faster. Look at his face.'

The kid was whining, his mouth turned down, close to tears. Dean clocked his parents, trundling along behind. Looked like they weren't speaking to each other.

Douggie giggled. 'This way.'

They parked themselves on a bench by some trees at the edge of a playing field. A crowd of Asian lads were playing footie, kicking a lightweight ball about using carrier bags and coats for goal posts. Dean leaned back, hands behind his head, looked up at the trees, watched the branches frame the sky.

'If you had two grand,' Douggie said, 'and you had to buy one thing . . .'

It was a game they'd played inside. If you had . . . ? A way of spinning fantasies, of daydreaming. They would add more and more conditions: it had to be red and only made in the US . . . it had to fit in a drawer, it had to make music. They became increasingly surreal until the game transformed to a puzzle. Trying to figure out what on earth could possibly fit the list of qualities the other guy had come up with.

'A suit,' said Dean.

'A suit?' Douggie looked at Dean. 'What the hell do you need a suit for?'

'Don't need,' said Dean. 'Want. Some of us have style, could have style.'

'Oh, aye?' Douggie laughed. The kids' football smacked him full on the back of his head. 'Oy,' he jumped to his feet.

'Sorry mister,' one of the lads yelled. Douggie kicked the ball back.

'D'you wanna game?' another lad shouted.

'Yeah,' Douggie stood up. 'We'll slaughter you.'

They raced about for half an hour. Douggie was a dream with a ball, bouncing it from knee to knee and then flipping it over his shoulder and onto his heel. Scoring goals from ridiculous angles. He'd clown about in-between bowing to imaginary audiences, pretending to weep with joy. It creased Dean up. The kids obviously thought he was a total nutter but allowed it because of his skill.

Dean was fast but couldn't do much to control the ball. When the umpteenth goal had been scored, Dean held his hands up. Enough. He was covered in sweat, his hair limp from it, his windpipe was burning from rushing about, his knees felt weak. The lads protested but Dean and Douggie quit. They went back to the bench. Douggie lit one of the joints. Dean took a hit. Man that was strong. Made him cough. Then he went dizzy, lovely and dizzy, and he felt lazy, hazy, like his blood was full of sherbet.

'If you could change one thing, just one, in the last year . . .' Douggie began.

Yesterday. Dean's mood shrivelled and soured. Stupid bloody question. Yesterday. Oh, man, yesterday would never have happened.

CHAPTER NINE

Janine got a text message, from Michael: *pls gt donuts ck chocsprd chili cola pudn*. She read it aloud.

Richard looked bemused.

'Michael, he doesn't speak anymore — just texts us.' Janine told him.

She started the car and took the road back towards the station. She noticed her petrol gauge was on red, reminded herself to top up soon.

Richard broke open a pack of Eccles Cakes and started munching.

She stared at him for a moment. 'Where d'you put it all?'

'Big brain. What was that diet you all went on — the grapefruit one?'

'Grapefruit and eggs. Dire. Only thing that produced was methane,' she giggled. 'About later — have you booked somewhere?'

'No, but if you think I . . .'

'No, no. Play it by ear. Have to get the kids.'

'Yeah.'

She patted her mobile. 'Do some shopping.' The kids would go bananas if they had to go another day without the essentials.

'Right. Rain check?' He asked her.

'Hope not,' she said quickly.

Richard grinned. 'What d'you fancy?'

Janine raised her eyebrows and he rolled his eyes in response. Mucking about. She laughed, enjoying the flirtation, and hit the indicator — only it was the wrong lever and the windscreen wipers clattered noisily across the screen making her feel completely foolish.

* * *

The bevy of reporters surged forward hurling questions and taking photographs as Richard and Janine got out of the car.

'Any news, Chief Inspector?'

'Any leads?'

'Was it a random attack?'

'Have you found the weapon?'

'Give us something, Chief.'

Janine held up her hand. 'There'll be a press conference tomorrow morning, time to be announced. No comment until then.'

Lesley Tulley seemed to have shrunk in the hours since they had last seen her. Already petite, she reminded Janine of a bird, fine-boned and nervy, on the edge of flight. Must be shattered, Janine thought, the shock easing now and the burden of grief settling.

They were in Lesley's lounge, asking about Matthew's friends and acquaintances. And enemies.

'Matthew didn't have any regular social engagements,' Janine summarised. 'Did you have your own friends, Lesley?'

'Had. You know how people drift apart, once you all get married, harder once people have children.' One hand gripping the other tightly.

'You're right,' Janine acknowledged. 'And you've none of your own?'

Lesley hesitated, she seemed shaken by the question. 'I can't have children.'

Janine cheeks grew warm, she was acutely aware of her own obvious pregnancy. 'Oh, I'm sorry.' She gave a pause wanting to allow Lesley to regain the fragile composure she had.

Richard spoke next. 'What about Ferdie Gibson, Mrs Tulley?'

Lesley stared at him, her eyes wide, confusion creasing her brow. 'Who?'

'He attacked your husband but you didn't say anything yesterday.'

She shook her head slowly, overwhelmed. As if she genuinely hadn't considered the possibility, thought Janine.

'I'm sorry. You think?'

'We haven't ruled him out,' Janine said.

'Oh, God.' Lesley Tulley bowed her head.

Richard looked at Janine — now they needed to ask the really tricky questions. The ones that, whichever way you phrased them, questioned the potential guilt or innocence of the bereaved family. Some people accepted this easily and were too stunned by their loss even to notice much; others went ballistic, the rage that accompanied sudden bereavement finding an outlet at those making the horrendous implication.

'If you'll just bear with us, it is usual in cases like this to establish the movements of family members,' Richard said.

'I told you,' Lesley looked at him directly. 'I was in town.'

'What time did you arrive?'

'Not long after nine.'

'You went shopping?'

She nodded.

'You'll have the receipts, parking ticket . . .'

Resentment flashed through her eyes then and she pressed her lips together. 'I'll see if I can find them,' she said quietly.

Janine glanced at Richard, feeling a little tense, watched Lesley go. Poor bloody woman.

* * *

When DS Butchers tried 7 Gorton Avenue for the second time that weekend, a reedy voice called to him to hang on and after a few, moments the shabby green door was open. The old man looked ill: his complexion grey, bleary eyes, smell of stale hair and unwashed skin coming off him.

'Mr Vincent, is it?' A nod.

'DS Butchers.'

'Is it about that murder? Mr Tulley?'

'That's right,' said Butchers.

'Come in. I hoped you'd call. I was going to come down to the police station tomorrow if no one had been.'

'We called before, sir,' Butchers muttered, anticipating a long-winded complaint.

'Only I've something to tell you about it.'

The room was shabby, a layer of dust coated everything, the low winter sun streamed in through grimy windows. Faint smell of gas. The floral carpet was worn threadbare in places. Old carpet tape curled away from one patch. Three piece suite, telly and table filled the space.

The mantelpiece, beige tiles, housed a gas fire and acted as shelf to a row of framed photographs. Wedding, holiday, group of men around an enormous table. Butchers remembered replacing a fire surround like that, in his last place. Did a lovely job with Welsh slate and a copper chimney breast. He waited while Mr Vincent lowered himself into his chair. Heard him gasp.

'You all right, sir?'

A grunt. 'Sit down,' he gestured for Butchers to choose a seat. Butchers sat on the edge of the sofa took out his notebook. 'Can I have your full name, sir?'

'Vincent. Edward Compton Vincent. Everyone calls me Eddie.'

'Date of birth?'

He reeled it off, noticed Butchers doing the sums and saved him the trouble. 'Eighty-three, come September.'

'Good age,' Butchers said and wondered where he found these platitudes. They seemed to spring from nowhere, fully formed and out of his mouth before he'd thought about it.

'Bloody awful age if you ask me. What would you know about it? Still you didn't come to talk about that.'

'Mr Tulley.'

'Yes. My house overlooks the allotments; well, you'll know that. Now, I can't actually see Mr Tulley's patch that well but I can see the gate that joins the back alley. 'Course, some of them climb the fences, some of these youngsters do, or come up the railway embankment.'

Butchers wondered where this was going. Wanted him to get to the point. Wanted to get some lunch.

'So, Saturday morning I was up late. Had a bad night. Not that I ever really have a good night nowadays. I got dressed and I drew the curtains and that's when I saw him.'

'Mr Tulley?'

'No. This lad, running he was, he runs up to the gate then he stops and looks out, like he's seeing if anyone's about, then he runs into the ginnel between the houses. I can't see him then but he was going hell for leather I can tell you.'

Butchers sat further forward, all ears now, a shiver of excitement making his hand shake slightly. 'What time was this?'

'Twenty-five past ten.'

Butchers looked at him.

'I'd just got up. I noticed the time, it being so late, like.'

'Can you describe him?'

'Youngish . . .'

'Teenager? Younger?'

'Older. Hard to tell an age.'

'Twenty? Twenty-one?'

Eddie shrugged.

'Younger than me?' Butchers asked.

'Yes.'

'Good. Go on.' Eddie hesitated. 'Short or tall?'

'Average, I'd say.'

Butchers stood. 'Like me?'

'But skinnier, wiry.'

'And can you remember what he was wearing?'

He could. 'A cap, baseball cap. Don't recall his top. And those . . .' he waved his hand about searching for the right name, 'sports trousers.'

'Jog-pants?'

'I don't know what they call them. They'd a stripe down the side.'

'What colour?'

'White.'

'White trousers?' Butchers thought of cricket. 'White stripe. The trousers were dark.'

'Black?'

Eddie thought. Shook his head. 'I couldn't say.'

'Anything else you remember?'

'No.'

Butchers thought of the crime scene, the details on the murder boards. 'What was he wearing on his feet.'

'I don't remember.'

'Right. This is very good. We'll come back to you, perhaps ask you to look at some photographs or attend an identity parade. Would you do that?'

'Yes, if I can. Funny, isn't it. Last time I'd anything to do with your lot, with the police, was at Agecroft colliery miner's strike. Trying to save the pit. I swore then I'd never trust a copper again. Place was thick with them, doing Thatcher's dirty work for her, protecting the scabs. Bloody tragedy.'

'Before my time,' said Butchers, who had had more than enough of this sort of crap from his father-in-law.

'Aye, but, you're paying for it now. Closed those pits, took the lifeblood from those communities. We import coal now, when we'd no need. Families broken up, people shoved on the dole. All comes home to roost.'

'You on the phone, sir?' Eddie gave the number.

'We'll be in touch. This lad, would you say you had a good view of him, what he looked like?'

'I did.'

'Perhaps you could show me where you saw him?'

Eddie balked. 'No, see, I'll not manage the stairs. I get up them at night and down them in the morning and that's it. You go up. Back bedroom.'

Butchers did. He pulled back the net curtain, gritty with dust, noted the corpses of flies strewn along the windowsill, the paint peeling and discoloured, tinged pink with mould. He looked out. Eddie's small yard surrounded by a six foot wall led onto the alleyway he'd mentioned. Directly opposite was the allotment gate, a metal frame covered in mesh, interrupting the jumble of old larch-lap and palings that ran the length of the allotments. The gate was probably twenty feet away. Near enough to get a good look at someone.

Butchers admired the plots. He could see one in particular with a pergola and a formal pool. More of a garden than an allotment. He wondered if there were by laws governing what you could and couldn't grow.

He turned away and took the stairs in a rush. Suddenly gleeful; it was he, not Shap, who had caught the call. Brilliant.

* * *

Lesley handed Richard a clutch of receipts and he thanked her. 'Anything else you remember about the morning?'

'No. Oh, I rang Emma, left a message.'

'We need to take the clothes you were wearing yesterday for our forensics, to help eliminate evidence from the scene,' he said.

'But I wasn't there,' she looked from one to another of them, incredulous, wounded.

'Your husband will have carried material from home, from you,' Janine explained. 'It's just standard procedure. We can take them when we leave.'

Lesley sat down, folded her arms across herself.

'How long had you been married to Matthew?' Janine saw the tears start in her eyes and heard the choked sob. 'I'm sorry, Lesley. I realise how intrusive some of the questions might seem but we have to ask them.'

Lesley nodded, wiped at her eyes and sniffed. 'Nine years. I gave up college to marry him.'

'And how would you describe your relationship?'

Janine heard the chatter of magpies from outside, loud in the quiet intense atmosphere of the room. Lesley Tulley struggled to speak.

'I'm sorry,' Janine apologised again. 'We're nearly finished.'

'He was a good man,' her voice trembled.

'Nine years is a fair while,' said Richard. 'There must have been some ups and downs?'

'We were fine, happy,' she broke down. 'I loved him, I loved him so much.'

Janine swallowed hard, moved by the woman's plight but determined to remain unruffled — at least on the outside.

* * *

Janine stretched, eased the seat belt round and clipped it shut. 'We need to have another look later.' Before she could turn the engine on a loud, rendition of the Birdie Song chirruped electronically through the car.

Both Janine and Richard waited, each assuming it was the other's phone.

'Oh, God!' Janine scrabbled for hers. 'Kids!' she hissed. They were always messing about changing her ringtone.

She listened while a triumphant Butchers related his news.

'Yes!' She turned to Richard, her eyes alight. 'Butchers. We've an eyewitness. Saw a lad running from the scene. Time's good and the description fits Ferdie Gibson.'

'We could go for a line-up?'

'Let's see whether Ferdie will come in tomorrow afternoon?'

'He'll probably tell us where to stick it.'

'Might see it as a chance to get us off his back?' She said. 'Who knows how a mind like that works. Probably does

89

shifts.' She spoke back into the phone. 'Butchers, see if the afternoon would suit Mr Vincent?'

'He's not a well man, boss.'

'Well, tell them to treat him like cut glass. Don't want him pegging out before he gets to the station.'

* * *

'Nearly there,' Jade encouraged her mam. Who had gone all quiet again and was walking so slowly.

'I know where we're going, Jade,' she snapped.

Jade said nothing. She was thirsty and she wanted a drink of fizzy. Sometimes Nana didn't have any and Jade had water or tea, dead milky with three spoons of sugar. They turned into Nana's street and Jade darted ahead. She could run really fast, nearly as fast as Carice who was the fastest in her year. She ran all the way to Nana's, seventy-six.

'Like the trombones' Nana always said. It was from a song about a band. Not a pop band, a band like the Boy's Brigade one that sometimes went down the road. All dressed in blue and playing things and kids at the back with no uniforms marching anyway.

She knocked on the door then pushed. Nana left the latch off when they were coming, in case she didn't hear them.

'Nana,' Jade called.

'Hello,' her voice sang out from the back. Jade found her in the kitchen. Jade sniffed, there was something in the oven.

Nana beamed, held out her arms and gave her a hug. She smelt of cigarettes and mints and baking. 'How's my little jewel?'

'Thirsty.'

'I've no pop but there's Lemon Barley or water. Where's yer mam?'

'Coming. Lemon Barley.'

'You know where everything is.' Nana let her do it.

Jade pulled herself up to reach across the sink for the bottle. Heard Mam come in. 'It's freezing out there.' Scrape of the chair across the floor. Jade wondered what was in the oven. Pies? Or belly pork and Yorkshire puddings? Or maybe hotpot? She poured some cordial in the glass.

'T'nt it awful,' Nana said to Mam, 'that murder, that Mr Tulley. They showed your allotments, on the news. They haven't caught anybody yet, then?'

Jade's belly flipped over. She turned on the tap, the water burst out fast, sprayed all over.

'Steady on, Jade,' shouted Nana.

'Bleedin' 'ell,' her mam jumped up and yanked off the tap. She thrust a tea towel with kangaroos on at Jade. 'Now wipe it up.'

'Someone must have seen something,' Nana continued. Jade rubbed at the water on the floor.

'Broad daylight, they reckon. You'd better make her play inside till they've caught 'em.'

'She's not allowed out the back, anyway,' Mam said, 'she knows she's not to go down there.'

Jade thought hard for something to tell Nana, anything, about school or telly but her brain was empty.

'Have you had the police round?'

'No.'

'You think they'd ask you, wouldn't you?'

'What?'

'If you saw anything. View you've got. What's the matter with you, you on them tablets again?'

Silence. Jade kept wiping. Sniffing noise. Mam kicking off again. If Nana was right and the police came round, what would she say? She couldn't tell them. She closed her eyes and prayed. Please God, please don't let them ask me. I'll be good, I'll never, ever go there again and I'll give all my money to the poor people. Please God, please.

* * *

Richard Mayne studied the chits of paper again and checked them off against the list he'd made. The car-park ticket and store receipts displayed the time so he could fix her parking the car at 9.22 but the first purchase was in Selfridges at 10.37. A gap of over an hour. Undermining her alibi.

While it might be improbable that Lesley Tulley had interrupted her shopping spree to carve up her husband, it was not impossible. Further investigation was required.

* * *

Janine was multitasking: trying to keep up with some of the mountain of paperwork that any case generated, eating her lunch and dictating notes for memos.

'And let the press know we're going for an appeal at eleven tomorrow, Monday.'

Someone knocked on her door and she paused the machine. 'Yes?'

Richard came in but, before she had chance to find out what he wanted, her mobile rang out. She snatched it up, cringing at the tune.

'Janine? Pete. Eleanor's making out that she doesn't eat fish. We've done it specially.'

'No, she doesn't,' she told him blankly.

'You said she was vegetarian.'

'She is vegetarian,' Janine gritted her teeth. 'Fish is not a vegetable, Pete.' What planet was he on?

'That's ridiculous — you'd think we'd made her raw T-bone steak the way she's carrying on . . .'

She was not going to get dragged into this. 'Just deal with it, Pete.' She pressed end call, rolled her eyes.

'Richard?'

'Mrs Tulley's receipts. Patchy. She didn't buy anything till after half-ten.'

'What about the parking ticket?'

'Twenty past nine, fits in with what she said.'

Janine considered. It would be best to be thorough at this stage even if it meant using up some precious time. 'Get that verified, CCTV'

She cleared the remains of her lunch into a wrapper, rolled it into a ball. 'I'm going to get some petrol.' She chucked the ball expertly into the bin and grinned at Richard.

She struggled with her coat, the sleeve was tangled. He gave her a hand. The attention was nice. If she hadn't been pregnant, recently separated, if she'd been looking for someone . . . the thought made her blush, stupid! She moved to the door, hesitated with her hand on the doorknob.

'The clothes you saw, in the Tulleys' washing machine?'

He nodded.

'We need to ask her about those, as well.'

He smiled. 'You don't think Ferdie's our man?'

'Keeping all my options open.'

* * *

'Bloody mess at the moment,' The Lemon pronounced, 'two suspects got you running in every direction.'

She wouldn't have put it quite like that.

'I'm hoping Forensics will narrow it down. And we've the press conference and line-up tomorrow, if we can get Ferdie Gibson in.'

'Who's top of your list, Janine?' He managed to make her name sound like an insult. She hesitated. Was he expecting her to back up her hunch with reasoned arguments or was he just after her gut feeling? She thought of Ferdie, broadcasting his hatred for Tulley, handy with a knife. Then Lesley Tulley, to all intents and purposes the grieving widow.

'I know we've motive and a possible sighting for Gibson but I'm not convinced, sir.'

'Women's intuition?'

Janine rated the skills she had in reading people: the ability to decode the patterns of words and silences, interpret body language, pick up on the tiny shifts in atmosphere that women were more attuned to because they'd been schooled to be from an early age. 'We've gaps in Lesley Tulley's account,' she pointed out. 'Not cut and dried.'

'Think she nipped home and committed murder and then popped back in to finish her shopping.'

'Not impossible, sir.'

'By all accounts the injuries were quite horrific. Is a woman really capable of that sort of thing?'

'You'd be surprised, sir,' she said dangerously.

When he released her she returned to the murder room to collect Richard. He was busy on the computer. She waited, fiddling with her phone trying to change the ringtone. Why did they make them so complicated? God, she was no Luddite, quite happy on the computer or setting the VCR but she'd barely mastered the basics on her phone. Never enough time. Better things to do. More important things. She pressed select and ended up with a diabolical marching tune.

'Boss.' Richard called her over. 'Dean Hendrix.'

She crossed to him, she recognised the name.

'He's one of the residents, yes?'

The screen was loading, criminal records.

'Denholme Avenue. Unaccounted for. Neighbours haven't seen him. There's a girlfriend, Paula, ex-pupil of Matthew Tulley's.'

'And Dean's got form?' She nodded to the monitor.

'You could say that.'

The page displayed.

Janine scanned the information. 'He's done time. Good God, three years in Young Offender's. GBH, weapon was a knife. Slit the victim's belly open. A Mr Williams, practically disembowelled him.'

She looked at Richard in horror, something twisting inside her, her throat suddenly dry. 'Oh, my god, he's done it before! Where the hell is he?'

CHAPTER TEN

'I want Dean Hendrix found. Top priority. Circulate a. description. And get Forensics to put him into the mix — tell them it's urgent.' She issued orders, her mind already running ahead. What should change, what not. Flexible but firm: adapt to new circumstances but don't let it throw you off course. *Don't overreact*, she told herself. *It's a lead, that's all, not a result.*

'Shap's found the girlfriend,' Richard told her. 'He's seeing her now.'

Janine printed off a mugshot of Dean Hendrix and stuck it up on the board next to those of Lesley Tulley and Ferdie Gibson.

'The Lemon's gonna love this,' she said, her heart sinking. 'He thought two suspects was excessive.' She thought hard and fast, they would expect her to give the lead.

'OK,' she called the room to attention. 'This could be a fluke — the lad's off having a holiday somewhere, not done a runner. Until we've something concrete we keep all the balls in the air. We keep after Mrs Tulley and Ferdie Gibson and we find Dean Hendrix.'

Richard had a smile hovering on the edge of his lips. Something amuse him?

'Look sharp, Inspector,' she said. 'Time we had a bit of a closer look round at the Tulleys'.'

* * *

Dean had shown Paula his photos. They hadn't been going together all that long, still working out the rules and getting the measure of each other. She had been asking about his family. He'd clammed up.

'I'm sorry, Dean,' she had said. They sat awkwardly on his sofa. He wanted to run. They both spoke together then. Mangled words. More embarrassment.

'I've got pictures,' he offered. He didn't want her to think he was a wimp, that he couldn't deal with it. Already he knew she was worth more effort than any of the others. She nodded and smiled at him. He brought them down. He never usually looked at them. He remembered Jean, his foster mum, showing him the album. Her rough smoker's voice, almost whispering, telling him who was who, reading the notes on the back.

Paula sat close. Dean cracked open a couple of cans. Gave her one. Took a swig. The album lay across their knees, half on his lap, half on hers. The first pages were his mum and her friends. Dean stared at the captured smiles, pointed out the skinny, dark-haired woman.

'I can see the resemblance,' Paula said. 'You're very like her.' Dean chewed his lip. He turned the page. Baby photos. A studio pose. Himself in white baby clothes against a shiny white curtain. Big, dark eyes and a bald head.

'Aw, Dean.' She nudged him gently in the ribs, 'you've not changed at all. Look at that.' Dean, a toddler, with bow and arrow. Dean with a dog in a back yard. Dean and friends round a birthday cake. Dean and his mum sitting on a swing.

'How old was she when she had you?'

'Dunno.' He had another drink. He didn't know how old she was when she died either. What did it matter?

'What about your dad?'

He shrugged. 'She never married.'

'Do you ever wonder?' She looked at him.

'Maybe when you're older.'

'Maybe.' He couldn't imagine it. Trying to find a non-existent father. A faceless, nameless ghost. It was all he could manage to consider someday finding out more about his mother.'

'What was she called?'

'Shirley he said.

'She looks nice,' said Paula. 'You look happy, don't you?'

He couldn't speak. Choked up. He turned the page. The last pictures. Dean with bucket and spade. With his mum and some other people at Christmas time. Tinsel on the table.

Paula realised. 'I'm sorry.'

He shook his head. Tried to shake the tears away. He lowered his head. Eyes stinging.

Paula slid the book away. 'I'm sorry, Dean. Too bloody nosy.'

'No,' he sounded strangled.

She put her arms around him. 'It's all right,' she said softly.

That did it, stupid bloody . . . he couldn't stop it. Her with her understanding. Had him scriking like a little kid. And it wasn't all right, was it? Not really. Later, she said sometimes it was good to let it out. Dean wasn't so sure. In fact he'd rather have left it where it was, ta very much.

Later still they drank some rum and smoked some grass and went upstairs. He had sex with her. He did it hard and fast. Not wanting to please her. Just wanting to take himself to a different place. She didn't complain. She let him drift asleep afterwards. She woke him in the night. Rubbing against him, coaxing him with her dirty sweet words, and he made amends.

* * *

'With your permission, Mrs Tulley, we'd like to look round the house?' Janine said.

'Why? Why do you want to look here?' Emma was suspicious of them.

'It's all right, Emma,' Lesley said.

'We might find useful leads among Mr Tulley's personal effects,' Janine explained. 'It's more than likely that Matthew knew his attacker.'

'What about Ferdie Gibson, has he been questioned? Have you searched his house?' Emma asked.

'He has been interviewed.' Richard answered. 'And we're continuing to investigate him.'

Emma handed out the tea, her mouth still set with disapproval. She leant against the counter with her mug while the others sat at the table.

'This press conference, Mrs Tulley, tomorrow morning, we'd like you to be there, to issue an appeal for help,' Janine said.

Lesley Tulley looked shocked at that, started to speak, thought better of it, tried again. 'What would I say?'

'We can help you prepare something later. We'll keep it simple.'

'Do they do any good?' asked Emma. 'These appeals?' Still in protective mode, defensive on her sister's behalf.

'Oh, yes,' said Richard. 'We tend to get a significant increase in information coming in from the public afterwards.'

Janine turned to Lesley Tulley. The woman's face was impassive, eyes lowered, cup to her lips. 'We should also get forensic results back tomorrow. I'm expecting those to move things forward a great deal. Without witnesses the forensic evidence is going to be vital — it will tell us, I hope, where we should be concentrating our energies. As yet, we've not found the knife that was used. Do you know if Matthew kept a knife in his shed at the allotment?'

Lesley ducked her head, paled and pressed a hand to her mouth.

'Are you all right?' Janine didn't want her throwing up again.

'I just keep thinking that someone did that. Why did someone do that?' She exhaled. 'I don't know if he had a knife, I never went there.'

'Are there any knives missing from home?'

'I don't know.'

'Would you check?'

'Now?' Emma scowled.

Janine nodded. 'Please.'

Lesley Tulley put her hands on the kitchen table and pushed herself to her feet. She opened drawers and cupboards and stared into them. 'There's nothing obviously missing.' She swayed on her feet.

'Lesley, you haven't eaten anything yet, have you? You must try something.' Emma told her.

Janine signalled to Richard. 'We'll start upstairs. We'll make a note of any items we need to remove,' she told Lesley. 'You might prefer to wait down here?'

Lesley nodded. Janine was relieved. It was harrowing enough to know someone was pawing through all your possessions without having to observe it.

They began in the main bedroom, it looked like something from a furniture showroom, smart and sterile. The room smelt of vanilla and lavender. Janine noticed the tiny bowl of potpourri on the dressing table. High quality stuff. Not the sort you get in the supermarket for next to nothing, that smells like toilet cleaner.

They were looking for anything amiss, anything unexpected, signs of illegal activity illicit affairs, financial problems. Looking also for a knife with a five inch blade, semi-serrated and some jog-pants. It wasn't an official search, for that they'd need a warrant, so they wouldn't be ripping up carpets or dismantling furniture. More a general look about.

It wasn't a hard house to search; quite the opposite, everything had its place. Drawers held neatly folded underwear, cupboards opened to reveal their contents without need for rifling through. Janine was impressed with Mrs Tulley's wardrobe; everything of impeccable quality, classic styles that would resist the fickle trends of fashion, nothing trashy or worn out.

Matthew Tulley's clothes divided into work (suits and shirts) and home (Land's End and Hawkshead). A penchant for check shirts and corduroy trousers. The books on his bedside table told them nothing new. *The Organic Gardener* and *A History Of Britain*. At her side a guide book to Singapore, a copy of *Elle*.

She and Richard took a side of the room each and worked systematically, replacing items carefully. She opened a drawer in the dressing table, found a selection of fancy underwear. Silk and satin slips, lacy bras and pants, camisoles, black suspender belts. She checked beneath them. Nothing. She picked up a pair of scarlet briefs, slippery fabric edged in cream lace. They were crotchless. She folded them quickly, suddenly embarrassed.

'The Lemon asked me if I really thought a woman was capable of such a thing.'

Richard smiled.

'No imagination,' she said.

Richard's phone rang. He took the call. 'The message that she left on the sister's phone is still there,' he told Janine, 'very precise: "it's only half past nine".'

'Neatly establishing time of day.'

'Exactly.'

'Too neat?'

'No motive.' He reminded her.

Richard Mayne knew, like a catechism, that there were three elements to look for in a murder case — motive, opportunity and preparatory acts. As yet Mrs Tulley wasn't known to have any motive for killing her husband (unlike Ferdie Gibson who had plenty), and they hadn't established any preparatory acts. As for opportunity she had access to knives like the rest of the population but whether she had the strength to gut a man was anybody's guess. People could surprise you. Until the CCTV tape showed them otherwise, she had the opportunity to return to Whalley Range and commit the crime. One out of three, maybe. Not great odds but you had to start somewhere.

On the landing Richard searched through the airing cupboard and came away empty handed. There were three other bedrooms, one of which was used for storage. All the boxes were neatly labelled; Christmas Decorations, China Tea Service, Velvet Drapes (Brown), Ski-clothes. A random check in some of the least accessible ones showed that each contained precisely what was written on its label.

'No point in going through them all,' Janine said. 'If and when we get a warrant . . .'

Of the other two bedrooms, one was being used by Emma whose hastily gathered belongings were still half in her overnight bag, and the other room with its twin beds looked as though it had never been used.

* * *

'Hello, Paula,' said Shap. 'Can I have a word?'

He'd been at Steel quarter of an hour, sitting on one of the high metal stools at the bar, sipping a strong lager and listening to chit-chat on the other side of the counter. Waiting till he was ready.

She frowned slightly. Broke off from stacking glasses on the shelves. 'Do I know you?'

Shap flipped his identity wallet open. 'DS Shap. Just a routine enquiry. We're trying to get in touch with Dean Hendrix. Thought you might know where he was.'

'Dean?' she said, frown deepening.

'Yes, Dean. Your boyfriend.'

She pressed her lips together. 'What's it about?'

'Nothing to worry about,' said Shap, 'we're talking to everyone who lives in Denholme Avenue, see if they saw anything in connection with the murder there yesterday. Matthew Tulley. Your old deputy head, eh?'

'Oh, right.' She nodded, wary but not panicked. There was a faint rattle as the beads in her hair knocked against each other.

'So, if you can tell us where we can find Dean?'

'I don't know,' she said, 'I don't know where he is.'

'Not at your place then?'

'No.'

'That usual? You not knowing where he is?'

She stared at him, eyes guarded. Be like pulling hen's teeth now. 'His place of work?' Shap asked.

'He's freelance,' Paula said, 'he hasn't got a regular place.'

Could mean anything, freelance. Good, bad or indifferent. 'Off working somewhere then, is he?'

'I don't know,' Paula said. Glancing to the left, two customers waiting. 'I've got to get on.'

'He'll be in touch though?' Shap lifted his eye brows. 'Not dumped you, has he?' Half-smile on his lips. She said nothing. 'If you hear from him get him to give us a bell.' He put his card on the bar, raised his glass in salute and drank it down. She pocketed the card, moved away to serve the couple. Shots of tequila, slices of lime, salt.

Shap watched, waited until she'd handed over their change. 'Paula. I was thinking, he'll have a mobile, won't he? Give me the number, I'll get in touch direct.'

She looked away quickly, blinked, looking up as though something in the air would tell her what to do. Swung her gaze back to his. 'I'll tell him to call you,' she said. Wheeled away before he could persist, through the door to the kitchens.

* * *

Downstairs, Janine and Richard explored the stylish dining room with its Moroccan tiled table, glass shelves and carefully arranged candelabras and glazed pots. They found nothing. The search of the lounge was fruitless too.

'You know what strikes me,' she said, keeping her voice low, 'is how impersonal it all is. There's no clutter, no letters and photos or mementoes,' she paused. 'No kids?' Could that explain it?

'I haven't any, either,' said Richard, 'but I still have stuff. Not that I've had chance to unpack it yet.'

'Photo there,' she nodded at the wedding snap in its fine golden frame. Lesley Tulley in a cream knee-length dress, short veil, leaning against her husband beneath a rose arbour, head against his shoulder. His hands around her waist. They looked very happy. Lesley Tulley said they had a happy marriage. Why did Janine have doubts about that? Something about Lesley's reactions? About the feel of the house too.

It wasn't just the elegance and the space; it was a mood, a tension in the atmosphere. Someone has just been murdered, she reminded herself; could have something to do with it.

The study looked more like what she was used to. Files and papers lay on Matthew Tulley's desk. All of it related to St. Columbus High School. Richard went through his briefcase.

She examined the shelves. A couple of silver flight cases and some padded bags containing camcorders and photographic accessories. The rest given over to books. She ran her eye along the rows; no fiction to speak of, some books on jazz and photography but mostly education and management books, papers from various examining boards, thick files relating to Standards and the National Curriculum.

Richard began to search the filing cabinet while Janine went through the desk. In the bottom drawer, underneath everything else, she found a pack of condoms.

'What have we got here?' She held them up to show Richard. 'He's playing away?'

Richard gestured. Could be.

Why else hide them? Janine thought.

When they checked in the kitchen, the washing machine was empty. Janine peered out, there was nothing on the rotary dryer in the garden. She went through to the sisters, now waiting in the lounge.

'We'd like to have a look in the garage.'

The double garage stood to the left of the house, its side entrance a few steps from the side door that led out of the kitchen. Lesley unlocked it and led them in.

'Thank you, we can lock up after if you leave the key.'

Janine waited for Lesley to go. There was a tumble dryer in the corner but it was empty. She looked along the workbench that ran across the back of the space. Tools neatly stored, nails and screws in containers. No knife. No empty place shouting 'here was a knife'. She shook her head at Richard.

They took a turn round the garden. It was a fresh day, cold enough for hats and gloves but the sky was a vivid blue, setting off the bare branches and the dark skeletons of the trees. 'No sign of fresh digging,' Janine pointed out, thinking still about the washing Richard had seen.

'Need a warrant to get a proper look.'

'No chance, yet.'

She crushed a sprig of conifer between her fingers, sniffed the pine scent. 'You got a garden, your new place?'

'Flat. Not even a window box.'

Janine nodded towards the side of the house and they turned that way. 'Ours isn't bad, Pete used to do a lot. The lawn's more of a football pitch now though, Tom practising his flying tackles.' She was curious about Richard; beyond saying that he was single again he hadn't volunteered anything else about his marriage break-up to her. 'Wendy still down there?'

'Yep. We sold up, she got her own place.' His voice was neutral, no clue as to whether he was sad or glad.

Janine nodded at the wheelie bin. Richard rolled his eyes but moved forward. Janine's phone went off, the lousy marching drill number, Richard recoiled.

'Hello?'

'DS Shap, boss. Paula, Dean Hendrix's girl — claims not to know his whereabouts. Not exactly falling over backwards to help us out.'

Janine sighed, another obstacle. 'Thanks, Shap,' she turned to Richard. 'No joy from the Hendrix girlfriend.'

Richard opened the top of the bin and they peered in. Bin liners neatly tied. 'Take it all away.' Janine said.

'Without a warrant?'

'With Mrs Tulley's permission, though she'd be an idiot to have dumped anything in that.' When would they get a break, some movement in the case? 'Christ, I hope Forensics have something we can get our teeth into. Or the eyewitness gives us a positive result. If we can just put one of them there.' Richard lifted the bags from the bin and placed them beside it.

'Right,' Janine said briskly, 'let's see what she's got to say about her dirty washing.'

Emma was just leaving when they joined Lesley in the house. She needed to call home for more clothes and to sort her flat out for the following days when she would be staying at Lesley's. Once she'd gone, Janine told Lesley, 'we're eager to locate some clothing that was here yesterday in the washing machine.'

'Sorry?'

'Sports clothing, jog-pants something like that. In yesterday morning's wash?'

Lesley's brow creased in a frown, she shook her head. 'I didn't wash anything yesterday.'

Janine glanced at Richard. An innocent mix-up or something more serious?

'You're sure? Please think very carefully.'

Lesley continued to shake her head. 'I'm sure.'

Janine stood up first, outwardly calm but thinking all the while that now they had something more to go on, now she had a place to start, a loose thread to pull on, and she couldn't wait.

CHAPTER ELEVEN

DS Shap knocked on Ferdie Gibson's door more loudly. 'Come on,' he said under his breath. He thought he heard sounds inside so he waited. He glanced down the road where two elderly women were in conversation. Bundled up in woolly hats, coats and gloves.

At last the door was pulled back and Ferdie stood there. Hair so short you could see the bumps on his skull and a smudged tattoo, some sort of moth or something on his neck.

Shap showed him his ID. 'Morning Ferdinand,' he said.

'Ferdie,' the lad replied.

'Whatever. Can I come in a moment?'

Ferdie looked as though he was about to refuse.

'Unless you want all the neighbours knowing your business.' He swung his eyes to the old women.

In the drab living room Shap explained that they had a witness who had seen a man answering Ferdie's description leaving the allotments where Matthew Tulley had been killed.

'Well, it weren't me,' Ferdie replied. 'I wasn't anywhere near there.'

'Where were you, Ferdie?'

'In bed, I told them others.'

'You sure about that?'

'Yes,' he said aggressively.

'Sure enough to prove it.'

'What d'ya mean?' His eyes narrowed, emphasising the feral look of his features.

'We want to hold an identity parade, see if this witness can pick out who he saw.'

'Well, it weren't me.'

'So you'd attend the parade?'

'Why should I?'

'Clear your name. There's a lot of people muttering about how you had a grudge against Matthew Tulley. You'd already gone for him with a knife before, hadn't you?'

'Yeah. And you know what he did, give me brain damage, that's what. I can't concentrate, I get these attacks. And he's still teaching.'

'Not now he isn't.'

'And I'll dance on his grave but I didn't do him.'

'Prove it. Or are you scared? Got something to hide?'

Ferdie clenched his fist. Shap could see a muscle in his jaw tighten. 'What time?'

'Two o' clock. South Manchester nick.'

'Right,' Ferdie said, his teeth still closed together. 'Maybe I'll show.'

'And we'll all know what to think if you don't,' Shap said.

* * *

Shap snatched the tenner from Butchers and murmured 'You won't see that again, mate.' He turned to DC Chen. 'Fancy a flutter?' She nodded, keen to be accepted by the more established team members. Before she had chance to put her name down for one of the three runners in Shap's book, Chief Inspector Lewis began Sunday evening's meeting.

Janine could sense the team were tired, getting ragged round the edges but she needed to use this chance to galvanise them. 'We all know we've had our magical 24 hours without a result but that doesn't mean we give up now. It means we work harder, we work bloody hard. Things are starting to open up.'

She referred to the photos on board. 'Three possible suspects. Lesley Tulley. Motive?' She was met with shrugs and grimaces. 'Exactly. Nada, nothing. Tulley claims the marriage was happy. No friends, barely any family. Married nine years. She can't have children. But there are condoms in Mr Tulley's desk.' She paused. 'Cherchez la femme? Could give us motive. No rumours of another woman but we're going through his email contacts. Mr Tulley's diaries, nothing obvious though we've some unexplained appointments. Other evidence?'

'The clothes that were in the washer,' said Butchers. 'Disappearing act. Lesley Tulley denies all knowledge.'

'Mr Vincent,' Butchers ventured, 'the lad he saw running, he was wearing sports pants, the sort with stripes down the side.'

Janine considered this. 'The sort my boys calls go-faster stripes. Inspector?'

'Possibly . . .' Richard answered. 'I only saw them briefly but they were something like that.'

Janine drew an arrow between the note up there about the clothes and the unknown suspect seen running from the scene by Mr Vincent.

'I don't believe in telekinetics,' Janine said. Butchers looked lost, an edge of panic in with his muddled expression. Janine waved her arms, mimed someone making an object move with brainwaves. 'They have to be there still. We're watching the place so they won't go anywhere.'

'Bins revealed nothing, nor the initial search,' Richard told them.

'Opportunity?' Janine asked.

Richard indicated the timeline he'd drawn up. 'Some blanks,' he pointed to the hour after Lesley had got her parking ticket.

'Shap will be checking CCTV footage,' Janine said.

Shap groaned.

'Ferdie Gibson,' she turned their attention to the second suspect. 'Unconfirmed alibi unless you believe his doting mother sat and watched him sleep.'

A chuckle rippled through the room.

'Motive?'

'Revenge,' Shap said. 'Ferdie never forgave him for the thumping.'

'Taken his time,' Janine pointed out. 'A year since Ferdie last had a go. Evidence?'

'Eyewitness,' Butchers said smugly, sitting back, arms crossed over his belly. Meaning Mr Vincent.

Shap rolled his eyes.

'Saw a lad running away on Saturday morning. The description fits Ferdie.' Richard summarised.

'Ferdie's got his invite for the line-up,' Shap said.

'Ferdie's mate Colin; he was well stressed when questioned.' Butchers added.

'Our weakest link. Might want another bite at Colin,' Janine said. 'And now a third suspect, Dean Hendrix, missing from home, previous form, same M.O. Last victim survived — just.' She held up a hand in warning. 'I don't want us to assume this is a series, not yet. We need to work away at all three candidates. Tomorrow, press conference at eleven plus forensics should be back before that.'

There was a muted cheer.

'Meanwhile, we keep doing what we do best: gathering evidence, checking statements. I want every house ticked off, every resident accounted for. We go over what we've got and we keep looking.'

She paused, looking over the faces of the team. Shap, one leg going, dying for a fag already; Butchers, plumped up like a hen with his lead on Ferdie; Chen, not giving much away but intent, learning fast; Richard, the two of them working well together, mutual respect and a similar approach to the case. 'I'm sure there's a bet on already,' she said. Shap grinned and Butchers squirmed in his seat. 'I don't need to know about that. But don't let it affect your judgement.' She pointed to the wall. 'That knife is out there somewhere, the clothes worn by the killer are out there, the person who owns that trainer,' she tapped the enhanced print with her hand. 'The one who left dabs on the tap. Matthew Tulley's murderer is out there. Find them,' she looked from detective to detective. 'The first 24 hours were crucial, the next are doubly so. Don't let me down.'

* * *

Emma had taken a key, so the knocking couldn't be her. The police weren't coming back, not till tomorrow. Lesley held the newspaper rigid in her fingers, pressed her feet tight to the floor, bit her teeth together. It was him. Coming after her. She remained frozen long after the knocking had stopped and the caller retraced their steps. The only movement an occasional blink and the tiny pulse which flickered fast in her throat.

* * *

Butchers and Shap came out of the meeting quarrelling. 'We see the CCTV stuff now, then we can go back there,' insisted Shap, 'get it done sooner.'

'Look,' said Butchers, 'you heard the boss, loud and clear, every resident accounted for. She couldn't make it plainer, could she? Nothing about me doing the CCTV. And I've Mr Simon to see. Split up.'

'Eh?'

'We're not joined at the sodding hip, are we?' Butchers retorted, though he couldn't have said why he felt so irritable. Apart from the fact that Shap was a smart-arse, who he'd not have chosen to work with. Who hadn't even had the grace to acknowledge that Butchers finding a witness had been a substantial break.

'The store will close in fifteen minutes, will customers please make their way to the checkouts.'

Janine was shattered, she could feel every bone in her feet and she had a dull ache in her lower back. She waited at the checkout with a trolley piled high. The man ahead paid and Janine began to unload her groceries.

Her phone sounded loud and brash, she was beginning to think that even the Birdie Song was better than this regimental tosh.

'Mr Simon, the guy who was first on the scene, boss. Wears slip-ons, never trainers.' Butchers told her.

'OK. When we've got the make confirmed, we'll have a look at Ferdie and friend. And Dean Hendrix when we find him.'

'Should I check the other gardeners?'

What did he mean? Loading items with one hand, phone in the other. 'Butchers, they'll have been covered in house-to-house.' Surely? Silence. 'You established no one used Tulley's tap? No one had set foot on the plot?' She couldn't believe she was having to ask this.

'Not, erm . . . exactly. We asked if they'd seen owt suspicious you know but not exactly whether they'd used Mr Tulley's tap . . .'

'Oh, bloody brilliant. So the dab and the footprints might be down to some Flowerpot Man filling his watering can. Good of you to share that with me, Butchers. Get back to all the allotment holders, now, and see exactly if anyone took water from Tulley's tap and when.'

The checkout girl and the customers in the queues either side, stared at her, eyes bright with interest. Janine slid the large milk cartons onto the conveyer belt.

'Yes, boss. Should I take prints for elimination, boss?'

'No, Butchers, you shouldn't. You'll only need to do that if someone says they used the tap, won't you. Christ!' If Butchers had been present she'd have been tempted to deck him. She slammed the ice cream down and began to unload several large pineapples.

'You favour one of the other gardeners for this, Butchers?' she said sarcastically. 'Know something we don't?'

111

'No, boss.'

'Sure? No one getting a bit carried away with his fish, blood and bone mixture?'

'No boss.'

'Fine,' she hurled the tins of beans down. 'Because I have got a dead man on my desk, Butchers, and I'd like him off it before the maggots start to hatch!' She pressed end call.

The checkout girl was gawping at her.

Janine shook her head, leant closer. 'Just can't get the staff,' she said confidentially.

The girl smiled uncertainly.

* * *

She asked Pete how Michael had been while the other two climbed into her car.

'Not seen much of him He went round to his mates after lunch. I told him to be back at yours for eight.'

'He won't report it.'

Pete shrugged. 'Not much point.'

'Pete!' They'd always been pretty much in agreement about the kids, the moral lessons to teach them, the rights and wrongs. Was it Tina's influence? Or just another form of needling that he'd discovered? Something to confuse the fact that he was the guilty one.

He turned and began walking away. 'You thinking about him, Janine — or how you look at work?'

'Piss off!' she flung after him.

* * *

It was on the box, they watched it at Colin's place. Ferdie called it the caravan. Ignored Colin who told him it wasn't a caravan — it was a static. Should have kept his trap shut. Something else Ferdie could wind him up with.

'Fame!' Ferdie shouted after and started clapping. He nodded his head at the whisky Colin had opened.

'Refill.'

Colin passed him the bottle. He'd had enough of the stuff last night, puked his guts up till there was nothing left. Ferdie — he could drink bleach and he'd not bother.

Colin lit another cigarette. Wondered how long Ferdie planned on staying. Need a cool head for the next day. Remembering, Colin felt his bowels loosen. He wasn't cut out for all this. Doin' his head in.

* * *

DI Mayne had spoken to Shap about the CCTV tapes that had been collected from the car park. There was only the one camera but it covered the entrance, which was where their interest lay.

Richard told Shap to study the tape between nine and eleven for Lesley Tulley's car. 'Fast search if you like but don't miss a thing, see if she doubled back. 'Course,' he went on, 'she could have got a cab in-between times and leave us none the wiser.'

'Don't,' DCI Lewis had groaned, overhearing.

Shap had been scanning the film for half an hour, and his eyes were going. He needed a fag an' all and it was past knocking off time. Rumour was The Lemon wasn't granting much overtime to the enquiry and Shap didn't do the job for the good of his soul. He saw a silver car, right sort of shape and paused the tape but it was the wrong registration, earlier model too.

Time to call it a day.

* * *

Janine had just lugged in the last two bags of shopping when Michael made his entrance. Staggering in with a silly grin on his face.

'Michael?'

The grin dissolved and he looked pale then, clenched his mouth tight. 'Feel ill.' His speech was slurred. He giggled.

'You're drunk! What have you been drinking?'

'Vodka — and cider.'

'Upstairs,' she pointed.

Tom jumped into the room and rolled across the floor. He peered up at his big brother. Frowned. 'What's wrong with Michael?'

'Now!' Janine told Michael.

He set off, his footsteps heavy and uneven.

Janine sighed. Praying he wouldn't throw up all over the carpets, or his duvet. The washing threatened to overwhelm her as it was. What if he's got alcoholic poisoning, needs his stomach pumping? Her heartbeat increased. Stop it! Bad enough without anticipating worse.

'I'm starving,' Eleanor wandered in. 'Mum, did you get the present?'

Janine held up a box of hair decorations from the supermarket. 'Thanks, Mum. Have we got any wrapping paper?'

It was never-ending. 'Dining room drawer.'

When Ellie had gone she rang Richard. 'Hi. Rain check time. I'm sorry. We're only just back and something's come up with Michael — or is about to.'

She gazed at a row of pineapples on the work surface. Did she buy them? Why on earth did she buy them? Maybe her body was telling her something. Some mineral she needed found only in pineapples. Or maybe her mind was going. Pregnancy could do that –addle the intellect.

Richard told her not to worry and they'd try it some other time.

Half an hour later and she was doling out spaghetti and garlic bread.

'I just want bread,' Eleanor said.

Janine was tempted to quiz her but she was sick of debating food with her daughter. Food had somehow become an area for argument instead of something nice to share. She wouldn't get drawn into it anymore. 'Fine.' She kept her tone light.

Sarah knocked on the back door.

''S open.'

'You not got your glad rags on yet?'

'Not going?'

'Why?'

Janine darted her eyes towards the two kids and said. 'Tell you later.'

Sarah caught on: not in front of the children. 'Right. See you then.'

'What's a beach whale?' Tom asked. 'Does it live on a beach?'

Janine felt her hackles rise, suspecting Pete of slagging her off to Tina.

'Who's been . . . Beached whale. It's one that's washed ashore and can't get back in the sea.'

'It's on my story tape.'

Ah. God, she was knackered.

* * *

Eddie Vincent had had a cup-a-soup for his supper. Not that he was hungry; as he got older and closer to the end he ate less and less, but it made a change from drinking tea. It had been growing dark by the time he'd finished. He struggled to his feet and went to close the curtains. He had turned the telly on. Eddie liked the wildlife programmes best. And science. There'd been a great series on about the universe and the planets. He could have watched that all day long. Whatever was on was just finishing. The credits rolling.

Yesterday's *Evening News* was in the kitchen but he hadn't got the energy to go and fetch it. He sat down, his hands wrapped round his belly for comfort. The pain wasn't too bad at present.

The titles came on for a documentary about the war, *My War, Our War*. He shuffled in his chair. Maybe he should turn it off? Save the upset. But he didn't move. He watched with a growing sense of fascination and unease as men his own age and older talked of their experiences. Of homesickness and conditions at the front, of letters home, and shrapnel and friendship. Two spoke of killing. One, chap, a little wizened man from Wales, could only estimate how many men he'd killed in fierce fighting in North Africa. Another, a blind man with a rough Yorkshire accent, spoke about killing a German, a boy his own age, and of losing his faith. 'I know it was a just war,' he said, 'we were fighting the Nazis, but it was hard to see any justice in that act.'

Eddie had closed his eyes and leant his head back against the chair. He'd never told anyone. No one to tell now. In those days you didn't speak of it. It was too raw. It wasn't dignified to spill the beans like that. Those that came home, it was like their secret. Not the stuff you told to sweethearts and kiddies. Not even your parents. He'd never even told Maisie. Best left unsaid. You got asked now and again. Young lads in particular. Did you kill anyone? What's it like to kill some-one? Heads full of heroes and comic books, the pictures at La Scala or the Empire, with Jimmy Stewart and John Mills being noble and decent to stirring theme tunes. You never told them. The youngsters. Shook your head. Never let on.

* * *

'He went out like a light. Absolutely rat-arsed. He's only fif-teen,' Janine finished telling Sarah as they sat lounging on the settees.

'He'll be fine.'

'I worry — I'm his mother. Young lads and booze.'

'They all do it. Probably won't even have a hangover.'

Sarah cut some more cake for them each and settled back, shifting the cushion to get comfy. This dislodged a pile of Janine's work, which slid off the couch and onto the floor. Gruesome photos of Matthew Tulley's corpse uppermost.

'Yeugh!' Sarah scrabbled away from them.

'Whoops!'

Eleanor, wrapping her present in the kitchen, heard the scream. 'What?' she shouted through the serving hatch, eager with excitement.

'Nothing!' Janine and Sarah spoke in unison.

'Sorry,' Janine mouthed and cleared up the folder, putting it in her briefcase. 'Bedtime, Eleanor,' she called out.

Sarah settled back and started playing with Janine's ringtones, trying to find something tolerable. 'So, the lovely Richard?'

'Had to put him off.' Janine shrugged. 'I'd forgotten what it's like. Someone enjoying your company.'

'Ask him over for a drink. It's not that late.'

'I don't know.'

'Why not?'

Janine dismissed the idea. 'How are you anyway?'

'Not brilliant,' Sarah gave a rueful smile. 'It's my mum's birthday, today,' she paused. 'Was. Fifty-nine.'

Janine nodded. She knew how hard Sarah had found the last couple of years since her mum's death. There had been countless evenings when Sarah had come round, just needing to be with someone. Janine moved over and gave her a hug.

Sarah sat back. Lifted Janine's phone again, scrolling through the directory. 'Ring him.'

'No,' Janine protested.

'Why not?' Sarah found Richard's entry and pressed call.

'I'm not going to ring him!'

Sarah gave a wicked laugh and handed the phone to Janine saying, 'You just have.'

Janine bared her teeth at Sarah but continued to hold the phone.

'Boss?' Richard answered.

Janine rolled her eyes and mouthed 'Boss' to Sarah. 'I wondered, if you still fancied . . . wanted a drink, you could always come round here. Taxi home?'

'Yeah, I'd like that,' he said. ''Bout half an hour?'

She ran round like mad trying to sort the house out a bit and make herself presentable. When she heard him ring the doorbell she opened the door with a smile on her face — only to find a uniformed policeman there.

Janine scowled. He held out his ID for her. 'Mrs Lewis? PC Durham. Michael Lewis your son?'

Janine nodded.

'Sorry, I tried earlier. Michael was involved in an incident at the Trafford Centre yesterday.'

'I know.'

The officer was surprised. 'He told you?'

'He didn't want to report it.' She was puzzled. If he hadn't reported it why were they here?

'The other lad did. The victim.'

Ah — a cock-up. She shook her head. 'Michael was mugged,' she said clearly. 'They were trying to get his mobile. Someone's got their wires crossed.'

'If I could have a word with Michael.' As if she was inventing this. Bloody, cheek.

'No. It's late and he's asleep.' And the worse for wear. 'You go back and get your facts straight and then you can talk to him.'

PC Durham gave her an ingratiating smile. 'Now, Mrs Lewis . . .' he began in a patronising tone.

'Detective Chief Inspector Lewis, actually,' she said curtly. 'Good night.'

* * *

Ferdie rang the mobile number that he'd been given while Colin watched. 'Hiya,' said Ferdie. 'It's about tomorrow — the delivery.'

'Oh, right. Everything still okay?'

'Cool. What time?'

'Where are you?'

Ferdie gave him Colin's address. 'It's under the fly over, a caravan.'

Colin glared at him.

'Second one along once you reach the end of the lane.'

'Yep. 'Bout two?'

'Right.'

'And we're still talking two grand?'

'Yeah,' said Ferdie. 'Catch you then.'

'Yep.' He closed his phone. He felt edgy. Not surprising with all the grief the cops were giving him. Substantial bloody harassment, that's what it was. Needed to chill out. Colin didn't help, the duhbrain, acting like a condemned man all the time.

* * *

Richard looked breathless when he arrived. For a moment she was amused, wondered at his eagerness. Then she clocked it — something had happened.

'What?'

'Just heard. We've got the knife.'

She threw back her head and raised her fists in a gesture of triumph. 'Yes!'

Richard opened the bottle of wine he'd brought and poured himself a large glass. Janine filled her orange juice up and they went through into the lounge.

'I'll see the bloke who found it first thing, rough sleeper on the booze.' He gave a grimace — might be waste of time. 'And Forensics will get back to us soon as they can confirm whether it's our weapon and see if we can link it to any of our suspects. If Mr Vincent picks Ferdie Gibson out of the line-up . . .' he speculated.

'Why would Ferdie wait till now?' She thought hard, turned to Richard. 'Try this: Lesley Tulley gets someone else to do the deed but the clothes are washed at her house and she gets rid of the weapon.'

'Motive?'

'The someone was a lover? In go-faster stripes?'

Richard laughed. 'Can you see her sleeping with Ferdie Gibson?'

He had a point. Would any woman sleep with Ferdie? 'She hired him then. A lump sum, he gets his revenge.' They both considered this for a moment. Janine pulled a face.

'Would you trust Ferdie with a mission like that? And why? Why would Lesley kill Matthew?'

'The other woman?' Richard suggested.

'We'll get there. It's a good enough team.'

'Butchers is not exactly a bundle of joy.'

'Not tonight he isn't,' she recalled the bollocking she'd given him when she was at the supermarket. 'And Shap's all mouth and trousers. Butchers is feeling the pressure, trial separation. You know what it's like, people outside the job can't relate.'

'And people inside are married to it. You and Pete, Wendy and I . . .'

Janine shrugged. 'We had a fair run at it — sixteen years.'

'And now?'

'The words skin and teeth come to mind. I couldn't give it up though. Couldn't pay the mortgage for a start, but I love it. I'm good at it.' Her mind roamed back over the case. 'What if Dean Hendrix was the lover boy?'

'Twenty-two? Bit young for Mrs Tulley?'

'Doesn't matter — does it?'

She was suddenly aware of Richard's eyes on her, a sense of intimacy that she hadn't been aware of before. She returned his gaze. He had nice eyes, bright, knowing.

* * *

Lesley watched as the flames took hold, the smoke blew towards her and made her eyes water. Oh, Matthew. Such a romantic. He had bombarded her with flowers and gifts in the two weeks after their very first meeting. She'd noticed him in the cafe bar, sitting alone, drinking coffee. She with two friends getting ready for a night on the town. He'd looked her way several times and not even bothered to glance away when she looked back.

He went to the bar and spoke to the waiter, handed over a credit card. She thought he was leaving but he returned to his seat. Billie Holliday singing soft, breathy blues in the background. Minutes later a bottle of champagne arrived at her table. A note: *love at first sight — Matthew.*

Her friends exploded with laughter. She blushed furiously, watched him raise his coffee cup in salutation. They popped the cork. Her friends called him over to join them. He pulled a chair up.

'Do you do this often?' Hilary joked.

'Never,' he said seriously.

'Well, Matthew, meet Lesley.'

He shook hands. When he held hers she felt warmth; long, smooth fingers. He wouldn't take his eyes off her. The drink made her giddy. He invited them all for a meal, his treat and no strings attached he said. Which they all found hilariously funny though Lesley didn't know why.

'We were going dancing,' said Lesley.

'Not till later,' said Hilary.

'That's agreed then. Have you heard of The Glade?'

They were first year students, new to the city. When they looked blank he said it was the place to eat in Liverpool. The meal was exquisite, the prices outrageous. Matthew encouraged them to talk, kept ordering more wine. He said little about himself but told them something of the town. Lesley thought he was wonderful. Relaxed and attentive. An older man, nothing like the overgrown schoolboys she had lectures with. After coffee the others went to the ladies; a fairly obvious ploy to leave her alone with him.

'When can I see you again?' he said.

'You could come dancing,' she replied.

'Not really my scene. Tomorrow?'

She laughed.

'Are you busy?'

She shook her head.

'Tomorrow then. I'll pick you up.'

She hesitated. Better to meet somewhere in town. Being cautious as a matter of course rather than anything else. 'I'll meet you at that bar again.'

He smiled, a beautiful smile, long curving lips, even white teeth. He was lovely. He reached across and took her hand in his. 'Yes. Seven thirty.' He was looking at her mouth. She felt a ripple of excitement, a flutter between her legs and in her stomach, tingling in her breasts. The song had changed, *Cry Me A River*. Poignant and melodic. For a minute she thought about giving in. Leaving the girls and going with him. Now. Soon. But he might think her easy then.

She squeezed his hand. 'Seven thirty.'

He found out where she lived, anyway. Asked Hilary on the quiet so he could surprise her. Flowers arrived the next morning. A huge bouquet. She filled two vases and a wine carafe. A card: *my love, Matthew*. She felt dizzy and happy and restless. She couldn't think about anything else. She thought she was falling in love.

'Lesley! What are you doing?' Emma, back from her flat, came out into the back garden where Lesley watched the bonfire.

Lesley coughed, the smoke was unpleasant, the burning plastic smelt toxic. She looked at the video cases, the curled and blackened cassettes twisting and melting.

'Memories, Emma . . . I can't bear it . . .' Lesley broke down.

'What are they? I don't think you should be . . .'

'Holidays. We were going again, Singapore, for Easter. And now . . .'

'Oh, Lesley,' Emma embraced her and coaxed her inside.

* * *

Jade turned round and the thing was chasing after her but when she tried to run her legs wouldn't work. It was like they'd lost their bones. She tried harder and harder but she couldn't move and it was just behind her . . . just . . . no!

Jade woke up. Her legs were wrapped tightly in the sheet like an Egyptian Mummy. The sheet was wet. She shuddered. They'd gone to see the Mummies at the Manchester Museum for their topic. They were all tiny and looked like brown paper with bones sticking up.

She wriggled free and slid out of bed. She pulled the sheet and cover off and took them to the wash basket. She put some water in the basin then pulled off her night-dress and wiped the flannel over her belly and her legs to get the wee off. She rubbed herself dry. Back in her room she put on a t-shirt and knickers then got a sheet and blanket from the box in Mam's room.

'What is it, Jade?' Mam sounded croaky like a frog.

'I wet the bed and I had a scary dream, a nightmare.'

Mam groaned.

'But I can change the bed.'

''Kay.'

She put the sheet on and tucked it in a bit and pulled the blanket over her. She didn't feel sleepy. She said some Hail Marys, that sometimes made her sleepy but it didn't work. Then she tried her eight times table.

* * *

'So you've not met anyone — since . . . ?' Richard asked.

'Give us a chance. Kids and work, work and kids. The job itself isn't exactly a turn on.'

'Oh, I don't know,' he said intently.

Janine wasn't sure what he meant. He was attractive, no denying it, his mouth, his eyes, the way he made her laugh. But she was six months pregnant. She spoke to mask her bewilderment, blethering on. 'That reaction you get at parties? Like you've just confessed to drowning kittens.'

Richard moved closer. 'Remember Hendon?'

She giggled.

'That night. I wish . . .'

She interrupted. Not wanting him to say anything he'd regret. 'Richard, I . . .'

'Mum?' Eleanor came in and the two of them sprang apart. She pulled Eleanor onto her knee. 'This is Richard, from work. You won't remember him.'

'What's that manky smell?' Eleanor frowned. 'You're wearing perfume,' she accused her mother.

Janine smiled inanely.

Eleanor scrutinised her. 'And eyeliner.'

'Let's get you back to bed.'

Richard got to his feet. 'I'll, erm — phone a . . .' he nodded.

Five minutes later the taxi horn sounded outside. Janine saw him out. She felt ridiculous, she must have misread the situation. She smiled at him, feeling brittle, nodded goodnight.

Richard stepped away then turned back to her, put one hand on her shoulder, bent a little. A friendly peck on the cheek. His eyes warm and bright, lingered on her face. She smiled. He bowed a little, she tipped her head and he went. Leaving her feeling warm and fuzzy and completely confused.

CHAPTER TWELVE

Day 3: Monday, 24 February

Tom sounded a bit wheezy, Janine watched him as he ate a bowl of cereal. He looked well enough and he hadn't said anything. Was she just fussing? It would be a nightmare if he had to stay off.

She had roped in her mum and dad to have them before school and to drop Eleanor and Tom there. Michael made his own way to high school. But if they had to mind Tom all day . . .

He noticed her eyes on him and beamed. She smiled back. He was fine. Don't go looking for extra problems, she admonished herself, you've enough on. She heard the mail arrive and went to pick it up. Bills, offers of a platinum card and a home loan, a letter. *Parents of Michael Lewis.* She ripped it open. Read the contents with mounting dismay.

Dear Mr and Mrs Lewis,

I am writing to you because I am extremely concerned about the deterioration in Michael's school-work and problems at school that have been brought to my attention. I would like to meet with you as a matter of some urgency and will be available during lunchtime recess every day this week.

Yours sincerely, Mr Corkland, Head of Year 10

She stuffed the letter in her pocket. She would try and get in today; the sooner she knew what was going on the better.

'Yer Dad had a terrible night,' her mum announced when they got there.

She felt guilty. 'Oh, Mum. Look, get a taxi, save him driving.'

'A taxi? It'll cost the earth.'

Janine pulled out her purse. 'I'll pay.'

Her mum put up her hand. 'We'll manage.' She was stubborn over money and would never spend anything she saw as unnecessary. Came from years of watching the pennies. Sometimes it drove Janine nuts — it wasn't as if she and Pete struggled. They had enough money — just too little time.

* * *

The Lemon reacted pretty much as she had anticipated.

'Three?! Good God, woman. The intention is to narrow down the number of suspects. Not keep adding to the collection.' He gave an exasperated sigh.

'Sir.'

'This case. If it's too much, in your condition . . .'

How bloody dare he! She gave him an icy stare. She noticed his computer had crashed again. Well, he could stay in virtual limbo for ever as far as she was concerned.

'O'Halloran's winding up the airport thing now. He should be clear by midweek. He can take the wheel if you've not made significant headway.'

She didn't trust herself to speak. He couldn't take the case off her. He couldn't! She sat mutinous, feeling her blood rising. Watching him sneer and carp.

'Cut to the chase, Janine. We are committed to an eight percent improvement in clear up rate, by next month. One cock-up and we'll all be under the magnifying glass. You've got forty-eight hours.'

126

She finally lost it. Not prepared any longer to tug her forelock and toe the line. Just what exactly was his problem? She got to her feet. 'Why are you constantly undermining me?'

He stared at her, incredulous.

'Rather we take it to Human Resources?' she challenged him. Knowing he'd loathe that, an internal enquiry asking him to account for his behaviour. Though of course she'd have to fight like hell to get personnel to touch it. Why couldn't he just let her get on with the job? 'I'm a detective,' she began, raising her voice, 'why can't you—'

'I was a detective,' he let rip, 'thirty-five years — and this,' he swept his arms at the computer, the piles of paperwork, 'performance reviews, financial audits, measurable outcomes. I'm buried alive.' The veins on his forehead stood out, his teeth were bared. He was livid. 'The force — you — it's all changed.'

'So, is that my fault?' she demanded.

Silence. Then he broke eye contact, acknowledging with a dip of his head that she made fair comment.

'I'll get back to work,' she said, and he made no move to stop her going.

It was like a double whammy. Still shaken by the confrontation with The Lemon, Janine walked into the murder room to hear Shap, in the process of scanning the CCTV footage, sounding off to all and sundry.

'Serial shagger, that's why Wendy dumped him. Anything in a skirt. Ten quid says he'll have scored by the weekend.'

She flinched. Was that what she was? Someone for Richard to practise his technique on. Anything in a skirt. She felt sick. Of course he didn't really fancy her. She should have known as much.

'Morning,' she announced her presence. Went over to study the board where Butchers was laboriously updating information in his slow, neat script.

Richard came in then. She nodded at him, keeping it cool.

'Two days,' she told them all. 'I've just come from The Lemon and we've got two days and then he's bringing O'Halloran in and your lives won't be worth living.'

They didn't like that. Shap cursed, Butchers flung his marker down, Richard groaned.

* * *

Jade was halfway dressed before the funny feeling came back. She could hear Mam moving around down stairs so she went into Mam's room and looked out of the windows. No police cars anywhere. She went back to her own room and peered out the back. The stupid tent thing was still there and there was a policeman near it. Her heart began to jump about. But he was just standing there. Guarding it, she realised. He had to stay there and stop people going in the tent. He wouldn't be allowed to come to the house and ask Mam and Jade lots of questions because then anyone might go in the tent. Jade wondered if the dead man was in the tent still, and if he looked like a skeleton.

She could set off for school really early and get there before the doors were open. Lots of people did that and you could play in the playground for ages. Jade was usually late and had to go and get her mark from reception. Miss Cornish always sounded tired when she saw her, 'Yes, Jade,' she said, with a big sigh, 'late again, off you go.'

She put her old shorts and t-shirt in her lion bag and clattered downstairs. Mam had made toast.

'I don't want jam,' said Jade.

'Now you tell me. It's jam or nowt. That's the last of the bread.'

Jade tried to decide. She picked up a piece of toast and closed her eyes. She was so hungry. She nibbled the edge, then pushed the piece in all in one go, chewed it quickly and swallowed it as soon as she could.

'Can we go early? Miss said we had to be early.'

'I haven't finished my tea yet.'

'We can't be late,' said Jade, 'I'll get in trouble if we're late.'

'Jade, we're not going to be late. Yer stressing me out! You're like an old woman. Mithering all the time.'

Jade went and sat on the sofa clutching her lion bag.

* * *

Not all murders made headline news but Matthew Tulley's did. A stack of newspapers, broadsheets and tabloids bore witness. Some had covered the murder in their Sunday editions but ran it again in more depth. To do with him being a deputy head teacher, Janine reckoned; doctors, lawyers, headmasters — always more interest when the victim was a professional. An added fascination with the stories of middle-class life gone horribly awry. The mighty fallen. Gloat factor in there for some but also the shock that violence could rip apart those with a well-paid job, private medical insurance, school fees and a two car garage in much the same way as it did anyone else.

The circumstances of Tulley's murder attracted interest too — the homely setting of the allotments, the fact that there was no clear motive or suspect as yet. She skimmed the headlines; *Allotment Slaying Mystery, Manchester Teacher Murdered — Police Hunt Killer, Tulley Killing Latest.* Most gave versions of the press release rehashed in their own house style. Photographs of the allotments, of Ashgrove, and a poor shot of Lesley Tulley and Janine hurrying into the house, were accompanied by the official photograph of Matthew Tulley.

Jenny Chen came in, clutching a pile of reports. 'Boss, forensics are back.'

Everyone stopped, all eyes on Janine as she took the reports. Her pulse raced and she was all thumbs as she leafed through to the appropriate sheet. Fingerprints:

the one on the allotment tap. She read it swiftly. Yes! Then read it again in case she'd made a mistake.

'We've got a match on the fingerprint.'

She regarded the expectant faces around her.

'One of them?' Richard nodded at the wall.

'Oh, yes!' She moved closer, looked at the three mug-shots: Ferdie Gibson, shaved head, his narrow face set with a cold, cocky stare; Dean Hendrix, looking lost; Lesley Tulley, her beauty impaired by the glazed disorientation that the press shot had captured.

Janine saw Shap smirk, thinking he knew who it was. Butchers frowned, uncertain, probably worrying about losing his tenner. Chen's eyes widened with the intrigue.

Janine tilted her head. 'What d'you reckon?'

'Hendrix,' yelled Shap.

'Ferdie Gibson,' shouted Butchers.

'Lesley Tulley,' called Chen.

'Inspector?' Janine invited Richard to cast his vote.

He spread his arms wide — no idea.

'Dean Hendrix, ladies and gentleman.'

The room erupted in uproar. She held up her hands to quieten them. 'Now our most wanted. Suspect number one.' They were nodding, shifting in their seats, ready to get on and catch the guy. She had to instil caution in them. 'But that doesn't mean we drop Lesley Tulley or Ferdie Gibson,' she said emphatically.

'But, boss, it's obvious,' Shap was outraged.

'One fingerprint doesn't make a case.'

'If we're looking at a serial offender . . .' Shap said.

'He's done it before, he's gone into hiding, he was at the scene. What else do we need?' Richard said urgently.

'Motive?' She flung back.

'He's a nutter!' Shap stood up. 'He didn't even know his last victim, picks a fight and bam, the guy's opened up and juggling his guts. Hendrix is the man!'

'He's got a taste for it and he'll do it again. We've got to stop him.' Butchers joining in now. Agreeing with Shap. Wonders would never cease.

'We've got to find him, first.' She raised her voice. 'Yes, we keep after him but we work just as hard on our other leads.'

They continued to protest, Shap shaking his head, Butchers flailing his arms about, Richard frowning.

'We've only got two days.' Richard said. 'He's good for it. Listen . . .'

'No!' They were like some Wild West posse intent on riding off into the sunset and ignoring the threat that lurked in the other direction.

'. . . if we concentrate on Hendrix . . .'

'Inspector!' She cut him off, using his title to pull rank. 'I'll allocate actions, I decide on priorities. We do the press, we do the ID with Ferdie Gibson and we keep watching him, we work away at Lesley Tulley and we find Dean Hendrix.' She rode over their objections, adamant that she spoke sense and determined to direct the enquiry her way. 'He may be top of the list but there are still three suspects up here and it isn't over until one of them is arrested and charged. Signed, sealed, and delivered. Got it?'

CHAPTER THIRTEEN

News had come in that Lesley Tulley had lit a fire in her back garden the previous night.

'What was she burning?' Janine asked.

'Holiday videos, if you believe that.' Richard said.

'She must think we're stupid. Get samples and tell the lab to fast track them. I think Mrs Tulley might just have burnt her bridges.'

Richard took a step closer. Lowered his voice, 'Look, last night—'

Janine moved away raising her own voice. In no mood to go into the mistakes of the night before. 'And you're following up on the knife too. Good.'

DS Shap rewound the film yet again and reviewed the frames showing the car entering the car park. He copied down the time from the bottom right hand corner of the screen.

'Boss. We've got something here.' They gathered round the monitor. 'Here she is arriving,' Shap froze the frame which showed Lesley's car at the car park entrance. 'Spot the difference?'

Janine looked, then smiled. Who said Dean Hendrix should be the only one they looked at? She nodded. Butchers scowled, struggling.

'Ten twenty-seven,' she gave him a clue reading out the time from the tape.

'And her ticket says nine twenty-two,' Richard said.

Another inconsistency which quickened her interest in Mrs Tulley. Burning things in the garden, missing clothes, and now a misleading parking ticket. What exactly was going on?

* * *

Dean had finally got his bottle up to ring Paula.

'Paula. Did you get my message?'

'Yeah.' Not sounding happy about it. 'Where are you?'

'Douggie's had this spot of trouble like, I said I'd, erm, stay for a bit, you know.'

'What sort of trouble?'

'You don't want to know,' Dean put a laugh in it.

'Wrong, Dean!' warning him.

'It's difficult.'

'Tell me about it. I don't need this, Dean. I want to see you.'

'A few days . . .'

'No,' she said sharply. 'The police want to talk to you.'

Aw, hell.

'They came to work, they wanted to know where you were.'

'What did you say?'

'What could I say? I didn't know, did I? Don't know if he believed me, even.'

'I'm sorry.'

'Dean.'

'What?'

'You haven't asked why,' she said quickly, like she was accusing him, 'why they wanted to see you.'

'Why?' said Dean, knowing it was pathetic, knowing it wouldn't wash.

''S not funny, Dean. I don't like this. I dunno what's going on and you're behaving like some prize dick-head. About that murder, Mr Tulley, you heard about it?'

'On the news. I was up here, left Friday. The police, what did they say?'

She sighed. 'They want to know if you saw anything. You've got to ring them. You can just say you were at Douggie's, can't you?'

'No, I can't.'

Silence. 'Oh, God. This trouble Douggie's in — is that what it is?' Horror dawning in her voice.

'No, no. Nothing like that. He owes some money. He'll have it soon but they've been threatening him, that's all.'

'So what are you? Bodyguard? Dean, they'll have you for breakfast.'

'Paula!' Outraged that she had so little faith in his ability to protect himself.

'Think about it. What are you going to do when they come calling?'

He thought of the bag in the cellar, what he could do with that. 'There's a few of us,' he lied.

'I don't like it, Dean.' He said nothing. 'You gonna ring the police?'

'Yeah, yeah.' He nodded as if she could see. 'Cos I don't want them coming round here giving me grief.'

'Yep,' still nodding, 'I'll do that.'

'When you coming back?'

'Dunno. Depends.'

'I wanna see you, Dean.' She paused. 'I can come there.'

'No.'

'Where then?'

If he put her off she might dump him.

'Dean?'

'Erm. I'll meet you in Oldham, the coach station.'

'Oldham?' Like it was Outer Mongolia.

He gave her directions. Paula's driving was good but her sense of direction was crap.

'All right. 'Bout three then.'

Dean came off the phone smelling so bad he needed a shower. Went upstairs. All her questions ringing in his head. One of his own banging like a big bass drum:

what the hell was he going to tell Paula?

* * *

Bobby Mac, the rough sleeper, was an irritable drunk. He'd been held at Bootle Street and that was where Richard interviewed him. It was the duty sergeant at Bootle Street who passed on the details to his opposite number at South Manchester. Told him about a vagrant, one Bobby Mac, no fixed abode, who'd been given bed and board after an affray in Market Street. Been rampaging around with a knife, a knife that matched the description in the bulletin that they had issued earlier that day. Long shot but you never know. The message was passed on to the murder room, both men aware that someone would want the knife sent for forensic examination and would probably want to discuss with Bobby Mac how it came into his possession.

'Where did you get the knife, Bobby?' Richard asked.

Bobby rubbed his hand over his mouth and over the pale bristles around it. He rocked a little in his chair.

'The knife,' Richard reminded him, 'where did you get the knife?'

'What's it to you?'

'Humour me. Did you buy it? Someone give you it? Eh?'

Bobby shook his head, an erratic movement, like he was trying to dislodge something. 'Found it.'

'Whereabouts?'

He shook his head again.

'Listen,' said Richard, 'you were arrested for threatening people with a defensive weapon. That's bad news. Get quite a stretch for that, Bobby. But it so happens we have a particular interest in how you came across that knife. Now, you tell us where you found it and they might take that into account when they consider your case.'

Bobby yawned then, giving the inspector a front row view of yellow-coated tongue and discoloured teeth along with a blast of fetid breath that caused Richard to sit back sharply.

'You don't wear a uniform.'

'CID,' said Richard, 'plainclothes.'

'I was in uniform, the army,' he waved a finger at Richard. 'Good soldier. It's a hard life, you know. This lot these days . . .'

'Bobby,' Richard broke in. 'This knife,' he pushed the evidence bag closer, the knife sealed within, 'where did you find it?'

'That place near Marks, where there's that stream thing?'

'Millennium Gardens?' Richard pictured the pedestrianised area, the Triangle at one side, Selfridges and M&S at the other, curving steps and a water course, where the stream bubbled between crazy-paving stepping stones, tall windmill sculptures. Part of the city's re-build in the wake of the IRA bomb.

'Whereabouts?'

'In a bin.'

'The knife was in a bin?'

Bobby looked at him, eyes bloodshot, blinking slowly. 'I was hungry,' he said, 'you've no idea. I was a soldier. Her Majesty's armed forces. Germany. The Falls Road, Belfast.'

'You were looking for something to eat and you found the knife?'

Bobby nodded at the carriers neatly folded in the second evidence pouch, the department store logo visible on one. 'I thought it was a sandwich.'

'What?' said Richard, lost now.

'The knife. I thought it was a sandwich. They have those bags. I was looking for some grub.'

'Did you see who dumped it?'

Bobby Mac considered this then shook his head. 'Nah,' he said. 'Didn't see nobody.'

* * *

Lesley Tulley sat in front of the blue partition screens flanked by her sister Emma on one side and Detective Chief Inspector Lewis on the other. Beyond Emma was someone from the police press office. Next to DCI Lewis was her boss, Mr Hackett.

They had all been rehearsed in where to sit and when to speak before the press came in. Then they had to wait in the anteroom until everyone was ready.

Lesley felt cold even though the room was stuffy. She wore a grey cotton blouse with long sleeves and a grey slim-line skirt to match, chosen for the occasion.

Mr Hackett was speaking first, describing the efforts of the police, the reason for the press conference, the faith he had in his officers. For Lesley the words droned together. She kept her eyes cast down at the plain white laminate surface of the table. Her hands rested together at the edge of it, two small, limp fists. It occurred to her that they looked posed, unnatural and she moved to fold one hand over the other.

Mr Hackett was sitting down now. DCI Lewis speaking, introducing her. Lesley could hear buzzing, her heart felt too big, her chest tightened. She waited for her cue. 'Mrs Tulley.'

A battery of flashes;' clicks, whirrs. Cameras like some flock of scolding, chattering birds.

'Please,' Lesley began, her voice surprisingly clear, 'if you know anything at all, anything that might help the police catch whoever did this to Matthew, please ring them up, tell them.'

She stopped, panic widened her face, she couldn't remember whether there was more. Had she said it all? More flashes. Emma put her hand out, squeezed hers in reassurance.

Chief Inspector Lewis was giving out the contact number, repeating the request for information. Lesley could feel the room bearing down on her, she wanted a drink but was fearful of spilling some, of not being able to swallow. She wondered if anyone ever had a drink on these occasions or was it just there for show?

Janine Lewis didn't give straight answers to most of the questions; just said they were still pursuing their enquiries or it was too early to say.

'Any news about the murder weapon?' one of the journalists called out.

'Yes,' she said, 'a knife matching the design of the one used on Matthew Tulley has been recovered. Forensic tests will be carried out to determine whether this was the murder weapon.'

Lesley froze, a picture of bewilderment. The flash bulbs erupted. This was the photo that most of the papers would carry the following day.

Hackett and the Press Liaison Officer thanked the family and said their goodbyes as soon as they left the conference hall.

'Why didn't you tell us about the knife?' Emma rounded on Janine. 'You knew when we got here. You trample all over—'

'Emma.' Lesley's protest went unheeded.

'Matthew was her life and you treat her like dirt, like she had something to do with it. She's never had it easy. You're not getting anywhere, are you? That's why you're messing us about?'

Janine ignored the remarks. She focused on Lesley. 'What was the bonfire for, Lesley?'

'You cow!' Emma said.

Lesley looked stung but upset too. 'I couldn't bear — we'd been so happy, holidays and I—' She began to cry. 'I never thought about evidence, it wasn't evidence.' Distraught, she pushed at her hair and then at her sleeves.

Janine saw ugly red weals, shiny puckered scars, across her inner arms.

Oh, Christ, thought Janine, she's cutting herself. What will she do if we push her too far? Be a bloody disaster. Janine wanted to catch a murderer, not cause a suicide.

'If Matthew's killer was known to him then we hope to find some information among his personal effects. Please leave everything else as it is at the house. I'll call round later. By then we should also have some results from the press conference, an idea of what level of response we're getting. It'll be going out on the lunchtime news and again early evening. Thank you again for your help.'

Emma still looked disgruntled. Lesley just looked worn out, thought Janine. Emma put an arm around her sister and walked her to the door where a uniform was waiting to take them to a car.

The Lemon had another axe to grind, complaining about her instruction to have the lab process the remains of Lesley Tulley' fire. 'You should have cleared it with me first. You know forensics cost a fortune.'

'I think it's crucial, sir.'

Her phone interrupted them, she blushed furiously and answered it with a hiss. Her mother!

'Janine, he can't get the video working! The news is starting any minute.'

'Mum, it doesn't matter.' She knew they were proud of her but honestly, watching re-runs of herself at the press conference was the giddy limit. Janine heard her mum shout to her dad. 'Press record.'

She was aware of The Lemon's eyes boring into her. 'Mum, really.'

'Have you got the tape in?' her mother yelled.

'Mum, listen—'

'Is it switched on?'

'I'll ring you back.' She ended the call. 'Sorry, sir. The bonfire — I believe that's how she got rid of the washing that was there on Saturday.'

'You're squandering resources on three separate tracks. Narrow it down.'

Back in the murder room, officers were fielding calls from the public. All the lunchtime television news broadcasts led with the press conference and among the calls flooding into the incident room were the usual number of hoaxers, attention-seekers and fanatics with their own personal agendas. These included one who knew that Matthew Tulley had been killed by aliens and another who saw the murder as God's sign to a corrupt society and predicted there would be one a week till the second coming of Christ.

All calls would be logged and anything that deserved closer attention was relayed to senior officers.

Janine made a quick call to reassure her mum. 'The press office can always get me a copy. And how's Dad?' Apart from in the doghouse?

'He's had a letter, he's an appointment next week.'

DC Chen came over with a memo.

'Good,' Janine said. 'I'll come with you, try and get some sense out of them about waiting times.'

'Oh, that'd be great.' She could hear the gratitude in her mum's voice and hoped that work wouldn't prevent her from keeping her promise.

'Bye-bye.' Janine finished the call and turned to the DC.

'Anonymous call from a woman,' said Chen. 'Claims Matthew Tulley was a right bastard and his wife should be glad he's dead.'

'Crank?'

Chen shrugged. Could be.

'Get a name?' Janine asked Chen.

'No, number withheld, too.'

Shap came over then, obviously excited about something, a glint in his eyes, smile playing round the edge of his lips. 'Matthew Tulley's parents. Back from a weekend in Paris and just seen the news. Want to know why we didn't try to contact them.'

'What with? A Ouija board? We were told they were dead!' Janine was astonished. 'When I asked about notifying close family on Saturday, Lesley Tulley said that both his parents were dead. Bloody hell!' She stood up and paced a few steps to the wall and back. She tried to work out the significance of this bombshell. 'So someone has been telling lies.'

'I said you'd ring them straight back, boss.'

'Of course. I'll want to see them as well. Where are they?'

'Lymm.'

'Right. I'm taking an early lunch, parents stuff, Michael's school. Then DI Mayne and I visit Ferdie Gibson's friend Colin, we'll see what Mr and Mrs Lazarus have to say after that.'

* * *

'We are very worried about Michael's attitude.' Mr Corkland, Michael's head of year, spoke gravely. 'His performance is disappointing and now these allegations of bullying have been made.'

Bullying! Oh, no. Her heart went out to Michael. The thought of him braving school each day. Waiting for the next attack. Had they hit him, verbally abused him or what? She'd had no inkling of it. 'No wonder his work's going downhill,' she said. 'You have an anti-bullying policy, don't you?'

'Mrs Lewis,. Michael isn't being bullied.'

'But you just said—'

'He's doing the bullying.'

Janine stared at the man, opened her mouth then shut it again. 'Michael?' She finally managed.

'There are four of them. They've been harassing two students in their year, sending text messages. There may have been thefts too. Mobile phones.'

'Why isn't Michael here? He should know what he's being accused of.'

'Michael's not in school, he appears to have left school after registration.'

Janine's heart sank. Bullying and now missing school. And the policeman last night, the one she'd sent away with a flea in his ear, who claimed Michael had been accused of an attempted mugging. She felt sick and dizzy. Michael. What on earth was going on?

She rang Pete from the police station car park where she was meeting Richard. 'Is Michael with you?'

'No. Why?'

She sighed. 'He's bunked off school. I've just been in. He's got in with the wrong crowd. Oh, Pete, they've been nicking mobile phones, bullying other kids.'

He exhaled noisily. 'So, he got a taste of his own medicine, Saturday?'

Janine closed her eyes. Wished this wasn't happening.

'Janine?'

Across the car park she watched Richard leave the building with Jenny Chen. He whispered something to her and the beautiful young woman flung back her head and laughed, put a hand on his arm to steady herself. Very chummy.

'I don't think he gave us the full story,' she told Pete. 'The police came round last night. Their version was that Michael was the villain of the piece.'

'Why didn't you tell me? Christ, Janine.'

Don't shoot the messenger, she thought. 'It was late and I thought they'd cocked it up, and,' she added reluctantly, 'Michael was drunk.'

DC Chen drove off and Richard scanned the cars. Janine waved him over.

'What! He's fifteen!' Pete sounded completely appalled.

'And how old were you, first time you got drunk?'

'I was never a thief.'

Janine gave another sigh. Richard reached the car, she nodded for him to get in. 'I expect he's with these mates. If you hear from him . . .'

'What?'

'Just, don't . . . don't go mad at him.'

Pete cut the connection, obviously resenting her for the comment. She just didn't think a full-blown row would help Michael.

Richard looked curious but she wasn't in any mood to share it with him.

'Any word on Dean Hendrix?'

He shook his head. Janine started the engine.

* * *

Even at school they were talking about it. Maria going on about how her mam knew the man that had been murdered. Then Megan saying that everyone who went to church knew him because he was there every week. He sat near the back with the Hennesseys. Jade couldn't remember him but she didn't go every week. Only when Mam felt up to it. And someone said the police had started a manhunt.

Jade wondered if the manhunt had horses or maybe they just used the helicopter because they could see where you were from that even if you were hiding. It was on the telly and they showed these men in some bushes and they were hot and the helicopter could see them with a special thing. They could even see you in a wheelie bin. Jade nearly told them what she'd seen. That would show them. They'd all want to sit with Jade at school dinners.

Then in assembly they had to say a special prayer for Mr Tulley and Mrs Tulley. He was a teacher at St Columbus. That's where you went to big school. They had the same colour uniform. At break, Anthony said Mr Tulley had his head chopped off but he was just making it up 'cos when Liam asked him how he knew he said he just did and he went red. Liam kicked him and said liar, liar, pants on fire and Liam said Mr Tulley had been shot with an AK-47. He pointed his finger at Jade and shot her 'pyew, pyew'.

'You are so sad,' Jade told him and she went to sit by the wall. She wondered if Mr Tulley would be in heaven already or if he had to go to purgatory for a bit. You only went straight to heaven if you'd no sins. So if you'd done something wrong and you died before your next confession then you went to purgatory and you suffered until your sins were cleaned up. Then you could go up.

If you had loads of sins, if your soul was all black with sins then you'd go straight to hell. Everlasting torment. If they were mortal sins. It was really hard, thought Jade, to be good all the time. Mainly remembering all the time was hard. Just one little thing and you'd committed a sin.

143

Even babies weren't pure. They were all born with the sins of the world. They didn't get sent to purgatory though, just limbo. They didn't suffer, just floated about like astronauts. But they stayed there. That was tight really, 'cos if you were a baby and you died and went to limbo and then your mam died and went to heaven then you'd never see her again. For all eternity. But a baby was all right if it got baptised. That took away all the sins and then they were saved. Jade knew how to save a baby. You could baptise it yourself. You needed holy water though. You put some on your thumb and you made a sign of the cross on the baby's forehead and you said, 'I baptise you in the name of the father and of the son and of the holy spirit. Amen.' Then it was safe. Jade had baptised all her dolls. It was good practise. Anyway, if Mr Tulley went to Mass every week he'd probably be okay.

* * *

Janine surveyed the tatty mobile home that Ferdie Gibson's mate Colin hid in. The place was near Northenden, tucked in between the motorway flyover and the steep banks of the murky brown river. A dismal place, she thought, the roar of the traffic night and day, the shadow of the concrete bridge and a dispirited ramshackle air to the whole site.

Janine wondered what sort of upbringing the lad had had to end up here, on his own. Colin blinked repeatedly and licked his lips as she and Richard stepped in through the narrow doorway and perched on the sagging mattress couch at the dining end of the space.

'Ferdie Gibson's down the station now, Colin. Helping us with our enquiries. We thought you could help, too,' Janine said.

'I told the other guy everything,' Colin meant DS Butchers.

'Tell us again,' Richard folded his arms.

'Ferdie came round about one. We went down the pub.'

'One o'clock?' Richard made it sound like the wrong answer.

Unnerved, Colin reached for a cigarette and lit it. 'Yeah, 'bout then.'

'You didn't see Ferdie earlier on Saturday morning?' Janine asked.

'No, I told you, I was in bed.'

'Really?' She didn't believe him. 'See, we know he'd attacked Mr Tulley once already. Probably talked about having another go. You've heard him saying he'd get Tulley, haven't you?'

'That was just talk. Everyone says stuff like that,' Colin puffed quickly on his fag.

'Ferdie follows through, though,' she said. 'We've a witness who's got someone like Ferdie near the scene of the crime. We're not looking at taking without owner's consent now, Colin. Murder.' She paused. The lad's face was tight with tension. His eyes darting all over the place. 'If Ferdie is charged and you withheld information then you could be done for obstruction or attempting to pervert the course of justice.'

Colin's hand shook violently.

'Be better for you if you're straight with us,' she said quietly. 'Much better. Well?'

In the pause before he spoke she heard the blare of a horn from the overhead traffic and the squeal of brakes. Come on, Colin, she willed, give it up, whatever you're hiding.

'I was here. I didn't see Ferdie till one. All like I said.' He spoke in a rush, pulled hard on the cigarette.

Damn! Any chance she'd had of persuading him had passed. She flicked her eyes to Richard. No score. Time to go.

* * *

Eddie Vincent took two extra tablets to help with the pain. He didn't want to be doubled up when he had his go at picking out the lad he'd seen. They had promised to send a car for him. He was ready, coat and hat on.

He didn't ever feel properly warm these days. Like the cancer was draining the heat from him as well as the life. His mother had lived to a ripe old age but Eddie's father died young. He'd been killed at work. An accident on the docks at Old Trafford. Six dead, several injured. Unloading cotton that had come all the way from India across the oceans and up the Manchester Ship Canal.

There was no compensation. His mother went before the Poor Board to try and get help with the rent. His sisters went into the mill as girls and he followed them. Till the war came long.

Knocking at the door. Eddie got slowly to his feet and went to answer it.

At the police station it was just like the television. A row of men sat behind the glass. They couldn't see him. They were dressed in similar casual clothing and wore baseball caps turned backwards. He took his time looking at each in turn. They were very alike. He'd expected it to be easy. That the face of the one he had seen would jump out at him, clear as day. But it hadn't and the more he studied them the more similar they appeared. Although one on the far end, a bit taller, looked most like he remembered, skinny too.

'Take your time,' said the policeman. 'Would you like them to turn to the side?'

'No, I saw him from the front.' He could hardly ask them to look desperate, haunted. 'But can you get them to look right and left, like they're watching out for something?'

The parade were instructed to do so. The movements were stilted and made Eddie more uncertain. He felt foolish for agreeing to come. When they had all finished he turned to the policeman. 'It's no good, the nearest is number one but I couldn't say he was the chap I saw. Couldn't swear to it in a court of law.' He had to be honest.

* * *

Butchers was adding to the boards again. All the bits of information they could verify and that might have a bearing were going up. He pinned the memo about the Tulley parents

146

up above the picture of the dead man. DS Shap sidled over. Butchers waited for some smart-arse comment. He didn't have long to wait.

'Dead loss, your old codger, Mr Vincent,' Shap said. 'Picked Andy from traffic.'

Butchers sighed and stabbed a drawing pin into the display and the whole thing clattered down, scattering papers and pins and the board landing with one edge on his left foot, the tender spot where he'd damaged a toe joint in a school rugby game. A sarcastic cheer rang through the room from the handful of staff working there.

'Piss off,' shouted Butchers, righting himself and looking at the holes in the wall. Some idiot had fixed it up with nails, instead of using screws and Rawlplugs. If a job's worth doing . . . thought Butchers. Be the bloody handyman cum caretaker. Had some fancy title: Building Resources Manager. Hah! Couldn't manage fuzzy-felt. Butchers sighed and began gathering up the bits of paper.

* * *

Janine pulled up outside the address where Matthew Tulley's parents lived. Nice bungalow, low-maintenance garden at the front, conservatory at the side.

'Lot chillier, today,' Richard looked at her. Not smiling. 'Not just the weather. Have I missed something?'

She tensed up. 'Can we just concentrate on the job?'

Her phone went. It was Shap.

'The line-up,' she told Richard, 'no joy.' She hit the steering wheel in frustration. It was disheartening, too many leads going nowhere. The Lemon was right, they did need to narrow it down but nothing concrete was coming out yet. She couldn't disregard Ferdie simply because the ID parade had failed. Eyewitnesses were notoriously inaccurate. Just because the old guy hadn't picked him out didn't mean Ferdie was in the clear. He still had the history with Tulley and she knew Colin had been lying about the morning.

Jack Tulley came out to greet them and took them in to meet his wife, Connie. They sat in the lounge. A room awash with floral patterns.

The couple looked shell-shocked, expressions slack with the impact of the news they had had, clothes flung on with little care, hair tousled.

'When we spoke on the phone you said you hadn't seen your son recently?' Janine began.

'Not for years,' Connie explained, her frame shaking. 'We didn't even know Matthew had got married again. He's got nephews and nieces he's never even seen. He just didn't want to know. And now—' her voice trembled.

'Matthew had been married before?'

'Awful business,' Jack patted his wife's hand, his voice husky. 'They were divorced before they'd even given it a go. They were far too young, still at college.'

'When was this?' Richard asked. 'Nineteen seventy-nine.'

'What was her name?'

'Laura, Laura Belling.'

'Do you know where she's living,' Janine said.

'No' said Jack. 'He told this Lesley we were dead, didn't he?'

Janine gave a small nod.

Connie made a mewling sound. Her husband shuddered.

Oh, God, thought Janine, aware of their pain and the awful humiliation. She took in the framed photographs on the wall. The sister they'd mentioned, young family, smiling parents.

'Julia and her crew — four grandchildren,' Jack told her, sniffing hard.

'And you've no idea who did it?' Connie's eyes shone with tears.

Janine shook her head.

'Or why? They said there was no idea why he'd been killed.'

'Not yet,' said Janine, 'but we're doing everything we can.'

The journey back from Lymm was turning out to be a nightmare. A lorry had shed its load of tinned goods just outside Manchester and traffic was backed up for four miles. The air was still and thick with the stench of exhaust fumes.

'So what does that tell us about Matthew Tulley?' she said to Richard.

'That he was a liar.'

'Why pretend they're dead? Why deny the existence of family?'

'Couldn't stand them?'

'But not a dickey bird in . . . what . . . nearly twenty years, eighteen years?'

'They cramp his style?' Richard suggested.

'Hardly Steptoe and Son though, were they?'

'Perhaps he was being economical with the truth in other ways; didn't want them blowing the gaff?'

'Like the first marriage? That was news. See if we can find her, see what she has to say about Tulley.'

'Yep.' Richard cracked open a can of Lilt. 'We're moving,' he gestured at the cars in front. His mobile sounded and he took the call. Relayed the details to Janine. 'Next lot of Forensics in.'

'The bonfire?' she said eagerly.

'As if! The trainer: Hi-Tec, Walklite, tens.'

'Get Shap to check out Ferdie Gibson's shoes. We know how unreliable ID parades are — doesn't mean he's off the hook. Anything from Lesley?'

'Hair and skin traces on his body and clothing,' Richard shrugged. 'Gets us nowhere: they shared a bed. Also the lab reckons the killer would have been awash with blood, and so would the knife — if they were carrying it.'

Janine tried to imagine the scene. The killer leaving the body, blood everywhere. 'Send Butchers back to Mr Vincent, take him through it, bit by bit. In minute detail. Oh, damn.'

They came to another standstill because of road works. Janine groaned. She was dying to pee, another symptom of her pregnancy. She put on the handbrake and shifted in her seat to ease the pressure on her bladder. She helped herself to a chocolate bar.

'One thing came up when I talked to the school,' Richard had visited St Columbus after seeing Bobby Mac, 'according to an old classmate, Gibson had been making personal comments about Tulley's wife. That's when Tulley went ballistic.'

'Jealous?'

'There's a chance.'

'We need to dig around some more. Did Ferdie Gibson know Mrs Tulley? I want to press her on the car park business, the times don't tally and cutting herself up — perhaps everything in the garden wasn't quite so rosy?'

Janine's phone went then. Her mum again. She was expecting more about the VCR but her mum's voice was full of panic.

'Janine, it's Tom, he's had an asthma attack. They've taken him to hospital.'

Tom! Her guts twisted in fear and she felt the blood jump in her veins. 'Oh, my god. Which hospital?'

'Wythenshawe.'

'Oh, Jesus, I'm on my way.' She turned to Richard, her face white with panic. 'It's Tom. He's had an asthma attack at school. They had to get an ambulance.'

Richard leant forward and opened the compartment, retrieved the magnetic blue light and siren from the glove compartment and wound down his window.

Janine looked at him, shocked. It was against all the rules to do that. Only ever police business, only ever a genuine emergency.

She frowned. Richard placed it on the car roof. Nodded at her. 'Go for it, Janine.'

She hesitated. He nodded again. She thought of Tom, her Tom, struggling to breathe. Took a gulp of air herself and shifted into gear as the siren began its wail. Prayers already tumbling through her head fast as her heartbeat.

CHAPTER FOURTEEN

She was breathless herself when she arrived in the ward. Tom in the bed, so small and fragile against the solid metal-framed bed, a mask over his nose and mouth. Pete was there, he stood and immediately reassured her. 'He's all right. He responded well.'

Janine sat down, unsteady, giddy with relief. She closed her eyes, put her hands over her mouth and took a minute. Then she reached out a hand to stroke Tom's hair.

Pete cleared his throat. 'It was—' he faltered. She could read in his eyes how scared he had been. 'They want to keep him in overnight.'

She nodded.

'You thought he was okay for school?' he asked.

She paused. Not knowing what to say. Yes, she had doubts but he'd seemed fit enough. Was it her fault?

Pete shot her a look of disgust. Stood up and moved away.

She tried to explain. 'Pete — it's not. Sometimes it's hard to tell.'

'And the job comes first?'

'That's not fair,' she said quietly.

'Really?' He was angry, the edge of his nostrils were flared and white, his jaw set. 'Michael's going off the rails, he'll be pulling some stupid stunt that lands him in court before long, Tom's left to fend for himself—'

Janine stood then, a flash of anger dislodging the guilt. 'Oh, come on. You can't say that. They're your kids as well. I can't do it all on my own though I'm having a bloody good try. You walked out on them, that has a lot more to do with it—'

'Oh, yeah. Back to that,' he spat the words out.

'Pete, you left them. It hurts.'

They stood, a few yards apart, the wreckage of their marriage all too apparent. Janine sighed and went back to Tom, cradled his hand in her own. She sat for a while and watched his chest rise and fall with the apparatus. He'd need pyjamas, some of his favourite toys.

'Can you stay till teatime?' Already thinking about the practicalities, who could cover when. Pete looked at her in horror. What did he expect? 'Or would you rather do overnight?' she continued.

He had the sense to look abashed and shook his head.

'Okay. I'll get Sarah to bring Eleanor home, stay at ours. I'll bring Tom's things.' She kissed Tom and told him she'd be back later. He slept on.

'If anything happens. Anything. Ring me.'

Pete nodded. He looked desolate. For a moment she wanted to hug him, to be back to before when they weren't on different sides, when everything wasn't a battle for the moral high ground.

* * *

Colin wasn't sure if he could go through with it. Ferdie should be here. If Ferdie didn't come soon he didn't know what he'd do. What if it was a trap? A set-up?

He wished he'd never got into it, any of it. Ferdie — all the drama, he got a buzz off of it, but Colin just felt like the stress was going to kill him. Must have a weak heart or something. If the police had still got Ferdie at the station . . . if they charged him with the murder . . . if he got sent down.

Colin had a glimpse of life after Ferdie Gibson and it was sweet. He'd better try Ferdie's mobile. If there was no answer then maybe he was still at the nick, 'cos they wouldn't let him take calls there, would they?

'Ferdie?'

'Colin.'

'Where are you? It's after two.'

There was knocking at Colin's door. His knees went weak. 'Shit! There's someone at the door, Ferdie.'

'It's me, Colin.'

'What?'

'Open the effin' door.'

He did. Ferdie stood there scowling with impatience.

'They let you out?' Colin said.

'They been here?'

'Yeah.'

'What did you say?'

'Same as before. They didn't believe me though. Kept going on, threatening me with being an accessory and obstruction and that. Perverting the course of justice.'

'They always do that. You didn't tell them anything?'

'No, honest.'

'They reckon someone seen me near Tulley's allotment. They wanted me in a line-up. Voluntary. So I went and they sent me home. Couldn't identify me, could they. Obvious innit?'

Colin nodded, no longer trying to figure it all out. Just wanting it to be over.

'Where's the money?'

'Bog,' said Colin.

Ferdie followed him to the minute bathroom compartment. Colin removed the floor panel from the peach-coloured shower which hadn't ever worked since he'd had the place and fished out a canvas shoe bag.

He handed it to Ferdie who grinned like a demon and swore softly with pleasure.

They counted twenties and tens into piles.

'There,' Ferdie set the piles aside. 'Two grand. And a bit left over for me pension.'

* * *

Dean heard Douggie and Gary leave. Knew it was Douggie by the whistling. Whistle like a bird, Douggie could. Do bird songs too and sound effects with his mouth; water pouring from a bottle, creaking doors and footsteps, MetroLink tram hooting. Brilliant. Hardly a career option though. Dean reckoned they must have used people like Douggie on the radio years back, when they still called it the wireless. Be all computers now. No need for a bloke in the corner knocking two coconut shells together or chugging like a steam train.

Douggie used to do his sounds when they were in Hegley together. Party trick. Douggie would play the fool, he got spared 'cos he entertained people. Even the British National Party nutters appreciated Douggie's talents.

Some of the lads in there had scared the life out of Dean. Hard men. Wound up tight, always ready to snap. Getting or giving a kicking on a daily basis. Violence the only language they spoke. Second nature. First nature. Only nature. Others, equally scary, got off on it. Sick. Not talking kinky sex, weekend S&M, hit me harder, baby. No. Not that at all. Talking some guy screaming, blood all over his face, bubbling from his nose, broken bone making his elbow hang all wrong. Battery and rape. It happened. He knew all about it.

One time, Dean had only been in there three weeks, he's in the bog and one of them comes in. McGowan they call him. Dean hears his voice. Then McGowan's climbing up the next cubicle, leaning over, looking down on him. 'Well, what have we got here then? Open the door. C'mon, open the fucking door.'

Dean, dread flooding his mouth, hand reaching for the door. Fumbling, pulling it open.

'Boo!'

Jesus! One of McGowan's stooges on sentry duty. Dean slams the door shut. Dean, flying on fear; everything sharp as razors, can hear a distant footfall: the squeak of rubber soles on the hard vinyl floor. He knows that squeak.

'Douggie,' he screams.

Footsteps. Squeak, squeak, squeak. 'Dean?' Douggie shouting.

'Douggie. Douggie.' No missing the need for help.

Glass breaking and then mayhem as the bell starts ringing and the sprinklers come on. McGowan disappears.

Later, sitting quiet with Douggie, he's amazed they haven't disciplined Douggie for setting off the alarm, not that anyone saw him but that didn't usually stop them. Douggie, sitting on the floor, his back to the bed. Dean lying curled on the mattress, arms wrapped round his belly, telling Douggie about what happened. What brought him to Hegley. Why he'd knifed the guy. Different from the statement he'd signed, the one they read out in court and different too from the story his victim had given. The first, last and the only time, that Dean ever told anyone the truth about it.

Dean finished and it's quiet. Douggie turns round puts a hand on Dean's shoulder, face tight with emotion, holding on. "S all right, mate,' Douggie says, husky throat. 'All right, Dean.'

He had the nous to go then, leave Dean on his own, door shut, so no one could see him weep.

* * *

Lesley heard someone at the door and then Emma's voice. Emma was asking them in. He was here! Lesley stood, ready to bolt, to plead illness, anything.

'Lesley, it's a friend of yours? I don't know if you feel up to it.'

Lesley froze then realised it wasn't him — it was another man. From the car park. Saturday, the man who'd stopped his blue van.

'Such an awful thing,' he was saying. 'I wanted to come and see how you were. If I'm not intruding.'

'No,' she said. All smiles. On the brink of tears. 'This is my sister, Emma. This is . . . John.' Very original. 'I'm pretty wobbly,' she said. 'Come through.'

He sat down on the sofa, stretching his arms wide across the back. She closed the door. Stood with her back to it.

He was sizing the place up. 'Very nice. Not the best area, though. Place like this in, Didsbury, you'd be looking at least 300K.' He sat forward. 'You were very good on the telly. Your appeal for information. I have some.'

She stared at him in confusion, then Emma interrupted them, 'Inspector Mayne on the phone.'

John got up. ' I'll be in touch.' She watched him leave, her heart thudding in her chest.

* * *

There was knocking at Colin's door.

'And that'll be our man.' Ferdie said.

Colin felt sick. He went and opened the door.

'All right, mate,' Douggie said and nodded a greeting.

'Right.' Colin swallowed. 'Erm, come in . . . in here.'

'All right, mate,' Douggie greeted Ferdie. He sat down and slid the rucksack from his back, retrieved two bags of cocaine wrapped in cling-film. 'Like a sample?'

Ferdie nodded.

'Help yourself.'

Ferdie opened one of the parcels, licked his finger, dipped it into the powder and rubbed it onto his gums. Nodded. Repeated the process and smiled broadly. 'Nice one.' He slid the money over the table. 'Two grand.'

'You don't mind if I—' Douggie pointed at the notes.

'No, best be sure,' said Colin hastily. 'Think it's right.'

Douggie counted the bundles. 'Cool. I'll be on my way. You've got the number if you want to place any more orders.'

'Yep,' said Ferdie, grinning inanely now.

Colin followed the lad to the door. 'See you, mate.'

'See you.'

* * *

DC Chen, parked in an unmarked car, watching Ferdie and Colin, noted the arrival and departure of the young man in the Nissan Sunny. She ran the number plate for identification. It was registered to an Oldham address, to one Douglas Connor. After talking to Oldham she established that they had Douglas Connor, aka Douggie, in their sights. He was allegedly shifting substantial amounts of stuff. There was an operation on and they were expecting some action soon. Chen reckoned Ferdie Gibson and chum were buying. But how did someone living in a dump like that caravan get that sort of cash? Oldham promised to keep them informed as and when.

* * *

On the way back to the station, Janine rang and left Michael a message, wherever he was, so he would know what was going on with Tom. She met Sarah at the house to give her the keys and to reassure Eleanor.

When she walked into the murder room the team gathered round her. Word had travelled fast and they wanted to know how Tom was.

'He should be fine,' she told them. 'But it's a horrible thing.' She could recall so clearly Tom's first bad attack. The feeling of helplessness. Tom, his face red with effort, the fear in his eyes. Her terror because although it was down-played she knew children could die from this disease. Every year the numbers of sufferers rose yet no one agreed about the causes. 'Terrible,' she shook her head.

She raised her eyes, braving a smile and caught sight of The Lemon looking through the glass room divider.

'Don't look now,' she told them, 'but we are not alone. Okay, Butchers is already knocking doors,' she nodded at Shap. 'You're back to Ferdie.'

She gathered up her things. The Lemon strolled into the room.

'Janine.'

'Sir?'

'Problems with the family?' She was suspicious, anyone else and she'd take the comment at face value, but she still didn't trust him.

She misinterpreted him deliberately. 'Skeletons in the wardrobe, sir. Tulley was married before and his dead parents are alive and well and living in Lymm.'

He didn't like that, a little flare in his eyes. Knowing her game. 'Your family,' he said crisply.

'Nothing I can't handle, sir. But thanks for asking.'

* * *

The tent had gone. Jade could see from her bedroom. All gone. The body must have gone too. And the police. She changed out of her uniform. Megan was coming round. Megan had a Top 40 cassette and a karaoke machine that you could carry around. Not with a screen or anything but there was a mike and you could sing while the tape was on. They could work out a routine.

It'd be brilliant to be a pop star. Jade was going to be one. She was growing her hair. It was nearly down to the bottom of her shoulder blades. She and Megan wanted their hair to look the same. When it was really long they could do it in plaits sometimes or up on top. It would depend if they were doing a concert or a video or what. She was going to do mainly the dancing and Megan would sing.

There was a knock at the door and Jade ran down to let Megan in. She pulled open the door. There was the police-man again. She slammed it shut and ran upstairs, went in the bathroom.

Rat a tat tat.

'Jade?' Her mam called from the back room. 'Jade?'

She heard Mam go down the hall and the rumble of voices. She was letting him in. She could hear them talking but not what they said.

'Jade,' Mam calling her, 'come here.'

'I'm on the toilet.'

'Well, hurry up and get down here.'

Jade had a wee and washed her hands. She looked in the mirror. There was all specks of toothpaste on the mirror, if you closed your eyes nearly shut and looked it was like you had white spots growing on you.

'Jade!' Her mother's shout made her jump. 'Get down here, now.'

She came slowly downstairs, her mam scolding her. 'It's the police. He's a nice man and he's not going to eat you. Just wants to ask you a couple of questions, then he'll be on his way.'

She steered Jade into the room.

'Hello, Jade.' He had a blue shirt on and a tie with Tweety Pie all over it. He was a bit fat. He looked like Megan's dad without the tattoos.

'Your mum says you're a bit shy of the police?'

Jade gave her mam a sulky look.

'There's no need. We're here to help. We have a motto. Do you know what a motto is, Jade?'

She thought it sounded like one of the Instants you got at the shop. She shook her head.

'It's a saying, like a promise. Our motto is to serve and protect. That's our job and people like you can help us do that. Now, you know a man's been hurt, been killed over on the allotments on Saturday?'

Jade found a scab on her knuckle that was nearly ready to pick. She pushed at it.

'What I want to know is whether you saw anyone on Saturday morning, anyone going to the allotments or coming away, anyone near there?'

'She's not allowed down there,' Mam said.

The policeman looked at Mam.

'There's been fires set and all sorts in the past. There's lads messing by the railway line, sniffing glue and I don't know what. All these perverts about it's not safe.'

He nodded. 'You don't play down there?'

Jade shook her head.

'But you might have seen something from your window or the yard. You could probably see quite a lot from upstairs.'

'No, I didn't see anyone. I was watching telly,' said Jade. Lying. One of the sins. Jade imagined her soul, a big satin cushion, all white and shiny with a mark on now. A black mark. Like where Mam burnt the hole in the duvet but a sin would be more like a smudge, more splotchy. There was another mark for breaking her promise and going onto the allotments.

'Thank you,' the policeman stood up.

'Can I go now?'

Mam nodded.

Jade ran up to her room. Everyone did wrong things. That's why Jesus had come, that's why they had confession to make it all right again. When you went to confession if you were truly, truly sorry your sins were wiped away. And your soul was made all clean again. Like Flash.

* * *

'What did Matthew tell you about his family, Lesley?' Janine was asking the questions.

'Well, he hadn't any. His parents had died in a car crash when he was at college; he was an only child. Why?'

'We've spoken to Matthew's parents today.' Lesley looked stunned. 'Oh, my god.'

'Have you any idea why he would tell you they were dead?'

'No, none.'

'And they have a daughter, Matthew's sister, married with children.'

'I don't know what to say, I don't . . . Did they know about me?'

'No. Matthew had been married before.'

'No!' she cried.

'We've verified the records, Lesley. Matthew was married in 1979. They separated a year later.'

'No!' She sniffed hard, shielded her eyes with one hand.

'Laura, she was called. He never told you?' Lesley didn't speak.

'Emma said you'd not had an easy time. What did she mean?'

'Nothing, just . . .'

Janine waited for her to fill the silence.

'. . . sometimes, I get depressed.'

'Yet you claim the marriage was a happy one? Did either of you have affairs?'

'No.' Lesley looked furious, appalled to be asked.

'What time did you leave your house on Saturday?' Richard took over.

'About nine o' clock. You know this.'

'So, you arrived in town at what time?'

'About twenty past.'

'Where did you get the parking ticket?'

She frowned, apparently puzzled at their interest.

'From the machine, in the car park.'

'The ticket doesn't correspond to the actual time of your arrival at the car park,' he said, his eyes intent on her. 'The ticket you gave us is for 9.22.'

'That's right.'

'Where did you get it, Lesley?' Janine said.

'From the machine.'

'What did you do with the clothes in the washing machine?'

Lesley shook her head, gave a hollow laugh as if to say this was ridiculous.

'We'll find them.' Janine told her. 'We can recover trace-able fibres even from ashes.' Janine pulled out a diary. 'This

161

is Matthew's diary, last year. Turn to March 17th. You see the asterisk there? The time eight o'clock. Do you know what that meant?'

Lesley shook her head.

'St Patrick's Day. Can you remember what your husband did that evening?'

'No, probably something with school or the church.'

'No, we've checked. June 7th, an asterisk again, 8.30. September 6th, November 29th. And this year,' she picked up a second book. 'This coming Friday. Did your husband have plans for this Friday evening?'

'Perhaps he didn't want you to know?'

Janine studied Lesley. She was shaking slightly, her mouth closed tight with irritation or fear 'We found condoms among Matthew's things. Why would he need condoms?'

'I've no idea.'

'You can't have children?'

'Was Matthew having an affair?'

'No,' she insisted.

'You're sure?'

'I'm sure.' A spark of anger in her response echoed by the flickering in her dark eyes.

'After all, he lied to you about his first wife.'

'So what!' she snapped.

'Perhaps he lied to you about this too.'

'I wouldn't know then, would I?' she shouted vehemently.

CHAPTER FIFTEEN

Paula wasn't there. It was quarter past three and Dean sat on the bench and watched people parade by. Maybe she wouldn't show? He could tell she was well pissed off but she'd kept asking to see him.

He hadn't worked out what to say. Hadn't worked anything out. Didn't want to lose her but he didn't know what would be worse; telling her the truth and losing her or lying and losing her anyway. Maybe go for something in-between. Like before.

She knew he had been in Hegley. He'd told her that not long after they first got together; three missing years not easy to hide. They had been for a meal, a busy Italian place on Deansgate. Lots of chatter and clatter, office party in the corner. Giant pepper mills that made Dean want to laugh, the size of them.

Afterwards they had walked along the canal. It was quiet there. Lights reflected in the oily water. It had been done up and there were bridges and places to sit, bits of sculpture dotted about. They found a bench and stopped for a while. She leant against him, easy and he felt warm and a bit scared because he had promised himself he would tell her tonight.

He spoke haltingly. 'Paula, there's something I want to tell you about . . . when I was younger I was a bit wild made some mistakes. I got sent down; Young Offenders Institution. I was there three years.'

She sat very still. She didn't pull away. He kept looking at the water, the lights dancing and stretching in there, and the shadows from the old railway arches that towered over them. 'I learnt my lesson. Places like that you grow up fast. I know what I want now, what's important.'

He had waited for the question that he didn't want her to ask. The question he didn't know how to answer.

'What did you do, Dean?'

A train rattled by overhead, the noise drowning any other sound. Dean listened as it died away. He took a breath. 'I hurt someone. Knifed him. It was stupid, I was pissed and he threatened me, acting the hard man and I just lost it.'

Telling her the same as he told everyone. Telling her lies.

'You had a knife?'

'I did back in those days. Paula, I was all over the place. Straight out of care, sixteen, hadn't a clue. I messed up but it's behind me now.' He paused. 'Thought you should know.'

'The guy?' she asked softly.

He had nearly died. They said it was a miracle that he had survived such a savage attack. 'He had surgery. He was all right.' He heard her release a breath.

'Since then?'

'What?'

'You ever hurt anyone?'

'No, never. I'm not like that. Paula, honest, it was a one-off. Anything happens I walk away.'

'Dean.'

He turned to her, his hands sweating, wound up like a corkscrew. Looked at her. Wanting to beg but knowing that it was down to her. Begging wouldn't help. She looked at him a long time, the light was dim but there was enough to see her eyes, gleaming in the dark, glinting with the reflections from the water. He held her gaze. Breathed in her perfume, smelling of hay and oranges. Then she had smiled and put her face close to his. 'Let's go home.'

She had trusted him then.

A bus swung into the station its brakes squealing, scattering pigeons. Dean watched them wheel up and round before landing on the surrounding roofs. He saw her then, crossing the road; long limbs, white coat and black pedal-pushers. He stood, foolish with excitement until the reason for their meeting came slamming back into his mind, squashing everything flat and leaving him stranded.

* * *

Ferdie and Colin had just started dividing the stuff, spooning it onto the little scales and then into baggies when there was loud knocking at the door.

Colin's eyes went round like marbles. 'Bleedin' 'ell,' he shrieked sotto voce, 'who's that, Ferdie?'

'I dunno, do I?'

Colin darted down to the cupboard under the sink and came back with a biscuit tin.

They crammed everything into it and he put it back under the sink, kicking the cupboard door shut with his foot.

The knocking came again. Ferdie nodded at Colin to answer it, stood beside him.

'Ferdie,' DS Shap gave a wide grin, 'thought I'd find you here. You must be Colin. DS Shap,' he flashed his ID. 'Just a couple of questions, Ferdie.' Shap stepped up into the caravan.

'Harassment, innit, that's what this is. Next time you'll have to arrest me, I'll want a brief and everything,' Ferdie complained.

'Fair enough.'

Inside Shap gave the place a once over and motioned for Ferdie to sit down in the living area. 'Colin?' He nodded to the sleeping quarters.

There was a slight delay, then Colin grasped he was being asked to leave. 'Oh,' he mouthed and went; though there was precious little privacy in the confined space.

'Now, Ferdie,' Shap gave another bright, insincere grin and leant carefully against the side wall. 'First off, what size feet have you got?'

'Ten. Why?'

'Those got the size on?' Shap nodded at his trainers. Ferdie slid low in his seat and lifted a foot. Shap crouched and peered closer. 'Forty-four, that a ten in English money, is it? Dunlop.' He straightened up. 'Got any other trainers?'

'Not made of money, am I?'

'How well do you know Mrs Tulley, Ferdie?'

'I don't know her.'

'Sure about that? Lovely looking woman. Out of your league, is she? Got a girlfriend, Ferdie?'

Ferdie sneered.

'That a no? You may know her as Lesley if you were on first name terms.'

'I don't know her.'

'Bumped into her at school perhaps?' Shap persisted. 'Open day, whatever?'

Ferdie shook his head, his fingers kneading at the blurred tattoo on his neck.

'She ask you for anything, Ferdie? Ask you to do her a favour, money in it?'

'You're off your head, you.' Ferdie retorted.

'And are you off yours?' Shap sniffed pointedly, rubbed at his nose. 'Colin.' Shap called the lad back.

Colin appeared, gnawing at his lower lip.

'What size feet you got, Colin?'

He stood there like a frozen rabbit.

'Hard question, I know. Phone a friend?'

'Nines,' Colin blinked.

Shap sighed. Stood up. 'Enjoy the rest of your day, won't you?' Giving two very distinct sniffs, he beamed at them and left.

'He knows we've got some stuff.' Colin hissed as soon as Shap had gone.

'He was taking the mick.'

'Why didn't he do us?'

Ferdie shrugged. Deciding to get on with the job any-how. Biscuit tin out again, scales, roll of baggies.

'But that's a good sign, isn't it?' Colin said.

'Are you mental? He knows we've got some stuff. He'll probably be back again after his share. That's all we need. A dodgy copper wanting a cut.'

'He never said . . .'

'They don't have to. That's how they work, innit. They do it more by what they don't say.'

Colin didn't understand. 'I meant about the murder, though,' he tried, 'if he was windin' you up then maybe they've stopped looking at you for the murder. I thought he was going to arrest you when he sat you down in here.'

Ferdie stared at Colin. Watched his friend go pale with unease. 'You think I did it, don't you?'

'No, I don't,' he said quickly.

'I was with you all morning. How could I do Tulley?'

'Not till half-ten you weren't,' Colin said resentfully.

''Kin' brilliant,' said Ferdie, shaking his head.

'That's it! Bag this and that's it. And I'm telling you Colin this is the last time I pull anything with you. Crappin' your pants half the time and dissin' your mates the rest. Forget it right? Divvy this up and I'm out of here. For good.'

* * *

Paula didn't touch him. Stopped just far enough away. No smile, no kiss.

'Dean.'

'D'ya get lost?'

'One-way system. Parked miles away.'

'Go for a drink?'

She shrugged. An awkward moment like they'd lost the script. There was a pub round the corner.

Douggie had given him fifty quid to tide him over. He bought himself a pint of lager, a sparkling water for Paula.

The pub was dead. Just a couple of guys drinking alone, wishing the afternoon away. One of them had a thin cigar, the rich smell mixed with the yeasty aroma of beer. The barmaid was bored rigid, eyes locked on the TV.

Dean and Paula sat in an alcove, out of sight and earshot of the other customers. Dean took a long swallow of his drink. Placed it carefully on the beer mat. Licked his lips. His throat felt tight. Like someone was squeezing it.

'Have you rung the police?' She kept her voice low, looking sideways at him. Straight for the balls.

'Why not?'

He rubbed at the back of his neck. Groped for words. 'I can't.'

She turned on the bench seat, swivelled round till she was facing him. 'But if you don't talk to the police they'll come after you Dean, it makes you look guilty, dunnit?'

He sighed, stroked at his throat and over his Adam's apple. Could hardly breathe. 'Paula . . .' but nothing followed.

'You're in trouble, aren't you?'

His eyes stung. He blinked.

'That's why you disappeared. That's why you haven't rung the police.'

'Don't do this, Paula.'

'You're keeping things from me. I want the truth, Dean. What's going on?'

'And if I tell you, then what?' Suddenly furious with her, frightened by her insistence.

Music started over the loud speakers, lifting beat, Cheeky Girls, Touch My Bum. She shook her head, the beads moving, a noise he loved.

Dean stalled, picked up his drink and downed half of it.

'What you've done . . . is it like before?' she said quietly.

'No. I haven't hurt anyone. I haven't done anything wrong. Why won't you believe me?'

'Why should I? You won't tell me. And the police aren't gonna believe—'

'You see if I do tell—' he clammed up.

'How long do you think you can hide for?' Her eyes shone hard and brown. -

'They might not believe me. It looks bad. I . . .'

He didn't want to say anymore. So much blood. And the guy's insides showing. Like last time.

'Dean, it's not about that murder, is it?'

He said nothing, stared at his knuckles.

'Dean.'

He took a look at her. Her eyes were filling up though her voice was steady. Oh, Paula. He wanted to let it all go, all the words and the thinking and just hold her. But he knew better than to make such a move.

She shook her head and stood quickly.

'Paula, don't. Paula.'

She left him.

He sat there for a while. Finished his drink. Went and got another and a whisky chaser, a double. Drank them. He felt raw, like someone had peeled his skin off or turned him inside out. He should never have agreed to see her, just stuck to the story about Douggie. She didn't know what the police could be like, the sneaky way they asked about things, mixing you up and trying to catch you out, the way they kept on and on, working away at you. She'd no idea.

Nothing mattered much now. He drained the last of the whisky and went to the gents. Left the pub and crossed to the bus station. The sun was too bright after the muted light inside, hurt his eyes. He leaned against the bus shelter to wait. His chest ached like someone had thumped him. It couldn't finish just like that, could it? With a row in a poxy pub in Oldham? Best thing he ever had, blown away. That couldn't be the end of the story, could it?

* * *

Butchers was having another go at Mr Eddie Vincent.

'I don't see as there can be more details,' said the old man querulously. 'I've told you what he looked like and what he was wearing and what he did. What else could there be?'

'Maybe nothing but if you don't mind we'll go over what you've already said and see what comes to light.'

'All right, then.'

DS Butchers took Mr Vincent through each item of the description; height, weight, build, clothing. 'Tell me again what he did.'

'He came down the path, he was running, that's why I noticed him in the first place. Then he stopped at the gate. He looked about,' Mr Vincent cast his own head from side to side. 'He looked . . . petrified.'

'I want you to try and picture him there, at the gate, looking about. Try and keep him in your mind. What's he look like?'

'Like I said. And he was out of breath, panting a bit, from running.'

'Any sign of blood?'

'Didn't notice any. But the clothes were dark.'

'Was he carrying anything?'

'Yes, in his hand.' The old chap sounded surprised.

'What is it?'

'Can't tell, it's like a bag.'

'What sort of bag?'

'Plastic bag, like from the shops. He wasn't holding it by the handles, not like a bag full of shopping, it was wrapped up and he had it in his hand.'

'Small enough to carry in one hand?'

'That's right.'

'Now, I want you to have a look at these photographs. See if he's there.'

'I don't know.' He complained.

Butchers spread the six mugshots out on the table.

'Need your glasses?'

'I don't wear them,' he retorted, 'nothing wrong with my eyes.'

Butchers rolled his own. 'Anyone you recognise?' Mr Vincent looked at them. He took his time, wanting to do a fair job of it. Studied every face even though his eyes had fallen immediately on the one he knew. 'This one,' he tapped his forefinger beside one of the photos in the middle. 'It's this one.'

'Brilliant,' said Butchers. Eddie Vincent had picked out Dean Hendrix. 'And you'd be prepared to come to court if the case went to trial?'

He sighed. 'How long would that take? For them to have the trial?'

'All depends. Few months, can be a year or more.'

Mr Vincent grunted.

'What?' Butchers asked.

'Well, I mightn't be here.'

'Go on,' said Butchers feeling uncomfortable at the plea for pity, 'you've years in you, yet. But you'd have no objections to attending, if you were able?'

'Righto, I'll take these,' said Butchers, eager to get back with the news, wipe the smile off Shap's face. 'Don't get up, I'll see myself out.'

* * *

Megan had gone for her tea. Jade was having chicken nuggets and oven chips. Mam said she didn't want any but she had quite a lot of Jade's when she was putting it out.

'Can I take it in?' Jade said. 'Neighbours is still on.'

'If you spill any . . .'

'I won't, Mam. Honest.' Jade loved *Neighbours*. And *EastEnders*. And *Casualty*. If she didn't end up as a pop star she was going to be an actress. Some people did both. The nuggets were hot so she cut them up to cool them down. *Neighbours* finished and the news came on. Boring.

When Jade looked up the lady was on telly. Asking people to help. Another lady said something about a knife and then the really pretty one looked like she was going to cry. Jade thought she seemed terribly sad. Jade hated it when grown-ups got upset. When Mam cried it made her feel all fumy inside like everything had gone wrong and it would never come right again. And if Jade had been different maybe Mam wouldn't be the way she was.

'We don't want this on,' Mam said. Then she shouted 'Jade!'

Jade looked down and her plate was leaning over and all the chips and nuggets were sliding off the edge and onto the chair.

'Take it in the kitchen.'

Jade cleared it up and took it through. If Jade went to confession then she'd be forgiven. Every Tuesday you could go from school to church next door, there was a weekly Mass, confession first. Jade hadn't been for a while but it was good if it was wet play. She went all the time when she had done her first holy communion but then it got a bit boring. She bet Megan would go with her. Megan's granddad was dying and Megan went loads to pray for him. Her chips had gone cold and spiky so she put them in the bin. She had a look in the cupboard to see if Mam had bought any biscuits or Coco-Pops. There was nothing new in.

'Mam, can I go to Megan's?'

'Straight there and back for eight.'

They always had biscuits at Megan's house.

* * *

Janine was trying to shift some paperwork, her mind circling around Tom and Michael, when Richard sought her out in her office.

'What did I do?' he said without preamble.

'Frighten the children?'

'What?'

'Last night we were getting on fine, today I'm pulling a shift with the Ice Queen.'

'Richard,' she straightened a pile of papers, 'can we discuss this some other time?'

'I don't like being messed about.'

Janine felt her cheeks grow warm. 'Steady on.'

'Put me straight, then.'

'Okay.' She sat back, took a breath. 'You and Wendy. You made out it was like Pete and I.'

'Yes.'

'Wendy chucked you out, didn't she? After numerous affairs.'

'What're you getting at?'

'Did she?' she challenged him. 'Numerous,' he stalled, 'what's numerous mean?' Janine said nothing, waiting for an answer. 'Yes, she chucked me out. You chucked Pete out, didn't you?'

'He had a choice.'

'You gave him an ultimatum, though. Her or me.'

'That's not the point.' 'You've lost me.' 'I wish,' she muttered. 'No. Explain.' 'You like to play the field.' 'I have done,' he said.

'Seen anyone else you fancy since you got back?'

'It's not like that,' he protested.

'Last night, what was I? A warm-up?'

'No!'

She shrugged her shoulders. 'I don't mind, Richard. Three kids and one on the way. I was surprised I was on your list in the first place!'

'List!' He exploded. 'List. Right! I'll cross you off my list, then!'

'Right!'

He shut the door without banging it.

'Good,' she shouted after him. She felt like throwing something. She was smarting from the encounter even though she'd made her point. The prospect of working with this tension between them was daunting. But, she stapled a report together, she was a professional, wasn't she? And she'd just damn well act like one.

* * *

Dean had been back maybe ten minutes. Feeling like crap and having to watch Douggie acting like a kid at Christmas. Good day at the office, nudge.

Douggie had dropped something and was out of his skull.

'Where's Gary?' Dean asked.

'Out,' said Douggie. 'Getting petrol. Busy week.' Dean wished he hadn't asked. 'You hungry?'

'Yeah.'

Dean looked in the kitchen. Found tins of tomatoes, a tin of tuna, some spaghetti. Reckoned he could rustle something up. He was searching for pans when someone started banging on the door, braying at the top of his voice.

'Open the door! This is the police!'

'Dean,' he heard Douggie shriek. Saw him fly upstairs. To his stash.

Dean couldn't think. How did they find him here? No one knew he was here. Had they followed Paula? Picked him up in the centre of Oldham and trailed him back? There could have been a regiment of them in full kit following him and he'd not have noticed. Too gutted.

More hammering. Dogs barking. Dean ran upstairs. Douggie was tipping stuff down the bog, ripping the plastic open, gasping like he's going to collapse.

There was more shouting. So much noise.

'Take this, Dean,' he shoved a roll of notes at Dean, 'put it in the tank.'

'Dead clever that, they'll never look there, will they?' he said sarcastically.

'Well, I don't know,' screeched Douggie. 'Shit, shit, shit!' Trying to get the toilet to flush. Downstairs they were threatening to use force to gain entry. Dean's stuff was in the cellar but there was nowhere to put it even if he had time to reach it.

He looked at the wad of money. Ran into Douggie's room. Wardrobe, chest of drawers, bed. If they were going to search they'd find it any of those places. Dean looked up, giving up. His eyes landed on Douggie's Chinese parasol; upside down, used for a lampshade. Dragons and flames on it. Dean lobbed the roll up and it landed, a cloud of dust puffed from the shade but with the light off there was no telltale shadow to draw attention. Cool.

Dean ran back to Douggie. There was a splintering sound from downstairs. Dean heard the door give with a loud crack, the sound of wood ripping and the tinkling crash of breaking glass.

'Here.' He grabbed the bags that were still on the sink and stuffed them into the airing cupboard as far back as he could behind the hot water tank.

The police came up the stairs and in the bathroom like the SAS. 'Freeze,' one guy barked. Watching too much *NYPD Blue*, thought Dean. There were loads of them. Dogs too. And when one of them read out the warrant and cautioned them he realised that it was a drugs bust. Not about him at all.

They put them in separate rooms. Dean in the kitchen, Douggie in the lounge. They were looking everywhere; methodically emptying the fridge, checking all the containers in the cupboard, peering under the sink. That was where the pans lived.

They found the gear upstairs and came down. They told Dean there'd be enough to make a case and it would be better if he cooperated now. Dean said nothing. One of the men went down the cellar, hauling a big Alsatian dog with him. Dean didn't like the way the dog barked at him. He felt his toes pressing down in his trainers, like he was trying to hold onto the ground. Tried to blank it all out.

They couldn't tie Dean to the drugs. No way. Everything's gonna be all right, he thought. Just like the reggae man says. Take it away, Bob.

'Sarge! Down here.'

Dean leant forward, head in his hands. He would pray if there was anyone to pray to. A big guy with a Groucho moustache and way too much aftershave came through the kitchen and clunked down the stairs. He could hear others above, moving furniture, opening drawers and tapping on the floor. Outside, Dean heard the chimes of an ice cream van in the distance. *Teddy Bear's Picnic.* A surprise in the cellar never mind the woods. The dog and his handler came up the cellar steps, the sergeant behind them. The men were wearing tight rubber gloves. The sergeant was holding Dean's stuff. 'This yours?'

Dean swallowed. If he said no he could be dropping Douggie further in it. Could well be his fingerprints on it. Then it'd be a done deal. To hell with Douggie. Dean was furious. He wanted to crush something. He never should have come here. Some bloody safe house. Chock full of drugs. Douggie and his dealing. All that bull about how careful they were. Douggie wouldn't know careful if it sat on his face. And he'd be looking at serious time. Whatever happened to Dean, Douggie would be going down. Possession and supply. Class A. Strangeways or Armley. Playing with the big boys. It'd kill him. And it'd kill Dean if they put him in there too.

'Well?' the man insisted.

Dean dipped his head.

'Oh dear, illegal weapon,' said the man. And he carefully withdrew first the flick knife and next the videotape from the thick plastic carrier bag and placed them all in evidence bags.

They led them out to the cars. Neighbours stood gawping across the way, and a string of Asian kids in bright tunics and trousers watched from their garden wall. A gaggle of lads on bikes looked on in fascination. Douggie was shouting and cursing. Not his usual style. Dean put it down to the pills and the stress. Douggie had probably clocked what was going to happen to him and he was falling apart.

'Don't effing push me,' Douggie kept on, 'I'll have you for assault.'

'Douggie,' Dean wanted to calm him down but Douggie didn't hear or he didn't let on.

Later, Dean couldn't ever get the sequence of things exactly right.

They were just by the cars, taking them in different ones. Dean was a bit behind Douggie and they led him to the black Vauxhall Omega at the rear. They were putting Douggie in a squad car parked in front. Someone shouted. Dean looked up and saw two things. Douggie bolting down the pavement, back past Dean, legs going like pistons, face rigid with effort and a red car turning into the avenue. A red Nissan Sunny coming round the corner. Douggie running towards it, shouting 'Gary!' Gary driving the car.

Gary swerved trying to avoid Douggie; he must have seen the police and then he was trying to turn the car, make a getaway. He hit the brakes, the noise was deafening. The car ploughed into Douggie who went up, flipped against Gary's windscreen like a puppet, a grisly crunch as he hit. Gary screeched to a halt and Douggie's body was tossed onto the road.

There was a moment of silence. Like the film had stopped. Then commotion as the police started for Gary and the car. He revved the engine in panic, and shot forward, driving over Douggie. Bumping over him, the engine howling.

'Douggie,' yelled Dean.

'Get an ambulance.'

'Jesus Christ,' someone called out.

A child on the wall started crying.

Dean stared at the street. At Douggie, Douggie's body. People moved closer, a police car drove off, mounting the pavement to skirt the little crowd.

Dean stayed very, very still. He felt very small. If he didn't breathe, he was thinking, then maybe it wouldn't be real. His teeth clattered and his knees gave way. He fell against the car.

'All right, son,' the man by his side spoke, 'you just get in here, sit in here.'

Later he wondered if he should have gone over to Douggie and said his goodbyes there. But Douggie wouldn't have heard him. He had seen the mess that Douggie was and knew you couldn't be like that and live. When he closed his eyes he could hear Douggie laughing his wheezy laugh and launching into a stupid impression of an ice cream van playing the *Teddy Bear's Picnic*.

CHAPTER SIXTEEN

Janine was in the murder room when she heard about Dean Hendrix. She sent for Richard. He looked guarded. Perhaps he thought she wanted to resume their altercation. His expression soon changed when she broke the news. 'There's been an incident. Drugs round-up in Oldham. Went sour. Main suspect got run-over.' She paused a moment — some young lad, not much older than Michael, dead on the streets. 'But they got Dean Hendrix. They'll transfer him first thing in the morning.'

'Excellent.'

'There's more, though.'

He looked questioningly.

'Guess who Dean's mate was selling to?'

'Tulley?' A drugs connection could give them some motive for the killing.

'Ferdie! And Ferdie needed some dosh to set up in business. So he and Colin went and took some.' She tilted her head, raised her eyebrows, inviting him to work it out. It didn't take him long.

'The off-licences.'

'That's why Colin was sweating,' Janine smiled. 'That's where they were Saturday morning.'

She removed Ferdie Gibson's photograph from the board. Looked at the two that were left. Lesley Tulley and Dean Hendrix.

'We know Dean was at the allotment, we've got the fingerprint, Mr Vincent has identified his photo—' Richard began.

'He also picked the wrong face in the line-up,' she countered.

Richard continued his thread. 'And Dean's done it before plus he goes AWOL. Now, all we've got on Lesley is a funny parking ticket and the washing.'

'He's no motive.'

'Nor has she.'

Janine looked back at the photos. Folie a deux perhaps? 'They plan it together. Dean kills Tulley and Lesley helps cover the traces. She takes the knife and burns the clothing.'

Richard shook his head.

'Be interesting to see her reaction to Dean being in custody,' she said.

'You going to tell her?'

'Tomorrow,' she checked her watch. 'And now I really must make tracks.'

'How's Tom?'

She hesitated. She was eager to keep things purely professional with Richard but he seemed genuinely concerned — and he had gone all out to get her to the hospital quickly.

'Sitting up and chattering.' Pete had rung an hour earlier, updated her. 'I'm on night shift.'

'If there's anything I can do?'

His offer disarmed her. It was what everyone said but she was tired, a bit vulnerable. She felt dizzy, had to look away because the last thing she wanted to do was to start weeping.

'Janine?'

'Just sometimes it feels like it's all unravelling, you know? Tom, Michael, work, this . . .' she nodded at her stomach, took a deep breath. Saying more than she'd intended. 'See you tomorrow,' she said briskly. He watched her go.

* * *

Ferdie was almost home when Shap and Butchers caught up with him. 'Ferdinand Gibson.'

Ferdie groaned. No more hassle. 'I've already talked to you lot. This is harassment, that's what this is. I'm going to make a complaint, you know. You want to talk — I want a solicitor.'

'I'm sure that can be arranged,' the new guy said. Fat bloke, stupid cartoon tie on. 'Ferdinand Gibson, I am arresting you on suspicion of being in possession of a Class A drug, namely cocaine, with intent to supply and on suspicion of armed robbery You do not have to say anything . . .'

Shap showed his teeth.

'Aw, Jesus!' said Ferdie, circling his head in hopelessness. 'Who grassed me up, eh? Was it Colin? I'll bleedin' 'ave him. Look,' he spread his palms wide, 'can I just tell me mam, I only live there, the blue door?'

'We'll tell her.'

Shap opened the car door, gestured him in.

'Can I just give her the shopping?' Ferdie held up his little rucksack.

'You heard that? Sonny Jim wants to drop his bag off,' Shap said with contempt. 'Must think we're bloody stupid. Who's been giving you lessons, Homer Simpson, was it? Eh? Hah hah hah.' He chortled at his own joke. 'Get in, Einstein,' Shap drawled. Slamming the door after him.

Butchers started the engine.

Fucked, thought Ferdie.

* * *

Janine was collecting an overnight bag for herself and Tom and making sure everything was all right at home.

Sarah had fed Eleanor and Michael and was holding the fort.

'You should have worn your black suit for the telly.' Eleanor had watched the press conference.

'Why?'

'You looked funny.'

'Funny?' She folded Tom's pyjamas and dressing gown.

'Your nose looked bigger.'

'Thank you, darling.'

'You know your nose is the only bit of you that never stops growing.'

Janine looked at Sarah. 'That's something to look forward to, eh?'

Sarah laughed.

Eleanor showed Janine a card. A child's drawing of a bed and a stick figure, balloons and dinosaurs. 'I made this for Tom.'

'That's lovely, he'll like that. Now, coat,' she nodded to the chair where Eleanor had dumped her coat. The girl picked it up and went to hang it up.

'Damn!' Janine knew there was something else to do. 'Packed lunch.'

'Whoa!' Sarah told her. 'I can do her lunch. Calm down.'

'I hate dumping on you like this.'

'I'd never have guessed,' she said dryly.

Janine pulled a face.

'I'll get you back,' Sarah warned her, 'you can defrost my freezer. So what's the story with lover boy?'

Janine sighed, surveyed the heap of stuff she was packing. Suddenly felt the weight of everything threaten to overwhelm her. 'Dunno really. Think he might be just messing about, playing the field. I've told him I'm not interested. And like I said, look at me.' She spread her arms wide, then let them drop. Began to put some of the clothes into the bag. 'Daft isn't it? Be nice, a bit of love and affection . . .'

Sarah gave her a brief hug. 'It's lonely, you know,' Janine said, 'having a baby on my own.'

Janine found Michael at the computer. 'I'm going back to the hospital now.'

He nodded, no other reaction.

'Michael, I went into school today. Mr Corkland wanted to see me. He told me there've been problems at school. And last night the police were here, wanting to talk to you. I don't know what's going on but we need to talk about it. Soon.'

He reached over and raised the volume.

A flash of anger warmed her face. 'Don't push it, Michael!'

'Or what? You'll lock me up?'

The doorbell sounded, preventing her replying. She answered it to find the police officer from the previous evening. Great timing.

Sarah came into the hall and, seeing the policeman, ushered Eleanor upstairs for her bath.

'Good evening, is Michael in?'

Janine stood aside, let the man in and showed him into the room.

'Michael,' she said.

He turned, saw the uniform and paled.

Janine nodded he should turn the sound off. He did.

'It's about Saturday, The Trafford Centre. You were involved in an attempt to steal a mobile phone,' PC Durham said.

'Someone tried to rob me.' Michael said.

'Don't mess about, lad. You're in enough trouble as it is. Now, what really happened?'

There was a pause. Janine wanted the floor to swallow her up. Feeling desperate for Michael, angry and sad at the same time.

'We were just mucking about.'

'Bit of fun? That's not how the other lad sees it; your victim.'

Michael blanched at the term.

'Wasn't funny at all. He hasn't been sleeping very well since.' He paused, letting Michael stew for a moment. 'Think yourself lucky, Michael, charges won't be brought this time but if there's a next time we'll pick you up before you can draw breath. Understand?'

'Yes.'

'This is an official warning. You look like a decent enough lad, sort yourself out. I hope we never meet again.'

Janine followed PC Durham to the door. 'The other lad?' she asked.

'Shaken up. They pushed him about a bit. There was a free for all, the security guards picked up on it pretty quick and this lot bolted.'

'I'm sorry.'

'Reckon he'll be all right. Learnt his lesson, they need a bit of discipline don't they, this age? I've seen it before.'

Janine resented the lecture, the implication that Michael hadn't had enough discipline. There'd always been clear rules at home.

When she'd seen him out she leant back against the wall, snatching a moment to recover. She didn't want to arrive at the hospital ragged and drained. Tom needed her; God, they all needed her. Never any chance for her to be the needy one.

CHAPTER SEVENTEEN

Day 4: Tuesday, 25 February

Janine had slept badly, the makeshift camp-bed that the hospital provided was narrow and uncomfortable and she'd had heartburn. Tom had been much better and seemed to shrug off the experience with the resilience of youngsters.

She was dressed and ready for work when Pete arrived at eight.

'How you doing, soldier?' He gave Tom a bear hug.

'I had chocolate cereal!'

'Chocolate!' He ruffled Tom's hair. Looked at her, 'What do they say?'

'They'll discharge him. We're waiting for the doctor,' Janine told him.

'How long's that going to be?'

'I don't know.'

'And then what?' There was a belligerent note in his voice. Janine didn't want Tom exposed to any bickering. She went over to the window, forcing Pete to follow.

'Stop it,' she said quietly.

'What?'

'Using this to pick a fight with me.'

He gave an incredulous laugh. 'You are so bloody selfish. I've got a life to lead too, you know, a job. I can't just drop everything either.'

She would not let him rile her. She kept her voice even. 'If you take him home, I'll collect him later. Sarah can get Eleanor.'

Pete hesitated. What else could they do? Janine wondered. Had he an alternative?

'Look, the kids don't know whether they're coming or going,' Pete said. 'Tina thinks we need to sort out fixed arrangements.'

Oh, she does, does she? 'Shame the pair of you didn't think a bit more about the kids in the first place. Christ, Pete, she'd barely got chance to get the polish out and her overalls on before you two were at it.'

Pete looked sick but continued. 'We need some routine.'

'I don't do regular shifts, I have to do overtime at a moment's notice,' she reminded him. 'You know that. And kids — things happen, life's messy. It won't work if you start being inflexible.'

'Won't work for you,' he accused her.

'For them,' she insisted.

'Dad. Mum.' Tom held up a model he'd made.

Janine glared at Pete. They couldn't sort this out now. They went and admired Tom's handiwork. Janine picked up her briefcase and coat. Gave Tom a big hug. 'Dad's going to take you to his, I'll see you later.'

'Yes-s-s!'

She looked at Pete — see how he loves you. Pete looked away, picked up the model and began to play with his son.

* * *

A doctor had seen Dean at the police station in Oldham. The doctor asked him some questions and talked to the other people there. They seemed unsure of what to do. He heard someone say hospital and then someone said Manchester and he guessed they were talking about the murder. They gave him an extra blanket and some tea which burnt his tongue. All night long they kept sliding the peephole back on the cell door and staring in. Dean didn't know if he slept or not. Every time he thought about it he was in the same position, hands together between his knees, curled up tight. When he was in care, after his mum died, they said he slept with his eyes open. Freaked the other boys out. He didn't think he slept that way anymore. Paula had never mentioned it.

When they had asked him if there was anyone they should notify about him being nicked he said no. Pretty tight that. The world fit to bursting with overpopulation and there's not one frigging person in the known universe who needs to know that Dean Hendrix is in trouble. He realised he was feeling sorry for himself but he reckoned he was entitled. He doesn't — who will? Not exactly the best day of his life.

* * *

'And the Gibson angle, the drugs?' The Lemon's eyes scrutinised her.

'No link to Tulley, sir. Ferdie Gibson and friend Colin were behind the off-licence robberies. They used the cash to buy cocaine from a firm operating out of Oldham. There was a connection, though; Dean Hendrix chose the house in Oldham to hole up in.'

'Two crimes for the price of one, eh? You'd never have got him without Oldham, would you?'

'Hard to say, sir.'

'Sheer fluke,' he said dismissively. 'Can't claim any credit for that. And one of the suspects was killed in the course of the raid?'

'Car drove over him, his accomplice.' Poor kid.

'Bloody mess, but that part's Oldham's problem. As for ours, I want a written report by the end of the day. Everything ready for O'Halloran. He'll be taking over from you first thing tomorrow.'

He couldn't take the case from her! Not after all this. A sign to one and all that he had no faith in her. 'Please, sir.' She'd beg if she had to.

He didn't give her the chance. 'You've run out of time, Lewis.'

She turned away, fists clenched, mouth set. Not trusting herself to say anything.

* * *

Butchers had traced Laura Belling, the first Mrs Matthew Tulley, to an address in Birkenhead and had used the directory to get a phone number. A child answered at the other end, burbling 'hello, hello' over and over down the line.

'Is your mummy there?'

'Who.'

'Is your mummy there?'

'Who is it?'

'Get your mummy.'

'Mummy. Hello.'

Shap, beside him, scrolling through records on the computer, sniggered.

'I want to talk to your mummy.'

'Who dat?'

'Mr Butchers. Tell Mummy to come to the phone.'

'No.' The child slammed the phone down.

'Hell,' Butchers pressed re-dial. Laura Belling answered. 'Ms Belling, I'm DS Butchers from Greater Manchester Police. You were previously married to Matthew Tulley?'

'Yes.'

'You are probably aware that Mr Tulley is the victim in a murder enquiry?'

'I saw it on the television.'

He could hear the child beginning to kick up a fuss in the background. 'I'll try and be brief; we're trying to establish what sort of man Mr Tulley was, build up a picture, talk to . . .'

'He was a bastard.'

'Sorry?'

'You heard. They say you shouldn't speak ill of the dead but he deserves everything he got.'

For one crazed moment Butchers wondered if she was going to confess to having done it. 'He was an out and out bastard.'

Butchers hesitated, uncertain as to how to frame the next question. The child was bawling now. 'When you say that, in what respect . . .'

'He was a pervert and a bully.'

'Was he violent towards you?'

'Oh, yes. That was the grounds for the divorce. Physical and mental cruelty.'

* * *

Dean Hendrix was on his way from Oldham and Janine was preparing to interview him later that morning.

'Bag his clothes when he gets here,' she told Chen, 'and if the trainers look likely, put them through as a priority request.'

Richard raised his eyes — more spending?

'I'm not going to see him walk for the sake of a few hundred pounds,' she said. 'Anything on Mrs Tulley's bonfire?'

Chen shook her head.

Butchers came in, his face alert; well, as alert as it ever got. 'The first wife, she cited cruelty in the divorce. Claimed he was physically violent.'

'Was he now?' Janine frowned.

'Nothing from Tulley's email addresses,' Shap said, 'but we did pick up something dodgy with one of the phone numbers in his diary. The guy, a Ronald Prosser, is no longer there, woman was very suspicious at first — turns out he's doing time. Found in possession of a class A drug, sentenced in May last year.'

'Connection with Tulley?' she asked.

Shap shrugged.

'Get some more on that Shap. I wouldn't have figured Tulley for drugs, but there's still the possibility that drugs could be the link between him and Dean Hendrix.'

'Hendrix was associating with known dealers,' Richard said. 'Maybe a deal gone bad?'

She left them to carry on the painstaking work of sifting details and checking facts and set off for Ashgrove.

* * *

'Come in,' Lesley looked pale, weary. Janine followed her to the kitchen.

'Would you like some tea? No milk I'm afraid. Emma's gone shopping. Or toast?'

'I'm fine. You go ahead. There's been a new development, I wanted you to know.'

Lesley turned, pausing in the activity of getting the bread out.

'We've arrested someone.'

Lesley's mouth opened in surprise, her brow creased. 'Who?'

'Dean Hendrix. You know him?' Janine stared at her, trying to gauge her reaction.

'No, erm . . . no, I don't.' Lesley turned back to the worktop.

'He lives locally, you may know him by sight. Matthew never mentioned a Dean to you?'

'No,' over her shoulder.

'What about a Ronald Prosser?'

A tensing of the shoulders. 'No.' She began to cut the loaf.

Janine didn't believe her. 'We'll be interviewing Dean Hendrix this morning. Is there anything you want to tell me, Lesley?'

Lesley stopped, turned, met her gaze. 'What do you mean?'

'I think you know.'

Lesley's lip curled with disgust. 'No.' Her tone became more aggressive. 'Do you enjoy this? Does it make you feel clever? Insulting me, trying to dirty my name?' She faced Janine, the knife in her hand. 'How would you like it? If someone kept on and on at you?' Her eyes glittered with emotion. 'On and on — nasty little minds.'

Janine's phone broke the tension. She watched as Lesley steadied herself against the counter then returned to her preparations while Janine listened.

'Janine? It's Richard. Dean Hendrix, we made a mistake. We know he was there but he can't have used the knife. He's left-handed. It can't possibly be him.'

She stared transfixed as Lesley Tulley sawed through the loaf. Richard went on, 'Ferdie Gibson's out of the picture, Dean Hendrix can't have done it. Leaves us with one suspect.'

She heard the faint tick of the clock, felt the hairs on her neck prickle.

'Janine?' He sounded worried. 'Where are you? Are you already at the Tulleys'?'

'Yes.' She tried to keep her voice level.

'Can you talk?'

'No,' she spoke softly hoping that Richard would too, trying to prevent Lesley from hearing the call.'

'Get out of there!' He said urgently. 'Janine? Janine?'

'No,' she said simply. She would not run away from this. There was a chance here, a chance to get a confession and then she'd show them all. The Lemon and all of them.

She pressed end call.

Lesley swung back her way, still holding the knife, an edge of instability in her manner. 'Are you sure you don't want some?'

Ambiguous. Janine felt a surge of vertigo but hid it. Shook her head.

'Bad news?' Lesley asked her.

Janine forced herself to ignore the knife. Resisted the urge to cover her stomach with her hands. 'You and Matthew, you had problems?'

'We were very happy,' Lesley said.

'But you had depression? And you cut yourself, Lesley, don't you?'

'No.'

'I've seen the scars.'

A flash of something crossed Lesley's face, a tightening round the mouth.

'You're not happy. Was Matthew?'

'We were fine.'

'Perhaps Matthew began looking for something outside the marriage.'

Lesley glared at her. 'That's not true.'

'You never had children.'

'I can't, I've already told you.' Her voice wavered. 'I had to have a hysterectomy.'

'Was that a cause of strain between you? Matthew may have wanted children.'

'No, he loved me, it didn't matter.'

'But it was all lies wasn't it?' She could see Lesley Tulley's breath come faster. 'He'd lied to you right from the start. About his parents. They didn't know you existed.'

'Stop it.'

'He lied to you about being the first. He'd already been married to Laura.'

'Shut up!' Her voice rose.

'He fooled you, didn't he? He kept it all from you.'

'Don't!'

Janine took a step closer. Knew Lesley was near breaking point. 'It was all a sham — your marriage. A pack of lies.'

'Shut it!' Lesley shouted frantically, her hand trembling, the knife glinting.

Janine felt her throat constrict. She'd gone too far. Misjudged it. Janine kept staring at her, saw the rage burning in Lesley's eyes.

The doorbell shrilled, startling them both.

'I'll be on my way.' Janine managed. She turned her back to Lesley, walked, her heart hammering, knees rubbery, to the door. Expecting Emma but it was Mr Deaking, the head teacher.

'Come to pay my condolences.'

'That's good of you,' Janine said, trying to sound normal. 'She's still very shaken up.'

* * *

She managed to rouse Richard who was already doing a cavalry stunt and breaking the speed limit. 'I'm fine, I'm fine.' Though that was actually a bit of an exaggeration.

At the station, she told the team the same thing after giving a detailed account of the stand-off. 'Alive and kicking,' she winced as the baby butted, 'being kicked.' She appreciated their concern but she needed to stay strong, in command. 'Now, we've all got work to do, let's get on with it.' The team dispersed.

She turned to Richard. 'You heard from the lab?'

'There's no trace of fibres in the ashes. All they've found is residue from the videotapes.'

She swore. She'd been sure that that was where the missing clothes had gone. 'I'm applying for warrants then. Search and arrest. The Lemon's given me till the end of the day. Let's hope Dean Hendrix will give us something we can use.'

'He's in room one,' Richard told her, 'and the trainer's a match.'

A moment of relief. At least they were making some progress.

'Plus they recovered a knife.'

She frowned. How did that fit? Two knives. His print at the scene but he couldn't have done the stabbing. She closed her eyes for a moment.

'You want a coffee?'

'Yeah, no — tea.' She was wired enough. 'What have we got? We know Dean didn't use the weapon but we know he was at the allotment.'

'Egging her on? Restraining Matthew for her?' Richard suggested.

'Could have just gone pear-shaped. Dean doesn't get chance in the commotion so Lesley stepped in? And Dean could have got rid of the knife.'

'And the one he had with him?'

'Maybe they had one each? Lesley got to strike first. Dean obviously likes to be tooled up. Probably feels naked without one.'

DS Shap came over. 'The guy you wanted the background on, boss. Ronald Prosser. They were also looking at him for distributing obscene materials. Charges were dropped. He was released last week.'

'Drugs and porn, you see a link to Mr Tulley with either of those?' Janine asked Richard.

He shook his head.

'Can't tell by looking, can you?' She was hit by a wave of fatigue. 'Get us that tea, will you? And a fudge brownie.'

* * *

A noise startled old Eddie, still sitting in his chair; woke him up. His head jerked back. The swill of fear coursed through him. He gasped. Listened. But there was no sound of intruders. His senses reassured him that he was alone in the house. Silly bugger, he chided himself. All this talk of murder getting to him.

He had woken earlier, near to daybreak, stiff and chilled. Dreams of the war, of killing, clogged his head. He'd done his duty, fought and killed and it had left him a lesser man, a damaged man. He wondered what the lad who killed Matthew Tulley felt? Remorse? Terror? Shame at what he had done or just fear of being caught?

He had made the trip upstairs to relieve himself. He contemplated going to bed but an early dawn was breaking so he had sat by his bedroom window instead and watched the light spreading over the allotments, saw the soft grey haze lift and give way to colours, heard the cacophony of birdsong fill the air. His favourite time of day.

Came from years back when his dad had taken him fishing. Leaving in the dark and walking all the way to the River Mersey. Never caught much, not many fish could survive the muck and waste that the factories and mills discharged into the river. It was his clearest memory of his dad, that was. Never said much, just the odd comment; teaching him the way the current worked, the names of the birds, even the stars when the night was clear. Cygnus the swan, the Plough, Orion with the row of stars for his belt, Cassiopeia the giant W.

Coming home Eddie would get tired, struggling to keep up and his dad would put the tackle down and swing him up onto his shoulders. Carry him back, big as a giant.

There was a pain in Eddie's head now. An awful pain. He tried to rise from the chair but he couldn't. He looked up and the sky was filled with stars, more of them than he had ever seen. Glittering and shining and rushing towards him. He could feel his dad swinging him up, up high and Maisie laughing, her breath hot on his face and the pain falling away as he spun round and round and soared among the stars.

* * *

There was an art to running an interview, building up the pressure, asking the right questions at the right moment, wrong-footing or confusing the person so they would make a mistake and give you a glimpse of the truth. It was a duel; she was good at it, quick to spot the body language, the tiny clues pointing to lies and half-truths. She was assertive, forceful but not aggressive; she used the power of her intelligence rather than the threat of violence to catch her quarry. And when the chase was on it was both exhilarating and exhausting.

Dean looked bewildered and on edge when Janine first saw him. His solicitor sat by his side and Richard made the formal introductions for the recording of the interview.

'Can you tell us where you were on Saturday morning, Dean?'

'Oldham, at my mate's,' his breath caught in his throat, 'Douggie's.'

'I was sorry to hear about the accident. You were good friends?'

He looked away, Janine saw his Adam's apple bob, realised how hard he was struggling to hold it all together.

'When were you at Matthew Tulley's allotment?'

'Never,' he said quickly.

'Don't lie to me. We've forensic evidence that puts you at the scene of a particularly nasty murder. I think you'd better consider your replies very carefully.'

'What evidence?'

'Hard evidence, Dean, and only you could have left it there.'

His eyes darted away again.

'And you know what also interests me?' Janine went on. 'Matthew Tulley had his belly slit open, top to bottom. You'll know about that, won't you? What it feels like to carve someone up like that?'

'I didn't do it,' he burst out.

'You were there.'

'Just to give Mr Tulley something.' An admission. Janine caught Richard's eye. He signalled back — keep going.

'Go on.'

'A tape that's all.'

'You knew Mr Tulley?'

'Only because of the videos. I'd collect them from him and bring back a master copy. He wanted his dirty stuff editing. Look at the tape — you'll see.'

Janine nodded. He knew more, she was sure. 'What happened Dean? Saturday morning. You weren't in Oldham.'

Christ! Knocking at the door broke her concentration. Richard sighed with exasperation. Janine excused herself and went to the door, ready to haul someone over the coals for barging in.

'Sorry, boss.' Butchers spoke before Janine got chance, lowered his voice. 'The video they found with his stuff — it's filmed at the Tulleys' place.'

This she had to see.

Shap started the VCR. There was a soundtrack playing, an instrumental of *Cry Me A River*, a haunting melody. The camera was taking the viewer through the shrubbery and up to the Tulleys' front door.

'Dean Hendrix said he ran errands for Tulley — getting tapes edited. Claims that was why he went to the allotments,' Janine told them.

Butchers took a call. 'The warrants, boss. Search and arrest. They've both been granted.'

A title sequence. *Lust Beyond Boundaries*. Oh, please! thought Janine. Though what had she expected? Pirated copies of Disney? 'Maybe Lesley stumbled on Matthew's home-made porn collection. Went for him in a fit of jealousy?' she said.

'Could explain the contact with Ronald Prosser,' Richard pointed out.

'Anything else, here?' She encouraged them to think like detectives — what could they learn? 'What about the tape, the quality?'

'Not as shaky as some,' said Chen.

'Yet,' Shap said quietly.

There was a burst of laughter, swiftly suppressed.

'Maybe using tripods?' Butchers said.

'Been edited,' said Shap, 'more than one camera, soundtrack added.'

Janine recalled the flight cases, photographic gear in Tulley's study. 'And that backs up what Dean Hendrix has been telling us so far. I think I'll leave this to you lot. Easy on the popcorn.' She had seen this sort of thing before, as a result of the job, but watching it made her toes curl and watching with a room full of men just added to the discomfort. Janine moved to go.

The scene on the video changed, the conservatory at Ashgrove. A woman, half-clothed. Janine stopped in her tracks. 'It's Lesley Tulley. Oh, sweet Jesus!' The man stood behind her, Lesley's face was pressed against the glass distorting her cheek and mouth. She was crying. The man had a knife.

'That's not Tulley,' said Richard, 'the guy with the blade, wrong build.'

On the tape Lesley began to beg. 'Matthew, please, no more, please! Stop him.'

'Tulley's filming it, he's the cameraman,' said Janine. 'The bonfire. This was what she was—'

Lesley's face contorted with pain and she began to scream, a horrific yelping sound that made Janine feel sick. No run of the mill porn video. This was torture. The sound that Lesley made left no doubt as to her suffering. She saw Chen flinch and Butchers turn away. 'Wait! Pause it!' Janine shouted.

Shap hit the remote. The picture froze, showing the man's arm, his hand around Lesley's throat.

Think. Janine told herself, resisting the temptation to turn from the image to leave the room. Analyse. How does this help us? What does it tell us?

'This explains the scars,' she said. 'She never cut herself.'

'This is sick . . .' Butchers said in disgust.

'I think we've got our motive.' Janine said. She looked again at the screen, there was something familiar. 'The guy's hand,' she said slowly. A copper arthritis bracelet, crabbed fingers. 'I'm sure I've seen . . .'

The truth hit her like plunging off a cliff. 'Jesus Christ, it's Deaking!' She raced to the door.

'Who?' Shap asked.

'The head teacher . . . and I've just left him at Lesley Tulley's house!'

CHAPTER EIGHTEEN

The car squealed to a halt, fishtailing on the drive. Janine and Richard jumped out and moved swiftly to the front door. Janine put her finger on the bell and pressed without let up. There was no immediate response so she moved back and signalled to Richard.

He smashed the glass in the front door and put his arm in to free the catch.

Where was she? Janine could feel the blood pounding in her ears and her heart bucking. Richard raced upstairs while Janine checked each of the downstairs rooms. Nothing, deserted, everything in order like the Marie Celeste.

'The garage,' she said, when Richard ran back down.

They were there. Mr Deaking had his hands tight round Lesley Tulley's neck, strangling her. She was like a doll beside him, petite, limp. Her face bloated and red.

'Let go! Let go of her!' Janine yelled.

Richard pulled him off and Deaking fell to his knees. Janine caught Lesley who was choking and shaking, her arms thin and frail, almost weightless; like lifting a child.

There was a pause, the only sound people gasping for breath: Deaking, bent double, his breath ragged and noisy;

Lesley shuddering, sobbing hoarsely; Richard blowing; Janine panting.

Janine looked at Richard, not hiding anything, a moment's emotion fired by adrenaline and the sense of shared jeopardy. He held her gaze, eyes wide open, unsmiling, gave a tiny nod. She wanted to hug him.

Richard turned to the teacher. 'Bernard Deaking, I am arresting you for attempted murder . . .'

Janine began to recite the caution, still breathless and wondering what the chase had done to her blood pressure. 'Lesley Tulley, I am arresting you on suspicion of the murder of Matthew Tulley. You do not have to say anything. But it may harm your defence if . . .'

'I didn't do it,' Lesley shook her head slowly, her dark hair swinging. 'I didn't do it. I didn't . . .'

'. . . you do not mention when questioned something which you later rely on in court.'

'You have to believe me.'

'Anything you do say may be given in evidence.'

A sound at the entrance and Emma came in, still holding their shopping, confusion on her face, trying to make sense of the situation.

'She was in town,' she said to Janine. 'You're making a terrible mistake. She loved him.'

Janine began to lead Lesley out.

'Emma,' Lesley said, 'it'll be all right, you'll see. I didn't do it.'

* * *

The team were gathered in the murder room and Janine briefed them on the arrests they had made. 'They're being processed now, we're taking Deaking first. The search at the house is underway.' With the warrant, the search would be completely thorough. Floorboards would be lifted, the roof space checked; dogs, detectors and staff would comb the

Tulleys' place inside and out. Janine remained convinced that somewhere there were the clothes that Lesley Tulley must have worn when she killed her husband. Clothes covered in his blood which she had then washed and concealed.

'We'll let them both stew for a bit while we have another crack at Dean. I want him to think he's still centre stage for this; maybe he'll admit they were colluding if he thinks we'll go easier on him.'

In the interview room, sat back, attempting to look more relaxed than he actually was, as Janine resumed the interview.

'Lesley Tulley,' she said briskly, 'tell us about her.'

'I don't know her.'

'Come on, Dean.'

'Straight up, I don't. I'd never seen her till I looked at the video.'

'You live just round the corner,' Richard pointed out, 'handy for popping in when Mr Tulley's at school?'

He frowned and then balked at the insinuation. 'No, no I never.'

The solicitor intervened. 'Mr Hendrix has answered your question, he does not know Lesley Tulley.'

'Even though he's carrying round a pornographic film with her in the starring role?' Janine turned back to Dean, his arms were trembling slightly. His eyes bloodshot. 'Let me tell you how I see it, Dean, then you can put me right. Mrs Tulley is a very attractive woman, perhaps she was lonely.'

'I've got a girlfriend, I only go with her.'

'What work do you do?' Richard asked.

The shift disconcerted him. He tucked his hair behind his ear, pulled on a strand.

'Freelance.'

'Freelance what?'

'Odd jobs. Backstage at the Lowry now and then, GMEX. Bit of driving.'

'Pay well?' he continued.

'Not really.'

Richard studied him. 'So it might be quite tempting if someone offered you a sizeable amount of money for your services.'

'I don't know what you're on about.'

Janine leant forward. 'Matthew Tulley was attacked with a knife and bled to death on Saturday. Where were you, Dean, when we came to call? Missing, in hiding. A witness saw you leaving the scene. Forensic evidence proves you were there too. A knife was found in your possession.'

Richard glanced at her. Careful now. They knew Dean's knife hadn't been used on the victim, it was a flick knife. Janine brazened it out, didn't hurt to let Dean think they had him every which way.

'You can see how someone might think you were helping her out, perhaps getting rewarded for your pains. Maybe you'd watched all the videos? Strong stuff. Can be addictive, can't it?'

'That's enough,' said the solicitor, 'these allegations . . .'

'It wasn't me, I didn't kill him,' Dean leaned forward, closer to Janine, his mouth stretching wide with emotion.

'But you've done it before.' Richard said.

'Yes. Oh, yes. Bit of a fight, out comes the knife.'

Dean was becoming more agitated. 'It wasn't the same!'

'Virtually identical.' Richard remained calm but insistent.

'Not the same, not the same,' the lad rocked back and forth. Tears started in his eyes. 'You don't know.'

'Tell me Dean.' Janine said. 'You get a taste for it? Give you a buzz?'

He gasped. 'No, no!' His breath was jerky, he kept rocking, his face wild. 'Last time, last time . . .'

'Last time what?' She pressed him.

'Last time, Williams—' He couldn't say it, he stared at Janine, on the brink.

'He struggle more?'

Dean broke. 'He . . . raped . . . me!' He drew it out like a howl of pain, face raised to the ceiling, the tendons in his neck standing out.

Janine's heart stuttered. The poor bloody lad. She put her face in her hands.

Richard stopped the tape.

'I'm sorry, Dean.' Janine said quietly. 'I'm so sorry. We'll get you a drink. You have a break.'

She thought of Michael then, if ever he . . . if any of her kids had to carry that violation with them. Stop it. She pushed back her chair. Richard looked as shaken as she was. They all needed a break.

They took fifteen minutes in Janine's office.

Janine sat with her feet up, her shoulders ached, she rubbed at them trying to release the tension. A good soak, that's what she needed. Later, she promised herself.

Richard was pacing about, still disturbed by Dean's story. 'Poor bastard.'

'He never spoke about it, never even used it in his defence, there was nothing in any of the trial reports, simply got put down to a fight. Too ashamed. Deep down he probably blames himself. Something he said, something he did.' She swung her feet down. 'I reckon he'll give us the real story once he's calmed down. Deaking should be ready now. Shall we?'

Mr Deaking sat rigidly upright his hands clasped on the table in front of him. He left the talking to his solicitor. 'My client would like to make a statement. He admits to taking part in the sex sessions with Mrs Tulley, which were filmed by her husband, but he strenuously denies the charge of attempted murder. He was simply trying to find out if Mrs Tulley knew where the tape was.'

'By choking the life out of her?' Janine raised an eyebrow. 'I don't think so.'

* * *

The canteen was busy, coppers coming and going, banter between them and the staff serving. Janine and Richard had got a corner table. Janine, feeling depleted of energy, had gone for a hot meal: lamb hotpot and braised red cabbage. Something to keep her reserves up for the ordeal ahead. Interviewing Lesley Tulley. Shap had joined them, avid for news about Deaking.

'They're always so normal, aren't they, the Deakings of this world. All that respectability and a shed full of porn.' Janine shook her head. 'He buys a tape from one of his suppliers and who's on it? Lesley, his deputy's wife. But he doesn't do anything yet — he waits until Tulley's in trouble.'

Shap listened, his eyes bright with curiosity.

Richard picked up the story. 'Tulley keeps his job after the assault on Ferdie Gibson because Deaking backs him to the hilt, in return for . . .'

'. . . a piece of the action.' Janine said.

Shap fiddled with his lighter. 'Was he really trying to kill her?'

Janine shrugged. 'He lost it. He was scared she'd talk, give us the tapes. She wouldn't see him, wouldn't take his calls. When Lesley said she didn't know where the video was he didn't believe her. Thought he could throttle it out of her.' She put her empty plate on the tray. 'Whatever he gets he'll never pick up another piece of chalk again.'

She drained her cup and grimaced at the rank taste. 'They ought to add that to the dangerous substances register.'

She stood up. Richard looked up. Got to his feet. 'Okay, let's do it.' She led the way.

* * *

It was hard to banish the brutal video images from her mind as she sat opposite Lesley Tulley again.

'Lesley, when we spoke earlier I asked you about this man. I am showing Mrs Tulley a photograph of Mr Ronald Prosser.'

A rapid blink.

'You denied knowing him.'

'I don't know him.'

'Are you sure? You've never met him?'

'No,' she said curtly.

'He's just come out of prison. Serving time for drug offences but there were some lesser charges for pornography. That's how Matthew knew him, isn't it Lesley?'

'I've no idea.'

'And Mr Deaking. We know all about it now.'

Lesley looked scared, her eyes rounder but she said nothing.

'We've got this.'

Janine glanced at Richard who slid the videotape in its evidence bag across the table and said. 'I am showing Mrs Tulley a videocassette, item 439.' Lesley sat unmoving.

Janine spoke gently. 'Lesley, we've watched the film.'

'Films, videos,' she tossed her head dismissively, 'it's crazy.'

'It's hard to watch. Unbearable. The violence. We know what Matthew made you do.' She lowered her voice further, creating the intimacy she required. 'What Mr Deaking did. It changes everything.' She could sense the other woman fighting to resist the empathy, avoiding eye contact, one corner of her mouth twitching. 'You can tell us now, Lesley.'

'I haven't got anything to say,' quietly.

'What about Dean Hendrix?' Richard said.

'Pardon?'

'What about Dean Hendrix? How well do you know him?'

'I don't.' She looked at Janine. 'You said you'd arrested him.'

'Dean is being very helpful.' Richard said. 'He gave us the tape.'

Lesley looked blank.

Janine spoke up. 'Perhaps you needed a friend, someone to share your troubles with? Or a lover?'

'No. I don't even know who he is.'

'The knife we recovered,' said Richard, 'the murder weapon, it turned up in town on Saturday morning.'

She remained unspeaking.

Janine sat back and regarded her. Began afresh. 'I'll tell you what I think happened. You followed Matthew to the allotments. You had the knife. You hurt him, badly.'

'Don't.'

'You went home. You'd blood on your hands, on your clothes—'

'No, stop it, it's not true, I loved Matthew.' The solicitor signalled to Lesley to keep quiet.

'You cleaned up, put your clothes in the machine.'

'No!'

'You know we are searching your property now?'

Her chin went up, she stared at Janine with defiance.

'You took the knife with you and drove to town. You got hold of someone else's parking ticket to try and give yourself an alibi.'

Lesley opened her mouth; lies, her face said, outrage burning spots of colour on her cheeks. 'It's not true. I can't explain the ticket. The clock on the machine—'

'We have CCTV footage,' Richard said flatly. 'How did you get to the Triangle?'

'Through Millennium Gardens.'

'Did you leave anything in a litterbin in Millennium Gardens?' he asked her.

'A sandwich wrapper.' She was indignant. 'I didn't kill Matthew. You can't do this to me.'

'Perhaps you had some help?' Janine said. 'Did Dean come with you to confront Matthew? Was he there in case you couldn't go through with it? Or did you send Dean to get rid of the knife?'

'This is completely crazy. I don't know Dean,' she shouted.

'Perhaps Dean had seen the videos? Seen some of the terrible things you had to suffer.'

Lesley covered her mouth with her hands. Tears splashed from her eyes.

'How long had it been going on? Months? Years? Did Matthew make you watch the tapes with him?'

'I didn't do anything. I didn't do it. I didn't.' She collapsed, her shoulders heaving, her words drenched in tears.

The solicitor leant forward to insist on a break but Janine pre-empted this by holding her hands up in surrender pose.

* * *

When Janine went into her office she was startled to find The Lemon lurking there. He was standing at the far wall, looking out through the glass partition. 'Your update?'

'Yessir. I'm sorry, there have been a lot of developments—'

'Which I expect to hear about from you, not from rumours flying round the office.'

'No, sir.'

'Gossip about serial killers and a drugs connection and the Tulley woman hiring an assassin. You nearly had her corpse on your hands too? And you're digging up the garden at the house?' His words laced with derision.

'I'm confident that the search at the house will turn up the missing clothes. We've now got her involved in the production of pornographic material.'

'Hardly a motive.'

'Not just blue movies, sir. The woman is being tortured while her husband films it. Deaking, the head, was an active player — he tried to silence Mrs Tulley.'

He took this in. 'And the serial offender — Dean Hendrix?'

'I'm going back in to him now. He's beginning to open up, sir. If he was in on it he'll own up.'

'If you don't find these missing clothes then you've nothing, zero.'

'The attempt to create an alibi—'

'Circumstantial, Janine. CPS won't wear it.'

'Then I'll get them to talk. Secure a confession.'

He turned to face her, questioning her confidence.

She smiled. She could do it. She knew she could. 'Communication skills, sir. I've done the course.'

The lad looked wasted, but he'd been offered drinks and he'd been seen by a doctor again. She didn't want to end up accused of interviewing him under duress so she had taken the precaution. She decided to begin with her questions about the tape, seeing as Dean had been happy telling them about that.

'You had prearranged to meet Matthew Tulley at his allotment. Did you usually meet there?'

'Yes.'

'You never went to the house?'

'No.'

'And you would take the tapes he gave you and bring back an edited version?'

'Yes.'

'You were there on Saturday morning,' Richard said, 'bringing him a completed tape.'

'Yes.'

'Did you ever meet with Lesley Tulley?' Janine said.

'No.'

'Did you conspire to kill Matthew Tulley?'

'You don't have to be the one holding the knife to be charged with the crime,' she told him. 'Murder, Dean, it doesn't get any heavier. And you are up to your neck in it. I've got you at the scene and you have previous form for an almost identical attack.' She sat forward, spoke with intensity 'You've got a porno film of the dead man's wife and you do a runner. Now why shouldn't I charge you with murder?'

'Because he was already dead when I went there,' he shouted in desperation.

Janine let a long breath out. Yes, this she believed. Richard stretched his fingers. Dean had closed his eyes.

'What time was this?'

'Half-ten, near enough.'

'How did you know he was dead?'

'You just know, he wasn't moving and there was blood on the ground. I tried to turn him, I saw, you know—' he wiped his hands on his chest, his face anxious.

'Where was he, exactly?' Richard said.

'He was lying on his front, by the shed. Sort of half in and half out.'

'Why didn't you call us, Dean?' Janine asked.

'I freaked. It was like before. The same—' Revulsion twisted his features. 'People would fit me up for it, my record. You all thought it was me, well didn't you?'

'Your heading for the hills didn't exactly help.'

'Did you see anything else at the scene?'

'No.

'The knife?' Richard checked.

'Anyone in the vicinity? Think carefully,' she said.

He shook his head.

'And you washed your hands — at the tap.'

He nodded.

Janine studied him, shook her head very slowly. If he'd only come to them then, told them. There was no trust, he had no faith in the forces of law and order. The dance he'd led them.

'I think you'd better make a statement now, Dean. We'll send someone in to write it down.'

He put his head in his hands.

'And don't leave anything out.'

CHAPTER NINETEEN

Janine looked eagerly at Shap for news from the search but he shook his head.

'No clothes yet. But they have found a hiding place in the fireplace in his study.'

'And?'

'Empty.'

Janine turned to Richard. 'We haven't enough to hold her.'

'Send her home?'

'One more shot, if we turn up something at Ashgrove,' Janine said.

'The solicitor's asked for a longer break,' Richard looked at his watch.

They couldn't go back into Lesley yet.

Butchers came in, 'It's your son, boss.'

Janine's blood froze. 'Tom?' Oh, God, no. Please no. She felt giddy.

'Michael. Downstairs.'

When she got down to reception he was standing by the doors. 'I'm locked out. Forgot my keys.'

'Shouldn't you be in school?'

'Review day.'

She was in the middle of a murder enquiry and he'd forgotten his damn keys. She looked at him. Should she just give him hers and let him make his own way home? No, that wouldn't be right. He was mixed up, sending him off would add to the chip on his shoulder. 'Timing!' she chided him. 'Come on.' It'd only take her fifteen minutes if the traffic was good. They couldn't see Lesley for another half an hour anyway. By then she hoped that they would have word from the search — some hidden clothes to confront her with.

Michael was staring out of the side window. Saying nothing.

'How was your review?'

A shrug.

'Mr Corkland said your work was suffering. You're a bright boy, you've worked hard and now . . . these so-called mates, where've they sprung from?'

'We have a laugh, that's all.'

'What? Stealing, pushing people about, sending nasty text messages. As a family we've tried . . .'

'What family? You expect me to be like you, don't you? Master Plod the policeman's son. Know what my nickname is? The Bill. They all think I'm a grass because of you.'

The strength of his outburst surprised her. She'd never imagined he got stick because of her job. But she wasn't going to start feeling guilty about her work. 'I'm proud of what I do, Michael. I'm not going to apologise for it.'

'And you ram it down my throat all the time. It is so uncool.'

'Oh, for God's sake, grow up. It pays the bills, it puts food on the table—'

He turned, about to challenge that claim.

'Takeaways! Whatever! People kill, I catch them. I don't care how deeply uncool it might be, it's a bloody important job.'

'And it's all you care about.'

That cut her to the quick. She pulled in to the side of the road and stopped the car. 'That's not true. I care about you.

I want you to be safe. I want you to be happy.' She struggled, feeling her chest tighten and not wanting to get upset in front of him. 'You're not a bully, Michael; I know you're not. I can't bear . . .' Tears sprang into her eyes. She sniffed them away. Cleared her throat. 'What made you do it?'

'It was meant to be a joke,' his voice was small. 'The messages — seeing how people would react. I didn't know they'd . . . just went a bit too far.'

'And the thefts?'

'Sort of a dare.'

'These lads. Do you like them? Really?'

He shrugged.

'Think they'll be good friends?' He didn't reply. 'They're not doing you any favours, are they? What will they be doing in five years' time, ten years? Picture yourself there.'

'Sorry,' he managed.

Janine put an arm round him. 'It's been a rotten year, I know. With your dad and all. But we both love you. Nothing can change that.'

He nodded. She pulled her arm back. 'We've a meeting with Mr Corkland on Friday. Think about what you're going to say. And I want you to write a letter.'

'What?'

'It's not me you need to say sorry to. Write a letter for the lad on Saturday. Tell him you're sorry.'

He looked aghast.

Janine started the car. Gave him a rueful smile.

'Turning it round, Michael. It starts here — putting things right.'

* * *

Jade was next. Megan was just coming out, she'd been dead quick.

'What did you get?' Jade asked as she passed her.

'Two Hail Marys.'

What would Jade get? A decade of the rosary? She hadn't any beads. The one she got for her communion had broken and she had saved them to try and fix the little wire back together but then they'd got lost.

She pulled aside the curtain and knelt on the small hassock next to the screen. The confession booths were dark with wooden walls and they smelt of Mr Sheen and when you knelt down it was red velvet. She could see Father Donovan a bit through the mesh, his head tipped towards her and his eyes closed. She looked away, you weren't meant to look at the priest, you had to look into your soul.

'It's four weeks since my last confession, Father.'

'I see. Will you say the confession prayer now?'

'I confess to almighty God that I have sinned through my own fault, in my thoughts and in my words, in what I have done and in what I have failed to do; and I ask blessed Mary, ever virgin, and all the angels and saints, to pray for me to the lord our God.'

'Now you can start your confession.'

Jade felt a bump in her chest. 'I promised my mam that I wouldn't play down the back and I went one day. Only for a bit, though.'

'Now, why does your mum not want you down there playing?'

'Not safe.'

'It's very important to keep those rules, the ones that keep us safe. Are you sorry for what you did?'

'Yes, Father.'

'And you won't be doing it again now, will you?'

'No, Father.'

'Good. Is there anything else?'

'And I told lies,' Jade said, then very fast so maybe he wouldn't catch it all, 'to the policeman. I said I didn't see anyone and I did.'

'See anybody?'

'On the allotments, on Saturday, you know.'

'Do you mean where that man was . . . found.'

'Yes, Father.' Jade's eyes had gone all hot now.

'But you did see somebody?'

'Yes. I saw someone running away. I'm sorry I was so scared!'

'Now, I'm glad you've told me, God is proud of us when we tell the truth, even if that means we have to be very brave about it. And I think it would be a big help for the police if you told them as well.'

'But . . .'

'I can have a word with your mum and make sure everything's all right on that score. What do you say?'

Jade knew she couldn't say no. Now she'd be in trouble. Big trouble. 'Yes, Father.'

* * *

'Nothing, boss,' Butchers shook his head. 'They've taken the place apart. Search completed.'

Janine felt like kicking someone. The clothes couldn't have disappeared, but without a break she could not hold Lesley Tulley any longer.

'Let her go.'

She was so disheartened. A few hours and her chance for a result would be over, passed on to O'Halloran. The Lemon would have something to gloat about.

* * *

Dean was remembering. Couldn't stop remembering, like someone scratching, the same sample over and over.

His first thought when the guy had shoved him was a mugging. Dean putting his hands up: 'Hang on, mate.' Saw the knife. Then the guy was holding it under his neck. A cool slice of metal against his throat. Dean was thinking please don't cut me, trying to keep his eyes calm so the guy wouldn't get more manic and top him.

'I've got money,' Dean had said to buy time but it came out quiet because he daren't move too much with the knife there.

'Turn round.'

Still not getting it. Turning, keeping his hands away so the guy can pat him down and take the bit of cash he's got left. Hand on him, pulling at his joggers, one swift yank, then his pants. The guy slammed him against the wall, he turned his face to the left to save his nose. The knife was by his chin, against the brick. Dean could smell the damp mortar, feel the moisture from the stone on his right cheek. He heard traffic and a girl laughing and a boom-box passing by and blood rushing through his ears.

Then Dean was crying with shock and pain, knowing what the guy was doing to him. The guy pulled away. His right hand on Dean's shoulder, left grasping the knife. Dean could smell the stink of the guy's deodorant and the grease on the air from some take-away. He felt this wildness in him, coming up, like something he couldn't stop. A roll of anger surfing away the fear. He didn't plan it, there was no time for that, he just moved.

He had swung round and threw his own body back against the guy, using the wall to wind him. Dean smacked the man's wrist against the brick until he dropped the knife. Breathing hard, Dean went for it. In slow motion, he watched his own fingers curl around the handle and lift it from the ground. The ground speckled with drops of light, a rainbow circle of oil and fragments of glass. The handle was warm. He was straightening up, saw the guy's fist come at him from the corner of his eye. Stabbed the knife in and pulled up. Easy motion, like ripping rotten cloth. Up and up till he hit bone.

When he got home, he sat rocking in the dark. Same as when his mum died and they took him into care.

* * *

Shap had taken the call from the priest while Janine was out with Michael. He'd left a memo for Butchers and gone to see what the story was. They both expected it to be a wild goose chase. Impressionable kid wanting fifteen minutes of fame or some extra attention.

He sat in the kid's house while she told him, her eyes wide, her mum looking on with thinly veiled dismay.

'It was the lady on telly. The one on the news that was asking for help.'

'What was the lady doing?'

'Running away.'

'What else can you remember about her?'

'Someone had hurt her.'

Shap looked sceptical.

'They did,' she insisted. 'They'd battered her and she was all covered in blood. Like a nosebleed.'

Shap pulled out his phone, asked the kid a couple more questions then rang it in.

At the station Richard answered the phone in the murder room. Listened to Shap and then reported to Janine.

'Kid at number three saw Lesley Tulley running from the scene, dripping blood on Saturday morning.'

Surprise rippled across Janine's face. 'Why the hell didn't we have this sooner?'

'They weren't home in the first house-to-house. When Butchers finally questioned her, the kid lied. She was forbidden to play on the allotments. Couldn't tell us without getting in trouble.'

'Oh, for heaven's sake. Time?'

'Definitely before 9.25. She saw . . .' he paused to check his notes, 'the end of Digit?'

Janine smiled at his mistake. 'Diggit. How old?'

'Seven.'

Janine winced. Very young. 'A witness, though. I'm bringing Lesley back in.'

She grabbed her coat.

'Is it enough?' Richard said.

'It's all I've got. I'm buggered if I'm going to let O'Halloran waltz in and get the credit. We've worked damn hard on this and we're nearly there. Well?'

Richard picked up his own coat. 'You're the boss.'

CHAPTER TWENTY

Lesley felt drained, her whole body ached as though she had been physically beaten. She stared at the mug in her hand. Let her thoughts drift.

'Lesley,' Emma startled her. 'It's your friend John again.'

The man from the car park. Tears stung her eyes.

'I'll tell him to come back later.' Emma said briskly, turning to go back to the front door.

'No,' she got to her feet, 'really, it's fine.' She daren't refuse to see him.

'Are you sure, you're exhausted?'

'Yes, I'd like to see him,' she said brightly, 'he won't stay long.'

She took him into the lounge. He shut the door. Stared at her. He came and stood very close. She could smell tobacco on his clothes and cooking fat.

'What I know. Could be crucial.'

'You just gave me a ticket, that's all. Don't be ridiculous,' she tried to deflect him.

'Just a question of whether I ring *Crimestoppers* or not.'

'What do you want, money?'

'Now, how do you cost a thing like that? Five hundred? Five thousand? What price freedom, eh?'

She waited. It was a nightmare. It was all a nightmare.

'And there are other things besides money,' he reached out and ran his finger along the edge of her jaw. She began to shake.

'Let's say a thousand cash, to start,' he whispered. 'And the rest, we'll play it by ear. Lady like you, just be a question of which card to draw it on, eh?'

'They won't—'

'Soon as you get chance. I'll call same time tomorrow. Be nice if we were alone.' He pressed the pad of his finger against her lips. She was rigid with fear and dislike.

A sudden commotion from the hallway and the door swung open. Chief Inspector Lewis came in, her mouth set. 'Lesley Tulley, I am arresting you on suspicion of the murder of Matthew Tulley . . .'

* * *

They took Dean to make his phone call. His chest hurt and he felt like he was losing it big-time but he had to try, one last chance.

'Paula,' his voice sounded dry and faraway. 'I'm in South Manchester police station. I want to see you, Paula, I know I've messed you about but I just . . . things are okay, you know? Just come and see us will you?'

'Dean,' she said, sounding unsure.

'I'll tell you, all of it, everything.' And he meant it. 'Will you come and see us?'

There was a long pause, then her breath, a little shaky. 'All right.'

Dean sniffed hard, wiped his nose with his hand and cleared his throat. He thought about the roll of dosh he'd slung up into Douggie's lampshade. If the Bill hadn't nabbed it, might be worth a trip to Oldham next chance he got. Nice little nest egg. 'It's gonna be all right,' he said, reassuring himself as much as her. 'Don't worry.' Be happy, like the man said.

* * *

'Is there anything you wish to say, Lesley?'

'If I could help, in any way, don't you think I would? I loved my husband.'

'Is that why you put up with his perversions?' Janine said calmly. 'The torture.'

'What about the man who was calling on you just now?' Richard said. 'Was he one of your husband's contacts?'

Janine sensed uncertainty in her response.

Lesley licked her lips. 'Just a friend of mine.'

'Really?' Richard said.

Lesley kept quiet.

'A witness has come forward.' He told her. 'They place you at the allotments shortly after nine a.m.'

Lesley recoiled with shock, shook her head in denial, her forehead creased. 'No!'

Janine spoke. 'You were covered in blood, you were running away. Later you get rid of the knife in a litter bin in town. We recover that knife. In other words, we can place you at the scene and we can link you to the weapon.' Stretching it a bit, Janine mentally crossed her fingers. 'We can also show that you consistently lied to investigating officers and constructed a false alibi. We have a motive, too — you were subjected to horrendous physical and sexual abuse in your marriage.'

Then Lesley Tulley looked at her, wounded eyes, mouth trembling. Speak, willed Janine, for God's sake speak. A rap on the door broke the spell. She could have screamed with frustration. What the hell were they playing at? They knew this was a crucial interview. Lesley Tulley sat, face averted and her eyes half-closed.

Janine stalked out. 'Boss.' Shap mouthed. 'Trouble!'

'But it's an eyewitness, sir.' Janine told The Lemon.

'An eight-year-old?'

'Seven,' Janine went on hurriedly, 'she gave us a detailed description, sir. as well. If I can just work at it—'

'No. No clothes, no forensics, no chance. Release her.'

'But sir, I think—'

'Release her.'

She nearly had her, why couldn't he see that? 'No. I'm sorry—'

'Chief Inspector Lewis!'

She left the room without another word, furious and disappointed.

* * *

A leaden sense of failure hung over the team in the murder room. She'd told them what Hackett had instructed, but she had not yet released Lesley Tulley. Janine couldn't sit still, her mind working overtime, her belly tense with the stress of the situation. If she only had the clothes. 'They searched the drains?' She went over it again.

'They did the lot. Nothing on the premises.' Richard said.

'It just doesn't add up. They were in the washing machine. The woman hasn't been out of the house without police escort. She's been nowhere. Why didn't she burn them with the tapes?'

'Too obvious?' Richard stretched his arms, folded them behind his head.

'The bonfire was hardly subtle,' she worked out the time, 'unless . . . she'd already got rid of them by Sunday night.'

'Where?' Richard thought she was clutching at straws. 'You said yourself she never went anywhere without—'

Sudden shocking realisation hit her like a cold shower. Jesus Christ! 'Wait! She did leave the house, we bloody took her! Oh, hell, we're going to be too late!' Janine said urgently. She ran, not easy with the weight of the pregnancy and the shortness of breath.

The others followed her through the corridors, across the car park and into the mortuary building. Along the corridor to the ladies toilets. She barged past the sign Cleaning in Progress and inside.

'Oy, closed,' the cleaner yelled at them all. Cream cleanser in one hand, she dunked her ciggie in the washbasin. 'Can't you read?'

'Have you done the bins?'

Janine went into the stall and upended the sanitary bin. One carrier bag, tightly tied! She undid it, her heart about to burst. Yes! There they were. Jog-pants, a stripe down the side, t-shirt, cap. She left them as they were, careful not to contaminate them.

She closed the bag, stepped out and swung it round her head.

Richard grinned. Shap cheered and the others gave her a round of applause.

'Right!' Her eyes sparkled. 'You two,' she nodded at her sergeants, 'keep The Lemon at bay.'

* * *

'We've found the clothes. At the mortuary.'

Janine saw the flicker of fear in Lesley's eyes, a blink, then she recovered. Richard had seen it too, he dipped his head a fraction.

'I still don't know what you're talking about.'

'I'm sure we'll get a conviction. The only question will be whether the act was premeditated or not.' Would Lesley go for the bait, try and persuade them it was in the heat of the moment? 'You claimed you loved him but his love had become a monstrous thing, hadn't it, Lesley? Destroying you.'

As Janine watched, Lesley Tulley appeared to crumble, her face dissolving in tears, her mouth taut with emotion. 'It wasn't like that.'

Thank God, Janine thought, she's talking.

The solicitor sat forward. 'Please, Mrs Tulley, I advise you most strongly to take counsel.'

'If I need any advice, I'll ask for it.' She paused, bowed her head as if gathering strength then began to speak. 'We had a row. A terrible row. He was hitting me and I thought he was going to kill me. There was a knife, on the table in the shed. The knife . . . I was so frightened. I didn't mean to hurt him.'

'Then what did you do?'

'I didn't know what to do,' her eyes were haunted. 'I was scared.'

'And the parking ticket?' Richard said.

'The man who came today. I took his.'

He frowned. 'You said he was a friend?'

'No, a stranger. I asked him for his ticket.'

'What was he doing at your home?'

Lesley gave him a look; defiance mingled with distaste. 'Blackmailing me. He'd watched the press conference.'

Janine exhaled and exchanged a look of disgust with Richard. 'We can do him for that. This row. What was it about?'

'About the filming. I wanted it to stop. He'd promised. He said I wouldn't have to do it again.'

'What were you doing at the allotment?'

'I went with him, to help out.'

She was lying but very convincingly, her demeanour all honesty now.

'Lesley. Matthew was seen arriving alone. You had no cuts or bruises.' Janine spoke softly. 'It wasn't self-defence.'

'Of course it was self-defence,' she said, anguish twisting her features, 'you know what he did to me? Remember the diary? Little stars? Film night. Friday was the next one. Prosser was coming back; he was so—' She broke off, pressed her hand to her mouth, struggled to stay in control. She looked up at Janine her eyes glittering. 'I can't have children. My hysterectomy? Matthew told the hospital that I'd been depressed and tried to abort myself. He was very plausible. Do you know what they had used on me that time?'

Janine swallowed her revulsion. You poor bloody woman. But I have to do this. This is what I do. 'You thought you could get away with it?'

'I couldn't think,' Lesley cried, 'I'd done a terrible thing and I felt guilty. And Matthew—'

Janine was measured, insistent. 'You followed him there, you took a knife and you took his life. There was a cut on his arm where he tried to stop you. Nine years, Lesley. Why didn't you leave him?'

'I loved him.' She paused. 'Once, one time I packed. I couldn't do it. I was scared.'

'That he'd find you?'

'Of losing him.' Raw emotion made her voice crack.

'Why Saturday, Lesley?'

'I told you. Matthew had promised me it was over. He broke his promise.'

'You could have gone to your sister's, gone anywhere,' Janine reasoned.

'No, no, I couldn't.'

'Why not?' Janine coaxed. 'Why not, Lesley?'

'Because he said he'd get someone else if I went,' she said passionately. 'That it'd be easy enough to find another girl and teach her, exactly like he had me. Break her.'

Janine felt the tension palpable in the room. The silence stretched. 'So you killed him?'

'I couldn't let him do that.' There was an ambiguity there. Had she killed him out of jealousy, unwilling to see him with another? Or out of altruism?

Janine nodded. 'The argument,' she said gently, 'when was it, Lesley? Last week? The week before? That's when you decided, wasn't it? You couldn't let some other woman go through that. You'd stop him for good.'

Lesley looked at Janine, her gaze confessing the truth, seeking absolution. A prayer in her eyes. She didn't need to speak for Janine to find the answer. The admission. And then like a shutter coming down, Lesley's expression switched. She shook her head.

'No,' she said.

CHAPTER TWENTY-ONE

Janine sat back, took a deep breath. Her work was done. Whether the crime was premeditated would be the business of the courtroom, as would the issue of whether Lesley Tulley deserved any punishment for killing the man who had used her so savagely.

Janine looked at Richard. His eyes steady on her, he adjusted his position. She began to speak. 'Lesley Tulley, you are charged that on the 22nd of February, year 2003, you murdered Matthew Tulley, contrary to Common Law . . .'

* * *

Janine and Richard were re-living the interview. A sense of achievement in the air despite the tragic circumstances of Lesley Tulley's life. There was a buzz to it that Janine savoured, knowing how hard they had all worked to get here. Aware that she had done it. Led the team and got a result.

'When you told her we'd found them. Her eyes, you could see it,' Richard's face was alight, his manner exhilarated.

Janine shook her head. 'But imagine that level of control. She can go and identify his body with the freshly washed clothes in her bag, right under our noses.' She sighed. Eased herself into her chair. She recalled the terrible cries on the videotape. The terror. 'What must it do to you? In your head, in your heart, living like that?' She broke off trying to take it all in. 'I can't . . . What she went through . . . horrific. No one should have to live like that. But . . . you can't go round killing people. At the end of the day she was clever,' she reflected, 'clever enough to buy a man's shirt for her husband an hour after she'd killed him.'

'Not clever enough to walk away.'

Janine stretched. 'Up to the jury now. With luck they'll find mitigating circumstances.'

'O'Halloran'll kill you,' he teased.

'Not if The Lemon gets there first.' She still had to face the music. 'Think I might need to go off on bed-rest.'

Richard chuckled. Then he stopped smiling. 'Janine . . .'

'Don't.'

'The affairs, Wendy — we were both unhappy.'

'That's not what I heard.'

'Well, you heard wrong. Wendy, she didn't want kids. I didn't think it mattered. But you get older — the affairs, it was a way out, that's all.'

'And I've got a ready-made family?' She said quickly.

'It's not like that. You and me, there was always that spark.'

'Richard . . .' She wished he'd shut up.

'You feel something.'

She didn't deny it but a thousand buts crowded her mind.

'We could be good together. The right wavelength.'

'I come with a lot of baggage.'

Richard observed her bump. 'I know,' he said wryly.

'Not just this. Three kids, Pete. It's not like before, it can't be the two of us. It's never going to be that simple.'

Shap stuck his head round the door. 'The Lemon, boss.'

* * *

'Sir.'

'Exactly which part of 'release Mrs Tulley' didn't you understand?' His words were clipped, sharp. 'Your promotion . . .'

'We got the clothes, sir.'

He stared at her, momentarily taken aback.

'And a confession.' She saw the venom in his glare. He loathed being bested. 'It'll fly, sir. CPS like it.'

He closed his eyes briefly. Then tight-lipped. 'Right,' a wave to dismiss her.

If that's how he wants to play it. As she reached the door, passing his computer with an error message on screen — Windows was not shut down properly — he spoke again.

'Janine.'

She turned, smiling, at last she'd get a morsel of praise, a crumb of appreciation. She'd solved the bloody case, after all. She looked at him expectantly.

'I need all your documents, evaluation, final budget,' he checked his watch. 'Five thirty.'

The bastard!

She nodded curtly. Then had a thought. 'The Chief Constable — he'll be delighted. Will you tell him, sir?' And may it choke you.

His face was like thunder. Then she glimpsed, just for a nanosecond, a hint of humour in his eyes. A slight inclination of the head. Touché.

* * *

Janine struggled to collate and copy all the relevant papers and the clock raced towards her deadline. Twenty-five past and he was still in his office. Half past. The last page printing. Beeping and the out of paper light started flashing. Damn. She stuffed more paper in, set resume. It was 5.37 when she got to his office. He had gone.

Janine had an infantile moment when she considered burning the lot before shrugging it off. He would not spoil her day. No, sir!

She dumped the pile on his desk and went off to join the rest of the team in the bar down the road.

They greeted her with a round of applause. As boss she did the honours and bought another round. She waited at the bar, tired but pleased with herself. Gazing into the mirror behind the bar she caught Richard's eye, held it a moment too long. Shook her head. What was she going to do with him? Nothing for now. Never make decisions when you are tired, stressed or emotional: that ruled out most of Janine's waking life.

He walked her back to the station when she'd made her excuses and left. Looked like Shap and Butchers were settled in for the night.

She and Richard stood beside her car. 'I could ring you; maybe do something later in the week? Go for a .' he tailed off.

'I don't know.'

'Not an outright no, then? There is a chance?'

She gave him a frank look. Shrugged.

'I can wait.'

'Some things are worth waiting for.' She smiled, opened her car door, got in and started it up.

He stood back and watched her pull away. Watched until the car disappeared from view. Then turned on his heels.

* * *

Tom was home, safe and happy and in bed. Michael had fallen asleep listening to his headphones. She eased them off and switched off his telly. Thought momentarily of Dean and Ferdie and all the young lads who had the odds stacked against them from the word go. The bubble bath was deep and just the right temperature. She slid into the water, leant her head back against the edge of the bath and breathed in the fragrance.

I did it, we did it. Oh, yes! Bone tired but home and dry — well, so to speak.

The weight off her feet was a blessed relief. She massaged her stomach, felt something solid to one side, head, hip? Stroked it. Boy or girl? Didn't matter, did it, so long as all was well.

She was drifting off when Eleanor's voice came bawling up the stairs like a banshee. 'Mum, the washing machine is leaking!'

Please, she thought, oh, please. Give me a break!

THE END

ACKNOWLEDGEMENTS

Adapting a book for television, and then back again, means many people helped shape this story. Special thanks to Carolyn Reynolds at Granada TV for the amazing opportunity and for encouraging me to write my first script and to Jane Macnaught for helping me through unfamiliar territory. For advice on police matters thanks to Inspector Roger Forsdyke, Inspector Peter N. Walker (Retd.) and Detective Superintendent Patsy Wood. Thanks to the cast of *Blue Murder* who made the characters theirs — and then some. A toast to Ann Cleeves from Murder Squad who first tipped me the wink and then kept nudging. And finally thanks to Tim — I couldn't have done it without you.

Thank you for reading this book.

If you enjoyed it please leave feedback on Amazon or Goodreads, and if there is anything we missed or you have a question about, then please get in touch. We appreciate you choosing our book.

Founded in 2014 in Shoreditch, London, we at Joffe Books pride ourselves on our history of innovative publishing. We were thrilled to be shortlisted for Independent Publisher of the Year at the British Book Awards.

www.joffebooks.com

We're very grateful to eagle-eyed readers who take the time to contact us. Please send any errors you find to corrections@joffebooks.com. We'll get them fixed ASAP.